Too Far
Too Fast

Trisha Pyle

ACKNOWLEDGMENTS

My gratitude to Scott for making my dreams become reality and my heartfelt thanks to my editor, Marilyn, for all her support and patience.

CONTENTS

CHAPTER ONE

Crushed gravel sprayed beneath the wheels and rattled against the taxi's metal belly as it drove between the tall, white, wrought iron gates and onto the wide circular track set into the lawn. Abby had arrived.

Stepping out into the late afternoon sunshine she breathed in the warm, fragranced air of her favourite holiday destination.

"Thank you." Exchanging her proffered case for a couple of euros she smiled at the young Greek taxi driver.

Happiness sang through her veins as she drank in the sight of the familiar apartments. At this time of day the sun shone on the balconies at the front, leaving the rear of the white, two-storied building in cool shadow.

A flight of stone steps led down one side giving access to the apartments on the lower floor. Beyond, a terrace and another set of stairs ended in a small garden and then the beach. Here, at the back, two matching sets of white painted steps, situated near each end of the building, climbed to the upper rooms. Everything looked the same as she remembered.

Short skirt billowing, bobbed, dark hair fluttering she enjoyed the pleasant balmy breeze, loving the way it made the tall spiky leaves of the palm trees, planted either side of the stairs, shiver and rustle.

A car door clunked shut, tyres crunched over small limestone chipping as the taxi departed. On her own at last Abby lugged her heavy case up the white concrete steps to the first floor.

As always the key sat in the lock waiting for a new tenant. Hand hesitating on the latch, she savoured the moment. A whole year ago she'd closed the door of this corner apartment knowing she'd be back. With sweet anticipation, Abby opened the door and stepped into the small kitchen area.

Puzzlement furrowed her brow as she peered through the arched doorway into the bedroom. Something wasn't right! The heavy, pale green curtains in front of the patio doors leading to the balcony hung partly open, as did one door. Sunlight poured in, spilling golden heat across the twin bed nearest the window. *Whew!* She fanned her face with her hand. The rooms were unbearably hot and, truth be told, a little bit whiffy.

Placing her suitcase in front of the fridge, she scooped a large, heavy frying pan off the floor.

What the hell!

Dropping the pan into the sink she slung her handbag onto the worktop and moved into the bedroom, intent on shutting the hot sun out of the room. Inwardly she cursed the maids for leaving the curtains open and herself for not stopping to pick up the remote for the air conditioning unit before coming into the accommodation - she'd planned to do it later.

Dazzled by the glare, she failed to see the tip of a shoe on the tiled floor a few steps inside the door arch. Stumbling she glanced down, swallowing a gasp, her body suddenly cold, her brain desperately trying to deny what her eyes were seeing. Heart thudding, scalp tingling fear held her immobile staring in horror at the man slumped between the wardrobe and the nearest bed like an abandoned puppet with it's strings cut.

Bloody hell!

Dark, bulging eyes stared sightless at the ceiling. A swollen, purple tongue protruded grotesquely between beetroot coloured lips. Dressed in light coloured chinos, a blue polo-shirt and white deck-shoes, the thin rope tied tightly around his throat was a superfluous, and unwanted, accessory.

Stirred by the warm breeze one of the balcony curtains fluttered. Nerves frazzled, Abby stifled a scream. Unable to take her eyes off the horrible sight, she pressed a hand over her mouth. Her stomach churning, threatening to disgorge its contents, she backed towards the small bathroom which lay just off the kitchen.

What was a dead man doing in her lovely rooms? How had he got here? Who had murdered him?

Questions buzzed, demanding answers.

The muffled creak of a handle turning, followed immediately by the sharp click of a door opening, sounded directly behind her. Gasping with shock she spun around, nerves jangling, fear spiking ever higher, her queasiness forgotten.

Oh crap! What now?

A youngish man walked out of her bathroom holding a bloodied hand towel to the crown of his head. Wet, light brown hair curled around his scalp, the collar and shoulders of his expensive looking cream shirt clung damply to his broad tanned body.

"Hi," a deep, rich, almost musical voice addressed her. "I thought I heard someone come in."

"What...? What the hell's going on here?" her voice bordered on hysterical.

"I can explain," his tone stated quite plainly that he intended to take charge of the situation. Casually daubing his head he stained the towel with more drops of bright red blood.

Abby's fear hiked up even higher than she thought possible. "Ex... explain?" she spluttered, waving a hand limply in the direction of the bedroom. "This I've got to hear, but you might as well tell the police at the same time." Snatching her handbag off the bench she groped in its depth for her mobile, her eyes never leaving his face.

A strong, masculine hand swept the bag from her. "I don't think so. At least, not until I've worked out what to say to them."

"What to say to them!" her words almost a shout, her legs threatening to collapse, she took a deep breath. "Why not simply tell them the truth?" she demanded, her voice still a few octaves higher than usual.

He gave her a lopsided smile. Some part of her terrified mind noted that he didn't look like a villain.

Alarm bells ringing, she realised why he would need to make a story up. Stuck in this tiny kitchen with a possible murderer blocking her way out, did she really want to hear the truth? Yes - nothing else would do.

Leaning a trembling hand against the wall she steadied herself. Terror dried her mouth, her tongue desperately wanted to attach itself to the back of her front teeth. Swallowing audibly brought some saliva back into her suddenly parched mouth, thereby freeing her tongue. It seemed like forever before he replied.

Balling the stained towel he flung it through the bathroom doorway into the tiny shower stall. A cheeky, half embarrassed smile tugged at his sensual mouth. He seemed to be considering what to say.

"I was trying for a blasé approach in an effort not to scare you further but you obviously need to know what I'm doing in your apartment. It is your apartment isn't it?"

Abby jerked her head up and down imitating the motion of a nodding toy dog normally seen in the back of a moving car. She preferred to let him do the talking for now.

"The problem I've got is I can't quite remember. I don't want to frighten you, but actually, I can't explain how I got here. I'm not sure what happened but about ten minutes ago I woke up on your kitchen floor with one hell of a headache and a cracked skull." He shrugged and immediately grimaced with pain, his free hand moved briefly to support his injured head.

"I recall visiting some friends earlier but nothing else. I don't even know how I hurt by damn head. It's bloody frustrating."

What a posh voice.

"Very convenient I must say." Surprised to find her natural no-nonsense attitude had reasserted itself, Abby pushed herself upright. "You had better put your thinking cap on and find some answers fast because I don't believe you. I'm not used to finding strange men lurking, or lying around, in my apartment." She tapped her foot while he stared at her, his blue eyes round with surprise at her sudden assertiveness.

Then he smiled - devastatingly.

Oh boy!

"Well?" she demanded, her temper at his cavalier attitude to the dreadful situation momentarily overriding her fear. "Have you remembered yet?"

Still looking bemused by the verbal attack, he continued to stare at her as though unable to think of anything to say.

"You're very loud," he managed at last. "Would you mind lowering your voice, my head is hurting like hell."

What?

"Loud, you think this is loud? You haven't heard anything yet," she raised her voice even more. Gulping in some much needed air she tried, unsuccessfully, to calm down. "Do you realise how frightened I am? I nearly died when you strolled out of my bathroom as though you had every right to. The least you owe me is an explanation. What – the – flaming - hell - happened - here?" She drew a shaky breath, realising for the first time that it might not be wise to berate a murderer with his victim laying less than a metre away.

He groaned, pinning Abby with a pained expression. "I don't need this," exhaustion laced his words, his, 'I'm in control' manner beginning to crack.

"You don't need this? I'm bloody sure I don't need it either. This is not what I expected when I booked this apartment." There was no way he was going to tell her to be quiet.

"Indoor voice please," he reasserted his dominance by raising his own tone. "What I do need is fresh air and a clear head." Standing straighter, he placed his feet further apart, bracing legs which seemed to be having trouble supporting him. Taking a deep breath he gagged.

Watching him alter his stance, Abby felt only less threatened. His body now totally blocked the only way out. She'd read somewhere that the best form of defence was attack. About to find out if the author knew his stuff, she squared her shoulders.

Bunching fists, hidden in skirts of her dress, she prepared to fight for her life. He looked strong. Muscles bulged beneath his wet shirt. She calculated, he was only a couple of inches taller than her own five foot nine, plus he was showing signs of being weakened by his injury - with luck and surprise on her side...

His smooth, cultured voice sliced through her thoughts.

"Look it's very hot in here do you mind if I open the door?" Without waiting for her answer he grasped the handle and pulled. "That's better; I was beginning to feel a bit faint."

With the door open she might get away from him. Altering her own posture she warned him. "You will have to secure it or the breeze will slam it shut again." She gestured to the fastenings. "When the balcony door and this one are both open it creates a through draught." Hoping for a chance to push past him and make a run for it she didn't want the door to slam shut in her face when the opportunity to flee came.

Using one hand, he grasped the metal hook on the back of the door and looped it through the ring attached to the wall.

Fresh air blew on Abby's face lifting her short, dark hair off her hot forehead. She eyed her escape route, mentally preparing to dash past the intruder at the first opportunity.

Anxiety over not making it accelerated her heart beat until if felt like a bird trapped in the cavity of her chest, wings beating frantically in an effort to escape.

"That breeze is great, it's stifling in here." Pulling his damp shirt away from his chest the man allowed the air to cool his body. "I'd love to be able to tell you how I got here. Maybe later, if you'll allow me, I'll be in a position too." He flashed another devastating smile. "I'm sorry to have made a mess of your bathroom but it couldn't be helped. God knows how I got here; it's a mystery to me. Hopefully I'll remember pretty soon." Giving her a quizzical look ending in a slow, sexy smile, he asked. "What's your name by the way?"

A charm offensive! How dare he?

Still there could be no harm in humouring him, getting him off-guard. Maybe she could persuade him to move away from the door by playing nice. If he thought she hadn't been in the bedroom yet, he might even want to get her out of the apartment before she saw the body.

"Abby. My name's Abby."

Pointing to her case he went on, "As you've clearly only just arrived I cannot be accused of trying to steal from you."

"What about my bag?"

God why couldn't she learn to keep her big mouth shut?

Surprise flitted briefly across his attractive face as he glanced down to where her handbag still swung from his hand. Giving her a rueful look, he placed it carefully on the worktop.

"Sorry about the towel,luv. I'm sure they'll give you a fresh one if you explain what's happened. I'd better go."

"Go!" Astounded, she frowned at him her heart beat slowing, her fear totally evaporating.

Surely a murderer would not be this cool? She'd seen his face and could give a description to the authorities.

Amazed, he didn't intend to kill her too, words again sprang unbidden from her mouth.

"How can you simply walk away and leave me to deal with the police?"

"Why would you need the police? I've only soiled a towel, its hardy a hanging matter." Tilting his head to one side he narrowed his eyes in puzzlement. Raising his hand he supported his forehead, his dark eyelashes fluttered, the movement had obviously caused him some pain.

"Did you hit me?" His voice barely audible, he moistened beautiful, sculptured lips with his tongue.

Abby followed the motion as though mesmerised.

"No, not you, I heard your car arriving after I'd come around." He sounded stronger as he answered his own question. "What is your problem? Do you want to find out who knocked me out? That's very kind of you but I don't intend to involve the police," he assured her, making an obvious effort to pull himself together. Providing a heart-stopping smile he stepped outside. "So if you're not going to take this any further I might as well go. I'll get myself checked out don't worry."

"You'll get yourself checked out?" she almost shrieked.

What a nerve!

"What about the other one? Don't you care what happens to him? I sure he'd love to get himself, *'checked out,'* only it's a bit too late for that isn't it? What am I supposed to do when the police question me about you and the dead body?" Giving an elaborate shrug she assumed her most sarcastic voice. "Sorry officer, the injured bloke with amnesia strolled off to get a sticking plaster for his sore head."

The audacity of the man!

"Dead body?" He blinked. "What dead body?"

"The one in the bedroom as if you didn't know."

"There's a body in the bedroom?" His startling blue eyes narrowed suspiciously.

"That's what I've just said." His acting skills were superb, Oscar nomination quality. "Don't tell me you didn't know about it?" Scepticism laced her words.

"Show me." Mr Bossy resurfaced, looking as though he couldn't believe his ears.

Walking back through the kitchen she led him into the large sunny bedroom.

"Jeez!" Staggering back a step, he gaped at the corpse. "God its Willy, I mean John. How did this happen?" His voice rose, his shock apparent. "He's my First Officer. Oh my God, who would murder him like this? It's so brutal! No wonder you were scared of me." Several colourful words escaped his lips.

Abby could have added a few extra - no bother at all.

"Poor Willie, I wonder when this happened?" Turning towards Abby, his bright blue eyes begged for some explanation.

"Don't look at me," she snapped.

Swallowing hard, he turned his attention back to the dead man, stepping forward to take a closer look.

Abby watched the changing expressions on his striking face - the foremost of these appeared to be disbelief.

"I've never experienced anything as stomach-churning as seeing a strangled man," she confided.

"Me neither. I guess it's a first for both of us." He rubbed his hand over his face as though trying to wipe away the horrible sight. "Willie was definitely strangled," he confirmed, studying his first officer's face. "He must have put up a fight, he's got a split lip, blood on his eyebrow and his cheeks are a bit bruised - look." Bending towards the body he stretched out his arm to show Abby what he meant.

"Don't touch him!" Abby warned, raising her voice yet again.

She really must stop bellowing - her grandmother had taught her that only fishwives shout.

"He's obviously dead, don't contaminate the evidence," she finished only slightly quieter.

He froze, seeming shocked by her advice. "I don't understand what's going on. What's he doing here?"

"That's what I'd like to know." She choked back a sob. Looking at the murdered man a second time didn't make the sight any easier to stomach. This wasn't how she'd planned to spend the first hours of her holiday. "Why did you call him Willy if it's not his name?" she accused, moving nearer to the open door. With a bit of luck she might be able to grab the key and get out. If she locked the door behind her, she could leave him with his late friend until the police arrived.

Straightening, he wiped sweaty palms down the sides of his cut off jeans.

"Jeez! What a nightmare! I think I'd better offer you some reassurance. My name is Jensen Stone, I'm a stockbroker and I live in London. You have nothing to fear from me. I sailed to this island on my yacht. I know that I'm not involved in this and I honestly didn't know that Willy had been murdered." Pointing to the corpse he continued, "He is John Thomas and he is, was, a member of my crew."

"John Thomas?" She frowned. "Oh! I get it." John Thomas, Willy, Charlie, Dick, were all nicknames for the penis. "That's why you call him Willy."

"Yes, everyone knows him by that name. Look, I need to escape from this dreadful sight." Walking swiftly over to the patio doors he stepped out onto the balcony.

Abby could hear him breathing deeply. Free to collect her bag and go, she made for the door. In the kitchen she hesitated. Jensen had looked so shocked to see the poor man lying there. Perhaps he was telling the truth and wasn't involved - she had to know.

CHAPTER TWO

"You said that Willy was one of your crewmembers. What did you mean?" Hovering in the doorway of the small platform Abby watched Jensen warily.

Standing with his body hunched and his hands resting on the waist high, white painted concrete wall, he nodded towards a luxury yacht moored in the sparkling azure waters of the bay. "That's my boat there."

For once the fantastic scenery she'd dreamed about all winter, failed to excite her. At the bottom of the garden tall, white, wrought iron gates, a match to the ones she come through less than half an hour ago, led to a small private beach with a little harbour for local fishing boats tucked away at one end. Set on the edge of a large curved bay the elevated apartments commanded a spectacular view.

"I've remembered something." Dusting his hands together, he turned to face her.

"What?" Fear rocketed. If he'd recalled killing Willy she could be next!

"My launch is moored in that small harbour. I came ashore with Willy and Neil Parks." He sighed. "I wonder where Parky is now. Maybe he could shed some light on the situation. God knows somebody needs to, I'm at a loss as to what's going on here." Placing a palm on his forehead he briefly closed his eyes. "If only I could remember how I got into this apartment it would be a start."

"This 'Parky' person could be waiting for you near the launch. Perhaps he might have some answers," Abby suggested, relaxing a little.

Jensen's hair took on a light golden hue as it dried, curling attractively against his forehead giving him an almost boyish look. Surely someone as strikingly good looking as this man couldn't be capable of murder? Looking away from the pleasing sight, she noticed the clothes dryer sitting in the corner of the balcony.

Moving closer she inspected the object. Folding metal legs in the shape of two X's supported a square frame with six lines of thin rope stretched across. A large stone lay over one of the two metal rungs fastened the bottom of the X's together, anchoring the flimsy structure against high winds. Mismatched, coloured clothes pegs dangled haphazardly, a bright yellow and a faded red lay on the concrete floor.

Oh God!

The short hairs on the nape of Abby's neck stood to attention. A sick sensation settled in the pit of her stomach. One of the lines was missing!

"That's what he was strangled with!" Hand over her mouth she twirled around to look at Jensen. "Did you kill him?" she whispered between trembling fingers.

"No I didn't kill him." His features tightened. "At least, I don't think so. There's nothing wrong with my long term memory, it's only the past few hours I'm having trouble with. I know I have no reason to harm Willy, and I'm definitely not in the habit of murdering people." Glancing around to see what she'd seen, he noticed the space on the dryer.

Coming forward for a closer look Jenson ran a tentative finger along one of the remaining lines. "You could be right. The cord around Willy's neck looks very similar." He gave a frustrated sigh. "I hope my memory returns sometime soon. I think it's time to call the authorities." Turning he took a long, yearning look at his yacht, as though wondering how long it would be before he could board her again.

Leaning against the kitchen sink, Abby stared helplessly at her mobile. She'd no idea how to go about contacting the authorities, or anyone else for that matter. Sensing Jensen coming towards her, she looked up. "Do you happen to have the telephone number of the local police station?"

"No. But I know a man who does," he informed her, taking his smart-phone from his pocket. "I'm going to call the friends I left - what now seems like hours ago."

"What's the name of these apartments?" he wanted to know after a while. Repeating the name she gave him into the phone, he glanced at the door to obtain the number. Finishing the call, he looked up at Abby.

"My Greek friend, Manolis, will send the police. We have to wait here."

Mr Bossy was back in the building.

Hands plunged into his pockets Jensen walked out of the back door.

Some of the apartments jutted out from the others at the front and Abby's was one of these, being at the end of the row a small, fairly private back balcony was created. Jenson paced like a caged lion.

"Come out here. It's not very pleasant in there," he called after a while.

Picking up the frying pan she remembered seeing earlier, Abby joined Jensen outside. "Do you know why this was lying on the kitchen floor when I arrived?" She waved the weighty pan at him.

"I've no idea." Gingerly he touched the back of his head. "Or maybe I do."

"You think someone hit you with this?" Horrified, she realised her fingerprints were now all over the handle. The damage already done, she flipped it over to peer at the base. "There should be traces of blood on here if they did. Maybe some hair as well, and even through I might have smudged a few fingerprints I'm sure the police will be able to find something."

"Christ! What are you? It's like being with Miss bloody Marple." Obviously stressed, his temper seemed to spiral out of control. "What with instructions not to contaminate bloody evidence, discovering the possible murder weapon and now a forensic investigation of the bottom of a bloody frying pan, what's next?" He uttered a number of choice words. "Why don't you get your camera and take photos of the crime scene? We won't need the police at all by the time you're finished."

How dare he be mad at her!

Hurt flamed through her entire body, tears gathered blurring her vision. Her holiday ruined before it began, she'd spent the last half hour in a state of fear. Now this stranger had insulted her. Biting her bottom lip she struggled to stop it trembling.

Jensen sighed. "Sorry, I didn't mean to bark at you. Please remember that's it's my blood and hair your talking about. I'm feeling a bit queasy as it is without you reminding me I've had my head bashed."

"And I'm not, I suppose!" Free hand on her hip, she faced him, burning with temper. "Don't forget it's my apartment you decided to get clobbered in. Please forgive me if I don't want any fingers pointed in my direction," she snapped.

What a cheek!

Hot fat tears scalded her cheeks as they escaped from her brimming eyes.

"Did you know your lovely green eyes blaze like emerald fire when you're angry?"

"Ooh!" Dashing the tears away she marched back into the kitchen placing the frying pan carefully upside down on the work-surface, her motions belying her still smouldering temper.

How dare he speak to her like that? Who did he think he was? Stuck up toff! Just where did he get off talking down to her then attempting to calm her with a few flattering words?

Sneaking a look through the open door she persuaded herself that he appeared to be sorry for his outburst.

The thought of the body sprawled in the bedroom was too much. No matter how much Jensen annoyed her, she would have to put up with him, she couldn't stay in here. Striding outside she prepared to give as good as she got.

Cooking odours wafted from one of the apartments, the smell of onions, garlic and locally made, spicy, village sausage filled the air. Jensen appeared to be swallowing repeatedly as though his mouth was filling with water, bending forward he took several deep breaths.

Holy crap - he was going to puke!

Close up his ashen face shocked her, her anger dissolved.

Please don't faint.

"Would you like some water?"

"Please." He managed a wan smile.

Dashing into the kitchen, she grabbed her handbag.

"Here." Taking out a half full bottle of water she handed it to him. "I've been drinking out of it I'm afraid."

"That's okay." He sipped carefully allowing the tepid liquid to settle his stomach.

Abby watched warily as he drained the last drop. "Better?"

"Yes thanks." Handing her the empty container he watched as she absently pushed it back inside her handbag. "How do you know so much about forensics anyway?"

So now he wanted to talk, he must have won control over his heaving stomach.

Thank goodness!

There'd been no need to be so horrible to her even if he was feeling ill, it was hardly her fault he'd been brained.

Convinced, he was about to mock her again, she lifted her chin and stood a little straighter. "I like watching programmes like 'Silent Witness' and 'Bones'," she admitted tartly. "It's amazing what you can learn."

Despite the appalling situation and his obvious discomfort, Jensen gave a grunt of amusement.

"I'm glad that you find me entertaining," she bridled. "You would be laughing on the other side of your face if you'd touched the body and left evidence of your DNA," she huffed. "I'd like to see you get out of that situation."

"I know, I know. I'm sorry; I understand you are only trying to help." Swinging away from her he slammed the flat of his hands down onto the balcony wall - hard. "Christ, how the hell did we get into this mess? I can't get my head around the fact that Willy is dead in horrifying circumstances," he sighed, "or that he was sprawled a matter of feet away without me knowing." He pulled air into his lungs. "I can't understand why the killer didn't simply finish me off.

"Then you've been dragged into this I can't imagine how you're feeling. You don't know me yet, as you rightly point out, I could have made my situation a hell of a lot worse if you hadn't been here. Then there's Parky, what the hell has happened to him? Please God let him not be lying dead somewhere too!" The last was a whispered plea.

Abby didn't know what to say, she stared at his broad, tense shoulders experiencing a ridiculous urge to run her hands up his back and massage the tightness out of his muscles. Confused by the rapid change in her attitude towards this man she was, for once, lost for words.

Jensen continued without turning around. "Suspicion will fall on me, of that I've no doubt. I'm aware by knowing the dead man I'll be implicated by association and, quite honestly, my gut is clenched with fear. Why can't I remember what happened?"

"Maybe you saw the murder and your mind is protecting itself by taking away your memory?" She squirmed, embarrassed by his admission of fright. "Or it could be you're the murderer and can't face the fact."

Oh no why couldn't she learn to guard her tongue? She hadn't meant to add that last bit - it just sort of slipped out.

Twisting his head, Jensen pinned her with a look of pure horror. "That's the second time you've accused me. I'm not surprised I'm the obvious suspect. Not only do I know Willie but you found me nursing an injury which could have happened during a struggle." Looking away again he seemed to regain his equilibrium. "The fact you've stood your ground and waited with me for the police to arrive is encouraging. Perhaps you don't really believe I murdered Willy."

"I don't honestly know what to think." It was true. All the evidence pointed to Jensen but in her heart of hearts she couldn't bring herself to believe he could have done such a thing.

"You're bound to be confused; you've walked into a nightmare. I'm finding it difficult to think straight at the moment. I'm stressed beyond belief. My head is pounding as though someone is repeatedly hitting it with a hammer and my stomach roiling worse than the last time I suffered a storm at sea." Turning his back on the scenery he leant his lean buttocks against the balcony wall, his amazing blue eyes surveying her with an unnerving intensity.

"You've been very brave. Most women I know would've had the screaming hab-dabs by now."

Flushed by the compliment delivered in such a rich, deep tone, Abby wondered briefly about the other girls. She imagined there'd been more than a few. He obviously had money, he looked like an angel and his voice made her think of caramel-covered ice cream. A perfect babe magnet if ever there was one.

Embarrassed by his stare, she looked beyond him out over the large, sparsely grassed area towards where the road ended in a turning point near the cliff edge. The sea gleamed serpent-like in the distance where the land wound in again, reminding her that these apartments were situated on a peninsular. In normal circumstances she would have enjoyed the view.

Jensen turned his head, standing a little straighter. "Well you don't need to play amateur detective any longer, it looks like the local cops are here."

The white police car drove between the gates at a leisurely pace. A cigarette butt arched gracefully from the passenger window as the vehicle ground to a halt. The overweight driver struggled out and reached into the back for his hat, holding the peak he pulled it firmly onto his head. A tall, youngish policeman unwound himself from the passenger seat. Adjusting his pistol belt, he slung it even lower on his hips like a Wild West gunslinger about to engage in a shootout, before donning his cap.

"They don't seem to be in any hurry," Abby remarked.

"Hmmm... They're so laid back they're virtually horizontal. Perhaps they think this is a hoax?" Jensen squared his broad shoulders. "Well, 'Laurel and Hardy' there, are in for a shock when they find out that it's not." He walked to meet the officers who were now on their way up the white concrete stairs.

CHAPTER THREE

Pressed against Jensen in the back seat of the cramped police car, Abby almost smiled to herself remembering the way the policemen had snapped to attention, like a pair of pedal bin lids, at the sight of poor Willy's lifeless body. The younger policeman had stayed with the victim until the coroner arrived, whilst the other now drove them to the police station, in the main town, to give their statements.

Abby didn't propose to speak to the odious man at her side unless she absolutely had to. She still hadn't forgiven him for mocking her attempts to protect the crime scene. His mirth at her explanation of how she'd gained her knowledge still rankled.

The car took a corner at speed. Off balance, Abby grabbed hold of the armrest. Jenson's warm body weight immediately pinned her against the window.

"Sorry luv." He pushed himself upright. "There's not much room in here with the goodies taking up so much of the space." He gestured towards the packs of bottled water, cola and cigarettes taking up most of the seat behind the driver. "Looks like our guys were out collecting supplies when they got our call."

Despite her intention not to say anything to him, the words, "I'd kill for a bottle of that water," sprung from her lips before she'd time to assess what she was saying. "Oh sorry, I didn't mean..." Embarrassment heated her cheeks, "God that was a terrible thing to say in the circumstances. I didn't think." Unable to look at him, she gazed out of the window.

"It's okay. I know what you mean. I could do with a drink myself. Although I think I need something a lot stronger than water."

"Me too." She turned to give him a brief smile. He might annoy the hell out of her but when he turned on the charm... Animosity melting slightly, she attempted to see the situation from his point of view. In a way she could understand his attitude. He'd lost a member of his crew, someone he probably knew quite well. He'd been knocked out and suspected of murder. Plus, he couldn't remember what had happened – or so he maintained. Perhaps her attitude hadn't helped either.

"How old was poor Willie?"

"Not sure. I think he was in his late forties but couldn't swear to it." He breathed deeply. "God it's hot and cramped in here."

"Who do you think killed him? Why would anyone do such a terrible thing?" Abby mused out loud.

"God knows! He was a nice chap and everyone liked him. He worked for me for several years and I've never had any reason to think he was anything other than an ordinary guy." He shook his head. "Ouch. Wish I hadn't done that, my head's pounding." Scowling, he rubbed two fingers over his forehead in an effort to sooth the pain.

Abby sighed. "I hope the police catch his killer soon."

"Me too, for both our sakes."

Nodding agreement, she resumed her contemplation of the scenery. White houses, many with bright blue doors, olive groves, glimpses of ocean and small herds of wild goats slid by without Abby being able to enjoy the sight.

Travelling in this police car was totally bizarre, the past hour so surreal, she was having trouble believing that she was actually awake.

"Are you on holiday on your own?" Jensen broke into her thoughts. His pained expression indicated he didn't really care whether she was or not. Perhaps he sought distraction to take his mind off returning queasiness? Abby pushed disappointment to one side. Why should she care whether he was interested in her or not? It wasn't as if she would ever see him again after today.

Still it wouldn't hurt to try and take his mind of his headache.

"I'm afraid so. My sister, Jenny, should be with me but she broke her ankle in two places the day before yesterday and the doctor told her not to fly in case of DVT. She insisted that I came on my own because we've had this holiday booked for months and she didn't want me to miss out." Realising this sounded a bit odd she felt the need to explain. "We've been here lots of times before so we knew I'd be alright. I refused at first, but when our mother added her pennyworth to the argument I gave in." She shrugged, sighing deeply. "I wish I'd stayed at home now."

At her side Jensen flexed the arm jammed up against containers and winced. His failure to comment led her to believe he hadn't bothered to listen to her.

How rude!

"God, I could do with some pain killers, my head feels ready to burst," he ground out.

A police car screamed past going in the opposite direction, horns honked in greeting, the noise vibrating around the small space. Jensen gasped in pain.

"Guess that's the cavalry on the way to the crime scene," Abby remarked, jerking her thumb at the retreating car.

The police car careered around another corner. Jensen's body crushed against her again, causing the door handle to dig into her side.

Hot, squashed, her side aching, Abby pushed Jensen upright. "Are you okay?" Concern laced her words – he didn't look too good.

"Apart from my head splitting," Jensen struggled upright, "and the fact I'm fighting the nausea that's threatening to overwhelm me."

"Oh no!"

"Oh yes! Earlier, when I awoke on your kitchen floor, I only just made it into the bathroom before throwing up several times. I felt half dead so I stuck my head under the shower to try to bring myself around. When I saw my blood flowing down the plughole, you can imagine my surprise. I was examining my wound when you arrived."

"Why don't you rest your eyes?" she suggested sympathetically.

Relaxing his head on the leather support he allowed his eyes to close.

Within seconds he sat up. "Oh God that's made me feel worse!"

"What's wrong?"

"Closing my eyes is like looking down a kaleidoscope. The colours I saw flickering behind my lids made my stomach heave even more." He swallowed and took several deep breaths.

"I've got some paracetamol in my bag if you could manage to take them without water," Abby offered, alarmed by the expression on his face and how pale he looked under his tan.

Even ill he retained a sort of classic beauty, his sculptured lips the only colour in his wan face. God, if he vomited in this small space, then she would too. She would not be able to help herself. She could not bear to see anyone being sick, she invariably joined in.

"No thanks, if you could just roll down the window."

"It's alright sir," said the driver, who obviously listened to their whole conversation. "We have arrived."

The car swerved into a vacant parking space, coming to a jarring halt in front of a sign marked, 'POLICE CARS ONLY', in both Greek and English.

Grateful the journey was over; Abby stepped out into a busy square. Early dusk cloaked the sky in a flimsy, pink tinted, grey mantle. Restaurants and brightly lit shops vied for customers. Small white lights adorned a number of trees, sparkling like bright stars as the branches swayed in the gentle breeze. Colourful goods crammed the covered areas outside supermarkets and gift shops alike, tempting customers to look and buy. The wonderful smell of Greek food filled the air. Abby's mouth watered. Planning to have an early dinner at her resort, she'd not ordered anything to eat on the plane.

Herded by the policeman, Abby followed a swaying Jensen into the police station which was sandwiched between a classy restaurant fronted by tall Grecian pillars, and a small, traditional taverna with a black-board menu outside. Glancing at the board she had time to note that their prices were reasonable. Perhaps she could eat there when the police had taken her statement?

Jensen's colour returned slightly as be breathed in the coolness of the police stations air conditioning system. Now they were no longer in a moving car he appeared to have his nausea under control. Abby watched as the police took him away, concerned by the slightly drunken manner in which he seemed to be walking. He disappeared into a nearby interview room and the door closed, blocking off her view.

The reception area of the busy station kept Abby well entertained. The miscreants were mainly tourists, most of them drunk. No-one appeared to have done anything too terrible. The Greeks sounded as though they were arguing. Abby knew from past experience that this probably wasn't the case, they often tended to talk loud and fast accompanied by extravagant hand gestures.

An older man wearing a dark suit and carrying what looked suspiciously like a doctor's bag, entered. A policeman took him to the room where Jensen was being held. Abby glanced at her watch. They had been interviewing him for nearly ten minutes. Hoping he had not taken ill again, she watched for the doctor's return.

Escorted to another interview room a few minutes later, she did not see the doctor leave. The small, almost square, windowless room, painted a dirty grey colour, felt claustrophobic. A darker grey table and four plastic chairs sat in the middle of the room.

Two small bottles of water glistened enticingly from the tabletop. Abby longed to lick the moisture beaded on the outside of the containers. She slid onto the seat indicated and, without being invited, picked up the nearest drink.

Gulping down the much needed liquid she listened to a policeman with three, six pointed stars adorning the epaulet on his shoulder, explain, in excellent English, the procedure for making her statement. A female officer sat watching her from the other seat. Bottle empty, her thirst sated, Abby turned her attention to the matter in hand.

Frustration mounting, she tried to give her account of events amid numerous interruptions and searching questions.

Why didn't they simply write down what she was saying?

Stomach plummeting, like an unwound yoyo, she suddenly understood what was happening.

They were treating her as a suspect.

"Am I under suspicion?" Abby stared across the small, scarred, plastic table in disbelief. "How can you think that, even for a moment? For God's sake my plane didn't land until after four o clock this afternoon. From the look of Mr Thomas he'd been dead for a good while before I arrived."

"It will be up to the pathologist to decide when Mr Thomas died. Until we have that information we cannot make any assumptions."

Eventually her statement was ready. After checking it carefully Abby signed it with a flourish. "Can I go now? I need to find somewhere to spend the night."

Sweeping the paperwork into a heap, the policeman, who'd identified himself as Captain Georgallis, noisily straightened them by tapping the edges on the tabletop before popping them into a manila coloured file. "I'm afraid you are going to have to accept our hospitality until we verify your story."

"What do you mean, 'verify my story'? I haven't been telling you any stories." Her voice rose, "I have only been in this country a matter of hours; you cannot treat me like this." Her temper rocketed taking her fear level with it.

This could not be happening to her!

Rising to his feet, the Captain tucked the folder carefully under his arm. The policewoman stood to lead the way out of the room.

"No!" she shouted. Chair legs squealed along the polished floor as Abby stood up in a rush. "Please listen to me, you cannot lock me up. This is ridiculous, I'm a British citizen. I demand to see someone from the British Embassy."

"Please remain seated, someone will come to take an impression of your fingerprints and then show you to your accommodation shortly. I'm sure this will all be sorted out in due course. In the meantime, it would go better for you if you do as you are told." He walked out into the corridor without a backwards glance.

"What...?" Abby stared at the closed door. Sinking back onto her seat she fumed. Within minutes, her anger spent, a type of post traumatic stress assailed her. Using the back of her hand she swiped away the tears of self pity gathering in her eyes and trembling on her lashes.

The hot meal the policewoman handed into her tiny cell tasted better than she'd expected. Sitting on the narrow bunk she wondered how many hours had gone by since they'd taken her watch and locked her in this small room. Sick of counting the squashed mosquito bodies smearing the, once white, walls while avoiding the sight of other nefarious stains she'd rather not think about, eating made a welcome distraction.

Scraping the last of the bolognaise sauce off the plate with a wooden spoon, the sound of keys jangling, accompanied by firm footsteps, brought her to her feet. Someone was coming her way. Heart pounding with anticipation, she hoped for some good news.

"You are free to go," the young policewoman told her, flinging the door wide. "Follow me. You can collect your things from the desk."

The Custody Officer handed Abbey a clear plastic bag containing her belongings.

"What about my suitcase?" She asked the desk sergeant a few minutes later. "I had to leave it at the apartments, when will I get it back?" Pushing her feet into her flat, cream leather shoes, she reached for her watch.

"I have a suitcase here that may be yours. Please describe it to me."

God this man could get a job scaring kids in the park - did he ever smile?

"It is medium sized, black with a pink bobble tied around the handle so I don't pick someone else's property off the airport carousel by mistake."

He nodded briefly. "Please sign for the items, here, here and here." He pointed to the relevant places.

Abby saw a full description of her case was already listed. The miserable sod knew it belonged to her all along. Perhaps a few hours in his own bloody cells would give him something to be depressed about.

"Thank you." Accompanied by a sugar sweet smile, Abby picked up her handbag and took the handle of her case. The reassuring thrum of trundling suitcase wheels followed her from the station.

CHAPTER FOUR

Outside, the humid Mediterranean evening enveloped her. Hesitating in the semi-darkness, she wondered what to do now. She could not go back to her accommodation. It would probably be cordoned off for days. Would a hotel accept her at this time of night? Having booked direct with the apartment owner, she didn't have a holiday rep to turn to for help.

The menu blackboard had disappeared, the taverna locked up for the night. Lights still shone inside the restaurant with the graceful pillars, although they were obviously closed for the evening. The subdued amber glow threw pretty shadows over the outside tables. The silhouette of a man uncurled from a pavement seat and came towards her. Light from the police station lit his dishevelled, caramel coloured hair – it was Jensen.

"I thought they would never let you go. I was beginning to think that they meant to keep you in all night," he greeted her.

"Have you been waiting for me?"

Silly question - he would not be here otherwise.

Relief surged, she was no longer alone in the virtually deserted darkness.

"Yes for about an hour." A warm hand slid over hers as he took hold of the suitcase handle. Unexpected tremors tingled up her arm at his touch. "I thought you might need somewhere to stay."

"Do you know of somewhere?" Haunted by visions of having to sleep on a sun lounger on the beach, the thought of being secure in a comfortable bed was wonderful especially with a killer on the loose.

"Yes, my boat." Carrying her case, as though it weighed nothing, he made for the nearby taxi rank where two drivers leaned against one of the vehicles smoking, their cigarette ends glowing bright red in the darkness.

Running to keep up with him, Abby croaked. "Your boat? You want me to stay with you on your boat?" How could she agree, she'd only known him a few hours? It wasn't as though she knew anything about him, apart from that he'd lost his memory - he might have conveniently forgotten he'd murdered his crewmember.

Surprised by her reaction he stopped. Swivelling to look at her he enquired. "Do you have a problem with that?" His blue eyes reflected a nearby amber streetlight; they glittered in the night like a cat's. Abby swallowed, suddenly intimidated by his stare. The man facing her oozed authority, a man used to people doing what he told them to do.

Oh lord!

"Yes... No... I don't know."

Placing the case at his feet he folded his arms. "What's the problem?" His stance dared her to argue with his suggestion that she stay with him.

Bloody hell, how to get out of this one?

"Only a few hours ago I thought you were a murderer. Now you expect me to calmly come with you. I don't know you," words spilled from her mouth as she spoke her thoughts out loud.

Anger flittered across his beautiful face. This was a man used to being obeyed without question.

"So you don't trust me." His expression changed to hurt surprise.

"Well no – of course I don't. I don't know anything about you."

What did he expect?

"You know I didn't kill Willy. If the police had one scrap of evidence I wouldn't be here talking to you now. Don't worry, we won't be alone, the rest of the crew are on board and I have more than one spare bedroom. You will be perfectly safe, I promise you." His voice sounded reasonable, his body language challenged her to defy him.

There was a murderer out there - if it wasn't Jensen then it could be the missing crew member. Dare she take a chance and stay on Jensen's yacht?

"What happened to the other man, did you find out?"

He frowned. "What other man?"

"The other crew member who came ashore with you."

"Ah! Parky! Well he's another matter. The police are out looking for him as we speak." He hesitated before admitting, "I don't want to go there. I've been worried about Parky turning up dead ever since I remembered the three of us left the yacht together. God I wish I could remember what happened."

"I would feel a lot happier if you could," Abby whispered.

"Look I'm frustrated, tired and my head's still aching, I'm past caring whether you come with me or not - so much for waiting for you and trying to play nice."

She got the impression he wasn't in the habit of 'playing nice'. "That's not very polite."

"Are you coming with me or not?" He suddenly ground out.

Abby dithered. *Did she really have a choice?*

"Well?"

"Will I really be safe?" Her thoughts escaped again.

"That's not very polite." He repeated her earlier words back to her.

"I'm just asking."

"And I'm just telling." He glared at her.

Abby quickly made up her mind. "Yes I'll take you up on your offer. Thank you." Wavering she continued to hold back.

"What now?" He almost snatched her case off the ground.

"Are we going to the little harbour for the launch?" She didn't really fancy making her way along the beach in the dark, or sailing at night on a pitch black sea in a teeny, little boat.

"No, I've asked my captain to moor her at a small town up the coast so we can walk straight on board from the quay." He tapped his foot. "Well?"

"Great. Thanks. Lead on." Quashing her misgivings, she took the last few steps to the taxi rank.

Fastening her seat belt, she glanced across at Jensen sitting at the other window seat in the back of the vehicle. Feeling more relaxed now she'd made her decision she wanted to talk.

"What sort of questions did the police ask you?"

Abby's stomach somersaulted at the brief lopsided grin he gave her before the interior light dimmed leaving them cocooned in semidarkness.

God he was one good looking bloke.

"One's I couldn't answer mostly." He rubbed his hand over his face.

"Funny." She smiled. "Seriously, I had a pretty hard time of it. My fingerprints were all over the frying pan handle, they were convinced I'd whacked you one although they doubted that I'd have had the strength to kill poor Willy. Apparently because you verified that I arrived at the apartments after you came around, I got off the hook and they let me go."

"You're welcome. As soon as I sat down in the interview room they gave me a bottle of water which I gulped down, it was so cold it when straight to my head and I passed out before they could begin interrogating me. Once their doctor confirmed that I was suffering from concussion and it was highly unlikely, if not impossible, that I'd brained myself with the frying pan then wiped my prints off it, they decided to let me go as soon as I told them what I could remember – which wasn't much. Apparently your prints were the only ones they found.

"Of course your statement that I'd been honestly shocked at the sight of Willie's corpse also helped. Thanks for that." He sighed. "Thank God. I don't think I could have got through a night in one of their cells. I still feel wobbly. My head hurts, my stomach's not at all happy and I keep thinking I'm going to faint." He gave a grunt of laughter. "God I sound such a whinge. Normally I would be trying to impress a beautiful girl like you."

Oh wow he thinks I'm beautiful!

"You deserve a good moan; you're obviously in a bad way."

"Cheers."

"What made them think you didn't hit yourself with the pan?"

"Because of where my injury is and the angle needed to strike the blow. I'd have had to put my left arm in an impracticable position to hit myself with any force, with a heavy frying pan in my hand it would be near impossible to knock myself out." Sighing he went on, "Thank goodness they brought the doctor so quickly, once he ruled out the possibility of self harm they did not keep me much longer."

"I was asked a lot of questions about the state you were in when I first saw you. I told them your wound was still bleeding a little and you could not remember anything."

He leaned over covering Abby's hand, lying on the seat between them, with his own much larger one. "The doctor assures me that my memory will return but it will probably be a little at a time. I will just have to be patient for now, apparently stress delays the process. I like the feel of your hand by the way. In fact I like all of you."

A brief squeeze and the warm, masculine hand moved away.

Flushed with pleasure and something more, coherent thought fled.

They travelled in comfortable silence for a while before Jensen spoke again. "What do you do when you're not on holiday?"

"Work." She could just make out his tired smile in the darkness. "I'm a secretary for a toy manufacturer," she continued. "I love it, I really do. It's fun mostly. Especially when one of the designers is working on something new and we all get to play with it to see what we think."

Chuckling she elaborated. "This one time, Leon, a junior designer who had not been with us very long, invented this whoopee cushion which made rude noises to the tune of 'Bob the Builder'." Laughing at the memory she finished, "Of course it wasn't suitable."

Jensen's smile flashed once more. "I would have liked to hear that."

He sounded weary, Abby looked across at him. Brow furrowed with pain, eye lids at half mast, he appeared exhausted.

"Why don't you close your eyes and try to rest?" She suggested.

Gratefully, Jensen did just that.

Quarter of an hour later they alighted from the taxi at a large marina. Fish restaurants lined the perimeter, all closed at this time of night. The faint, delectable aroma of recently cooked meals wafted around them. The dark outlines of several large boats loomed offshore, their mooring lights glistening on the water as the vessels danced sedately in the light wind.

Cabin lights shone from only one boat, casting long shimmering rivers of radiance over the sea.

"Is that your yacht?" Abby pointed to the lit boat.

"Yes that's her. I can't wait to get to bed, I'm sure I'll be fine after a good nights sleep." He looked bushed. "Watch your footing, I've been here before and some of this planking is uneven," he warned.

Carrying her case Jensen led the way along the wooden jetty towards his yacht, which was even more striking up close than it had looked from her apartment balcony. A small ramp gave access to the main deck.

Bloody hell, this guy was seriously rich.

"Wow, I'm impressed. What's she called?" Abby tried to read the name bobbing gently in the darkness just below the walkway underneath their feet. Jensen seemed to be taking a long time to answer. Glancing at his chalk white face she grabbed his arm. Straining to keep him upright, she shouted for assistance. Her case thudded onto the planks as he slumped against her.

The jetty dipped marginally as a large man leapt ashore. Pushing his shoulder under Jensen's other arm he took most of his weight. Abby struggled to hold up her end as together they helped him aboard. Another man quickly took her place. Supported between the two men, his feet barely touching the ground, Jensen was propelled across the deck.

Stepping back onto the short pier Abby hauled her suitcase aboard. Pulling up the handle she swiftly set off in the direction she'd last seen Jensen. Hurrying through a huge dimly lit stateroom, she followed the men through a lighted doorway into the bedroom beyond.

"You must be Abby," the big man said after depositing Jensen's prone body on the huge bed. "I'm Captain Simms. Mr Stone said to get a bedroom ready for you. I told him he should have spent the night in hospital but you can't tell him anything. He always does just as he wants." He shook his head. "This way Miss, I'll show you to your room."

Taking a last look at Jensen she quickly averted her eyes. The other crew member, wearing a similar outfit to the one Willie had worn, was busy undressing Jensen's apparently unconscious body. The brief glimpse of a toned, tanned torso wrung a mental 'wow!' from her tired brain. Jensen was all muscle with not a pick of fat in sight.

The captain wore a jacket and shirt in the same colours as the man undressing Jensen and the newly dead, Willie had worn. Abby realised it must be some sort of uniform. At close range she could see a name embroidered in gold across the top of the dark jacket pocket, 'Cassandra Rose'. Her earlier question answered, she now knew the name of the yacht.

CHAPTER FIVE

Warmth and sunlight streamed in though the window, Abby stretched languorously loving the feel of the soft mattress beneath her. Turning over she snuggled down in the large bed again. Amazingly after all the trauma of the previous day she'd not expected to be able to sleep, but she'd gone out like a light. Still feeling tired she closed her eyes again. It was no good, her bladder refused to allow her to rest.

Sighing she swung her feet onto the floor, which thrummed and swayed softly beneath her soles. Wiggling her toes with pleasure, she picked up her toiletry bag and made her way to the roomy en-suite bathroom.

Showered and dressed in lightweight blue crop trousers and matching sun-top, she picked up her hairbrush. In the mirror her unusual, emerald green eyes stared back with more than a hint of trepidation. Brushing her jaw length, dark, bobbed hair she wondering what would happen next. Should she go and find Jensen?

A brisk knock at the door took the decision from her.

"Come in."

The large captain, she'd met last night, entered the room. "Mr Stone would like you to have breakfast with him in the main stateroom, Miss," he announced.

"That sounds good to me. I take it he has recovered." With a last glance in the mirror she followed the captain into the short corridor.

"That remains to be seen, Miss."

"What do you mean?" Grasping the beech wood banister she prepared to mount the stairs to the upper deck.

"Concussion can be a strange thing, Miss. To my mind he should have spent the night under medical supervision."

"I expect you're right. He looked dreadful before he passed out." She thought a moment. "I am sorry about what happened to Willy. It must be awful to lose a friend like that."

"He was a really good man, everybody liked him, he didn't deserve to die like that, Miss."

"I'm sure he didn't." The smooth, gleaming, warm wood under her hand came to an end. They'd reached the upper deck.

"Has the other man been found yet?"

"Parky? No, not yet. We are all pretty worried I can tell you, Miss. He's a very pleasant, clever young man with his whole life in front of him." He shook his head sorrowfully.

"I'm very sorry I seem to have forgotten your name."

"Simms, Miss. My name is Bob Simms."

"Mine's Abby." She smiled at him. "I'd prefer you used my name rather than call me Miss."

"As you wish... Abby." He smiled. "Here we are."

In daylight, the stateroom took her breath away. Pale cream carpet, buff coloured leather sofas and armchairs, glowing walnut woodwork with matching coffee and occasional tables. Two places were set at one end of an outsized oval dining table around which ten high backed chairs stood like toy soldiers on parade.

Lounging in a large easy chair, Jenson smiled at her.

"Oh this is lovely." Abby exclaimed as she noted the classy décor.

Grinning, Jensen rose, moving forward to greet her.

"Hi."

"Hi." Sudden shyness assailed her. It wasn't every day she found herself on a posh yacht with a handsome, sexy and obviously rich man she hardly knew. "You look a lot better today." *Understatement! He looked gorgeous.*

"Yeah, just a small headache this morning. Sorry I passed out on you. Bob told me what happened."

"It's okay. Have you remembered anything yet?"

"No. Not yet. Racking my brains only makes my head hurt more. The doctor who examined me last night at the police station said not to rush things," he reminded her.

They stared at each other, mutual attraction initiating a slight tension.

China rattled, cutlery jangled. The small silence broken, Abby glanced towards the sound. The polo-shirted man, who'd undressed Jensen the night before, placed cereal bowls on the table.

"I hope you're hungry. I ordered cereal followed by a full-English." Jensen grinned again, looking more like a small boy than a high flying stockbroker.

"Famished," she admitted, admiring his boyish smile and the way his tanned skin crinkled slightly at the corners of his eyes. "I would have thought you'd be steering well clear of frying pans," she joked.

Laughing, he replied, "Well I did wonder about that but I never could resist the smell of bacon cooking." He pulled out her chair and made sure she was comfortable.

Abby loved the gesture, enjoying the luxury of being treated like a lady.

Seeming only half interested in his food, Jenson stared as though having difficulty taking his eyes off her.

Abby squirmed with embarrassment under his piercing blue gaze. What was with him this morning?

Seeming to realise the effect he was having, he gave his signature lopsided grin. "Yesterday concussion clouded my vision. Today I can clearly see what a lovely young woman you are."

Her slight blush of confusion deepened when his steward, Mark, placed the pale gold, damask napkin over her knees.

"You're not used to being pampered are you? You know you're a refreshing change from the women I normally date." He grinned. "Not that this breakfast constitutes a date of course," he added hurriedly.

Embarrassed and painfully aware of Jensen's continued appraisal, Abby glanced out of the window while the steward cleared the cereal bowls. Frowning, she pivoted to look out of the window on the other side of the room.

What the hell?

"We are no longer in the harbour." Horrified surprise laced her words.

"No," he confirmed, digging into the hot food Mark placed before him.

"Thank you." Distracted, she accepted the full plate from the steward and automatically cut a small piece of egg. Worry gnawed, how could he sit there so calmly?

Leaning forward she hissed at Jensen. "I don't know about you but I was ordered not to leave the country."

"So was I." He chewed and swallowed. "Don't worry; as long as we stay within the three mile limit we aren't breaking the rules."

Unbelievable!

"I hope not." Alarm jangled as fear of the possible consequences of this little trip caused her temper to surface. "A few hours in a Greek prison cell made me realise I don't want to repeat the experience." She waved her knife at him.

He grinned at her anger. "I wish you wouldn't point that knife, it's taking me all my time not to cross my legs."

"I mean it," she threatened. "Turn this boat around at once."

"I don't need too. There are a couple of policemen on board who are currently questioning the crew." Lifting his coffee cup he took a small sip.

She knew a moment's relief before alarm resurfaced. "What? Why?" The piece of egg still perched on her fork slid down to her plate with a soft splat.

"Because they believe it's quite possible Parky, or one of the other crew members, murdered Willy."

"Oh!" Food forgotten, a knot of apprehension filled the space where her stomach should be.

Shivering at the thought of being trapped on the yacht with a possible murderer, her voice quivered. "Who do they suspect?"

"Everybody at the moment," smiling in an attempt to reassure, he continued, "it's okay, honestly. Just relax and enjoy the trip. Once the crew have been eliminated, and I'm sure they will be, we are going to pick up the launch and have a scout around for Parky." Pointing his fork at her meal, he suggested. "Eat your food before it gets cold luv. I believe its cook's turn to be interviewed next so he won't be available to warm it up for you."

Slightly mollified, she did as he recommended. The way he pronounced the word 'love' did funny things to her insides. His diction so correct the rest of the time yet that one word with it's slightly Northern inflection seemed to fit him perfectly.

Later, arms folded on the deck rail, Abby stood drinking in the pretty scenery as the land slid slowly by. Although fairly barren, the Greek countryside had a raw beauty that never failed to impress. Imposing cliffs dropped down to secluded beaches where turquoise waters gently lapped golden sand. Dropping her gaze to the sea she watched the foamy seawater arrow alongside before disappearing behind the boat. Jensen leaned beside her, so close his body heat warmed her arm.

Terribly aware that being so near to Jensen did funny fluttery things to her stomach, she sought for something to say.

"How will you get a boat this size into the small harbour? The entrance is narrow and only small fishing boats can cope with the shallow water. There are also some large rocks to navigate." She showed off her knowledge of the area.

"We'll use a smaller boat to go ashore."

"Will you go?"

"No."

"No?"

"Some of the other members of the crew, his friends, have offered to go and help the police search."

"Shouldn't you join them?"

"I'll go later if they don't find him first time around." He sighed. "I hope to God they do."

"So do I..." She hesitated. "You don't think...?" She allowed the rest of the sentence to hang. Jensen didn't answer, his body tensed at her side. Abby rubbed the arm next to her in a gesture of comfort, loving the feel of the fine soft hairs of his forearm under her fingers. Her eyes still on the scenery she absently started to play with them, gently running single strands between her thumb and forefinger. His low murmur of appreciation snapped her back to the present.

"Oh, sorry!" Mortified, she snapped her hand away as though stung, her cheeks burned.

"Don't apologise, I was enjoying the sensation." He sounded a little husky.

Twisting around, Abby stared into brilliant blue eyes only inches away. Long dark lashes swept down and back as he blinked.

God he was so sexy!

Hot blood scorched her cheeks. Suddenly breathless, warmth surged through her veins to pool in her groin. Unable to look away she watched his eyes darken, knowing that his obvious longing must be mirrored in her own.

Mesmerized, she leaned towards him. Warm male lips engulfed hers with undisguised hunger, moving and shaping until their mouths fit perfectly. Desire sizzled like molten lava. Large hands grasped her waist pulling her against his hard chest.

Wow!

"Excuse me Mr Stone." said a voice from behind them.

Her lips suddenly bereft, Jensen's sigh of annoyance blew warm air against her ear, sending another quiver of delight down her spine.

"Yes Bob. What's the problem?" He spun to face his captain.

"We are nearly there. Do you want me to ready *Waverunner Two?*"

"Yes please. I will be there directly." Turning to Abby he whispered. "Later."

Still trembling with the promise of that deliciously evocative word, she watched him walk away. What was wrong with her? She wasn't in the habit of kissing men she hardly knew. In fact she hadn't been in the habit of kissing men for a while. *Bloody hell!* What had possessed her to blatantly offer her mouth like that?

Placing her fingertips lightly on her lips she relived the experience. Never had a kiss affected her in the way Jensen's had. He managed to covey not just sexual need but also gentleness and respect. Something special had just happened and she wanted more, much, much more!

Curious, Abby followed the two men to where other crew members waited beside a smart motorboat. Watching Jensen dishing out orders with easy authority she was only too aware of the differences between them. This was a man born to be obeyed. A man who wore responsibly with the casual confidence that came with experience and long term wealth. What would a man like him know about having to choose between buying lunch or bagging a bargain pair of desperately needed shoes? Sighing, she acknowledged that a romantic relationship with Jensen could only be on a short-term basis. Did she really want that? Holiday romances had never been her thing.

The launch was placed in its own little niche tucked into the side of the yacht. An electronic crane and winch stood ready to swing out and lower the boat into the sea. Jensen touched the control panel and the door lifted out and up in a somewhat jerky manner. A warm breeze swept through the area dispelling the faint smell of diesel.

"We seem to have a problem." Stretching, Jensen reached up and pushed the juddering door fully open. His shirt rode up giving Abby a brief glimpse of his hard, flat abdomen. Her own stomach clenched as a rush of hot lust stabbed her innards.

Taking a deep breath she controlled her surprising reaction. Nothing must be allowed to happen again. A rich, handsome man like Jensen could have any woman he wanted, and probably did. She did not intend to be one of a string of conquests even if he did draw her like a moth to a flame - everyone knew what happened to the poor, hapless moth.

"Over there. Look," Bob suddenly shouted.

Snapped out of her reverie, Abby followed Bob's pointing finger to where a pale blue launch skimmed gracefully over the glittering, turquoise sea towards them.

Unable to believe his eyes, Jensen's hand dropped, swinging around he dashed out of the garage-like room with Abby and Bob close on his heels.

Waverunner One sped nearer, a lone man at the wheel.

"It's Parky!" Bob cried. Relief etched his lined, weather-beaten face.

CHAPTER SIX

Several crew members rushed to the other side of the yacht, Abby realised that there must be a matching mooring-garage-thingy over there. It seemed everyone wanted to help bring the incoming boat aboard.

At her side Jensen whispered. "Thank God. Oh thank God." Relief lit his handsome features. "I've never been so pleased to see anyone in my life. Now I might get some answers to what happened at the apartments yesterday."

Shortly, a tall, slightly dishevelled young man appeared over the side of the boat. Dark hair, long on top, fell over one brown eye giving him an engaging, rakish look.

"Are you okay, Parky?" Bob was the first to reach his side.

"No worse than any other morning after a good tank full the night before." He grinned.

Seeing Jensen, Parky hesitated giving him a slightly puzzled look, followed by a disarming smile, before walking across the deck. "I'm sorry Sir. I believe I owe you an apology."

"You certainly do. However glad I am that you've finally turned up, there are some things I need to say to you." Jensen's tone brooked no argument.

"Of course, I can explain everything." Shrugging, palms upward Parky attempted to look contrite.

Several crew members started talking at once. It appeared everyone wanted to hear what he had to say. A valued crew member and friend had been brutally murdered and anything Parky could tell them that might point to who had committed the crime was important.

"That's enough," Jensen barked, effectively silencing the commotion.

"It's only natural, we all want to hear where he's been," Bob reasoned.

"Yeah, that's right," a tall gangly man spoke up.

"In private. This way," Jensen addressed Parky. He jutted his chin at the men standing around grinning at the newcomer. "The rest of you back to your duties. Bob kindly have the launch checked over." Noticing Abby, he hesitated as though wondering what to do about her. His inherent good manners surfaced. "Abby, as you've probably already guessed, this is the elusive Parky." He waved his hand towards the young man. "Neil I'd like you to meet Abby... she's a... friend of mine."

"Hello, I'm pleased to see you alive and well." Abby smiled.

Neil raised the one eyebrow on view. "Thanks... I think?" He gave her a puzzled look.

"Perhaps you had better come with me too." Jensen suggested to Abby.

Reaching the stateroom, Jensen nodded towards a leather chair. "Sit down Neil," he ordered, seating himself opposite.

Abby flopped down on a nearby cream coloured sofa, grateful for the large ceiling fan whirring above her head. The temperature had risen sharply as the morning progressed. It would be lovely to be lying in the sun reading her book but she wasn't going anywhere until she heard this young man's story. His temporary disappearance had caused her problems. She deserved to hear what he had to say for himself.

Fingers tapping the arms of his chair, Jensen stared across at Neil Parks as though wondering where to begin.

"You looked surprised to see me. Why was that I wonder?"

"When I saw the Waverunner in the harbour I assumed you were ashore for the day." He grinned. "So who have I stranded by taking the launch?"

"No-one. Why did you take it if you thought someone might need it?"

"I figured that I was late enough already and it would be better to report in as soon as possible. Someone could easily take the launch back to shore to pick you up." Parky spread his hands.

"You've been gone since yesterday afternoon. Would you like to tell me what you've been up to?"

"Yes of course. Sorry sir." He brushed his wayward hair away from his face. "How did you get back to the boat without using the launch sir?" Neil casually leaned back in his seat crossing his long legs.

"It's a long story. I'd like to hear what you have to say for yourself

44

first," Jensen reasserted.

"Where do you want me to start, sir?" If he realised the trouble he was in, he showed no sign of it.

"What happened after I left you and Willy at the harbour?" Jensen leaned forward, eager to glean any information that might help him to recover his memory.

Appearing confused Neil sat upright, automatically uncrossing his legs. At last he seemed to realise that there was more to this cross-examination than his extended shore leave. "Excuse me sir, but have you asked Willy?"

"I'm asking you."

Neil pushed his errant hair out of his eyes again revealing a serious expression. Staring straight at Jensen as though trying to figure out what was so important, he began to speak. "We tied up and walked into the village for a drink. There was a taverna overlooking the beach, it was hot and we needed a drink so we had a couple of beers.

Being thirsty, I soon downed mine. Willie likes to take his time, so I decided to have a few ouzos while I waited for him to finish up." he gave an appealing smile, looking like a naughty child caught with his hand in the biscuit tin, "quite a few ouzos in fact."

"And then?" Jensen prompted.

"And then..." Briefly he hung his head. "Willy said I'd drunk too much to be useful." He sighed. "It was hot... We were sitting in the shade looking at a fantastic view... I guess I got carried away," he excused himself. "Anyway he told me to wait where I was while he made sure the launch was still alright. We weren't due to meet you for nearly an hour and I was to try and sober up. I think he was disgusted with me.

"After maybe half an hour I went after him. I'd left my mobile phone in my cabin so I couldn't contact him. He wasn't at the launch so I decided to return to the taverna and wait. Err..." He glanced at Abby before continuing. "Actually sir on the way back from the harbour I noticed you going up the steps of those apartments which overlook the beach next to the harbour."

"You actually saw me?" Jensen's voice rose in astonishment. "Whereabouts was I? Who was I with?"

Looking baffled by the quick-fire questions, Neil cleared his throat.

"You were on your own around the back of the building, sir. When I noticed you, you were nearly at the top of the stairs leading to the upper floor."

"My God!" Jensen sprang to his feet, a brief image of himself hurrying towards Abby's apartment swiftly imposed itself on his mind like a light being flicked quickly on and off in a pitch dark room. There was no time to take in details and he was left with a general impression that he was meeting someone.

"Is there a problem sir?" Neil used the armrests to lever himself out of his chair, concern lacing his words.

"No, I'm fine." Jensen motioned for Neil to resume his seat before lowering himself back into his own. In control again, he asked. "So then what did you do?"

"Well you can't sit in a taverna and not drink so I hit the ouzo again. Figuring you and Willy were obviously busy and Willy would come and collect me when you were ready, I sat back and relaxed.

"Then this really pretty English waitress I'd been flirting with for most of the afternoon, said she was nearly finished her shift and would I like to go back to her place... Well put it this way I didn't need asking twice." He gave Jensen a cheeky grin. "I don't know what she gave me to drink but I didn't wake up until a couple of hours ago. Sorry sir, I can see you are very annoyed that I didn't turn up. I hope my absence didn't cause you and Mr Thomas too much inconvenience."

"In a way I suppose it did." Jensen leaned towards Parky concern showing in his bearing. The ceiling fans whirred softly in the short silence before he spoke. "Neil, I have to tell you that Willy is dead."

Abby had never believed that, apart from playacting, jaws actually dropped, but Parky's did. He gaped at Jensen in disbelief.

"Dead? Willy's dead? How? When? Why?"

"He was murdered. Strangled in fact." Pain washed over Jensen's face. "I found him in Abby's apartment."

Parky glanced at Abby before turning back to Jensen, puzzlement creasing his brow. "I don't understand. What was he doing in your friend's apartment?"

"That's what I'm trying to find out."

"I understand Mr Parks has materialised," A deep voice said in very slightly accented English.

Jensen and Parky rose in unison. Abby stood a few seconds later.

"I'm Mr Parks," Neil told the policeman who'd interviewed Abby the previous evening.

CHAPTER SEVEN

Abby stretched out on the sundeck covered in her favourite sun-cream and agreeably aware that the comfortable, coffee coloured, mattress on the lounger set off her new cream and brown striped bikini beautifully. Hot sun danced along her skin, glinted off the yachts brass rails and sparkled across the sea.

The gentle hum of the boat's engine reverberated rhythmically in her ears and the mixed aroma of warm leather and salty sea filled her nostrils.

This was the life!

Jensen had a few things to do before he was able to join her, giving Abby a chance to enjoy a little bit of peace and quiet.

"Can I get you anything? Drink? Snack?"

Opening her eyes, Abby found Parky ogling her, the long bar of his shadow shading her neck and face. Sitting up, she placed her hand protectively over her cleavage.

"Where's Mark?"

Surely it was the steward's job to offer refreshment, not this good looking, over friendly young man?

"The police are speaking to him. Cook asked me to see if you were okay." Parky dropped onto the adjacent lounger where he sat fanning his face with his hand. "It's pretty hot out here today," he remarked, his role as steward obviously forgotten, his bold look taking in her nearly nude state.

God another man too nice looking for his own good! Forcing herself not to blush at his admiring stare, she asked. "Did the police give you a hard time?"

"Pretty much. They are checking out my alibi. God, if I'd known I would need one I'd have made myself more conspicuous. Maybe started a fight or something." He grinned before sobering swiftly. "Sorry I didn't mean to be flippant, I'm gutted Willy has been murdered. The police wanted to know if Willy had any enemies on board the yacht. Of course I told them that he hadn't.

"They asked about recent arguments and such. I had to tell them about the dressing down the Boss gave him the other day for sloppy work though. Willy was mad and answered back, saying that it hadn't been his fault. As First Mate it was his job to make sure we kept the decks and outside stuff clean and tidy. Typically, Willie wouldn't tell Mr Stone who'd made the mistake. It turned into quite a row."

Heart sinking at hearing the words argument and Boss linked to Willie, she had to ask. "So Jensen and Willy had words?"

"Yeah that's putting it mildly. A few of us thought Willy would walk, he was so mad. Course no-one came forward to admit blame. There was a stinking atmosphere for the rest of that day and most of the next." He grinned again. "If you don't want anything I'll get myself off, I'm already in the bad books." Standing he placed his hands on his thighs and shook his slacks straight. "Maybe we can talk again later."

Noticing Jensen's head and shoulders emerging from the stairway, she quickly gave Parky a reason for being on the sundeck. "I'd like a glass of iced water please." Having only met him a few hours ago, his penchant for getting into hot water was already becoming apparent. His obvious youth together with his cheeky, easy manner invoked her protective gene.

"Everything okay?" Jensen gave Abby an appreciative look, taking in the delightful picture she made in her eye-catching bikini.

"Would you like anything Sir? I'm standing in for Mark at Bilbo's request."

"Bilbo?" Abby immediately imagined a small man with big hairy feet. She'd read 'The Hobbit' several times.

"Bill Bowman." Jensen and Parky answered together.

"The cook," Jensen supplied.

"Oh yes, I see." She smiled. "Does everyone on this yacht have a nickname?"

"Pretty much." The younger man grinned.

"That will be all thank you," Jensen interrupted before Parky could elaborate.

Suddenly shy, Abby sat up linking her arms around her legs; she rested her chin on her raised knees. "Have you come to join me?" Now that they were alone the memory of their kiss warmed her cheeks, sending spirals of heat to every part of her body.

"Sorry, no. Not yet. I'd love to be able to." His eyes darkened, dampened down desire apparent. "You look gorgeous in that brief bikini."

Face heating at the unconcealed need showing in his tense features, Abby looked down pretending to examine her bright pink, nail-varnished toes.

"I love it when you blush." His sexy voice grazed her nerve ends sending scorching heat to her groin.

"I suppose you're very busy." She hardly recognised her own voice, she sounded so husky.

"Not by choice. I came to tell you the police want to speak to me again. I guess Neil must have told them that he saw me going towards your apartment. I've asked Bob to turn the boat around and head back to port. Apparently after talking to me they will be finished their investigations for today."

Looking up she said. "It's not looking good for you is it?"

Sighing, Jensen shook his head. "I'm not sure. They already know that I was there. I think they might be hoping I've remembered something new."

"And have you?"

"I have a vague memory of walking towards the apartment, but nothing more. When I saw Parky I half expected he would be able to tell me what happened. Guess I'll have to wait for my memory to return of its own accord."

"Do you think they will need to speak to me again?"

"Nothing has been said but I wouldn't rule it out. I have a feeling we will all be asked to repeat our stories many times before they are satisfied we're telling the truth." He smiled sadly. "I hope they catch Willy's killer and string him up."

"I heard you and Willie argued recently," Abby probed, hoping for a reasonable explanation.

"Yes. Someone had carelessly left a broom lying across one of the top steps leading down from the upper deck. The handle had somehow jammed itself sideways. We found the brush head later at the bottom of the stairs. In the dark the handle would have been nearly impossible to spot by anyone descending.

"If someone had tripped they could've broken their neck or at least had a nasty accident. It was Willie's job to ensure the deckhands kept the walkways clear. In the end I had to admit that I admired him for protecting his team, although he was really annoyed the culprit didn't come forward to admit that he was to blame."

"So Willie was mad at the person who left the broom there and not you?"

"Yes." Narrowing his eyes he looked at Abby suspiciously. "Who told you about the incident?"

Oh no!

"I don't like to say." Her earlier blush was nothing compared to the heat in her cheeks now. Lowering her head, she gazed at her feet again.

Jensen chuckled. "I've guessed. There are a few big mouths aboard but the biggest one is always Neil."

Relieved he wasn't annoyed, she smiled up at him. "It's good Parky has turned up isn't it?"

A genuine smile lit his face. "Yes. Yes it is, very good indeed."

Beyond Jensen a man appeared carrying a tray. "Here's my drink. It looks like the police are done with Mark."

Glancing at his steward, placing Abby's water on a low table, Jensen nodded. "Yes. Well, I'll go and see what the Captain wants with me. I'll catch up with you later." An apologetic smile lit his face before he strode away.

Later, wrapped in a large, multi-coloured beach-towel, Abby walked to the upper deck rail to watch the yacht dock. Jensen hadn't returned. She could see him deep in conversation with the policemen waiting to disembark. Even from this vantage point she was in no doubt as to who was in charge. Jensen emitted an aura of leadership that was impossible to miss. His boat, his kingdom, his stance proclaimed.

Boat secured, he shook hands with both of the policemen as though they had been invited guests. Courteous to the last, he waited until they got into their car before turning away. Abby couldn't help but be impressed by his lovely manners.

Dressed in an apricot and green, tie-dyed dress, Abby adjusted the thin shoulder straps lying on skin glowing from hours basking in the sun. Bending over the open suitcase lying on the bed, she concentrated on pushing the last item, her hairbrush, into an already crammed corner. It hadn't taken long to repack the few things she'd used.

Her nerves jangled at the sudden rat-a-tat on her door.

"Come in," she called, fully expecting to see the bulky outline of Bob Simms filling her doorway.

"Going somewhere?" Jensen moved further into the room to peer into the overstuffed suitcase.

"Yes." The sight of Jensen standing by her bed quickened her pulse. He looked so handsome, cream chinos hugged his lean hips, the dark blue shirt brought out the wonderful blue of his amazing eyes. Her heart raced as though she'd been running. Glancing down at her case she was relieved to see that none of her underwear was on show.

"Now we are back in harbour I need to find myself some accommodation for the rest of my holiday."

"You can stay here as long as you like," he offered, taking hold of her hand. "I like your company, and I think you like mine, so why not?" His eyes loitered on her lips.

Flustered, she liberated her hand using it to close the lid of her case. "I don't think that's a very good idea. I don't really know you and I'm not used to living on a boat with a lot of strange men." Even to her own ears she sounded like some sort of Victorian maiden aunt. "I need to get back to my resort and see if the owner of my apartments has anywhere else I could use."

"At least stay tonight, it will be dark in a few hours. Tomorrow I could run you back to your resort and help you find somewhere to spend the rest of your holiday. Please, please say yes, I want to get to know you better." His beseeching look could melt butter.

It sounded enticing. She'd not been looking forward to finding her own way back to her resort tonight.

Jensen watched her keenly, as though he could see the first signs of her capitulation. Smiling, he pressed his advantage. "Come on you know you want to," he encouraged. "Bilbo is already planning a special dinner for us."

"Bribery and corruption," Abby said through her laugher. How could she resist the look in his beautiful blue eyes? "Okay, okay I'll stay, but just for tonight. Promise you will allow me to leave tomorrow."

"As Scarlet O'Hara once famously said, 'Tomorrow is another day,'" he said, with a bone melting smile that scorched her very flesh.

CHAPTER EIGHT

Much, much later, relaxing in an enormous armchair sipping a delicious cool glass of white wine, Abby wanted to stay forever. The dinner had been wonderful and the company... Oh the company! Discussions, both heated and amusing, on books, movies, television programmes and politics, left them both surprised at how many things they had in common. Their tastes and attitudes fitted perfectly. Unfortunately, their lifestyles could not be more dissimilar.

Her eyes greedily devoured him over the rim of her glass. Sprawled in a facing, matching armchair, one leg draped over the wide arm, head thrown back and eyes half closed, he looked incredibly sexy and a little bit dangerous, like a large tawny tomcat.

Longing smouldered deep within her, the magnetic pull of his attraction dragging her thoughts into deep, sensual waters. Taking a cooling drink she sought to extinguish the sensation.

No way! Sleeping with Jensen wasn't an option.

A knowing smile played on his sensual lips, his sleepy lids opened a fraction more revealing smoky blue eyes.

"Time for bed?" he suggested with a wicked look.

Holy hell! He'd been watching her, watching him!

Mortified she straightened in her chair. "It's early yet," she managed, attempting to sound casual despite her fluttering stomach. *What did he mean by that comment? Did he expect her to sleep with him?*

"It's nearly one. I'm beat." He looked too exhausted to move - but looks could be deceptive.

"Of course, I don't expect you slept too well last night after your ordeal, you are bound to feel tired." She searched for something to say that would not sound banal, and failed. "I've really enjoyed tonight." Rising she placed her empty wineglass on an occasional table. Time to beat a hasty retreat! "I'll see you tomorrow. Thank you for a lovely evening." She ran a nervous tongue over her full bottom lip.

"I'd like to do that." Jenson pushed slowly to his feet.

"Do what?" Puzzled she waited for him to elaborate.

"Trace your lips with my tongue."

Oh! Heat seared her cheeks, her heart rate accelerated.

"Don't make fun of me." Flustered, his words had actually made her blush, she took refuge in anger.

"I'd like to have fun *with* you. God you're beautiful, I've spent this evening desperately trying to keep my hands off you."

"I bet you would like to have *fun*! That's what this is all about." She waved an angry hand at their sumptuous surroundings.

Mystified he couldn't help asking. "That's what all what is about?"

Her voice rose. "Luring me onto your yacht, wining and dining me, kissing me earlier today... Hah! You're trying to seduce me," she accused.

"And you're objecting to that?" The corners of his eyes crinkled – he was laughing at her.

Only because I'll end up getting hurt!

"I certainly am." Folding her arms protectively across her chest she flashed him her most defiant look.

"If I remember rightly it was you who kissed me." He raised an eyebrow, daring her to deny it.

Oh God she couldn't argue with that - time to change tactics.

"You promised not to do this." Her voice dropped to just above a whisper.

"When? What's happening here?" His puzzled, petulant, boyish look was almost her undoing.

"You told me I would be safe on board your boat." Standing her ground, she fought the desire to step into his arms.

"You are safe. Christ, I only want to kiss you - not kill you." Wrong thing to say in the circumstances but it was too late now - the curt words had already left his mouth.

"I hardly know you," she countered, ignoring his reference to the reason she was here.

"That's what I was planning to correct. I thought we could get to know each other a lot better." His grin was pure sex.

Too tempting! Abby took a half step back.

"Oh lighten up, I get the message," he sighed throwing his hands up. "Go to bed."

Feeling really stupid she muttered. "Sorry. I think I overreacted."

"I'll say." Jensen tried to reassure her. "You're quite safe with me you know."

Nodding she acknowledged. "Yes I know."

But am I safe with me?

"Friends?"

"Friends." Wanting to be much more than friends had made her act so prickly, she'd made a fool of herself in an effort not to let him see how she really felt.

Holding out her hand she expected him to shake it to cement their truce.

Taking her unresisting hand in his, Jensen drew her towards him. Abby allowed herself to be pulled gently into his arms. Masculine lips brushed her cheek in a soft kiss.

"Goodnight luv," hot breath whispered against her ear.

Scalding awareness ran riot at both the sensation and 'that' word - uttered in an undeniable Northern accent. Then she was free but still standing much too close.

Long seconds crawled by as they stared at each other, neither one wanting to be the first to turn away. Hypnotized by his darkening blue eyes she leaned towards him. His mouth skimmed the sensitive area at the side of hers. Previously banked down embers fluttered back to life at the first touch of his warm lips against her skin. Traitorous arms wound around his neck without her permission. He gathered her close, so close she could feel his reaction to her.

Oh my! I'm in trouble – big trouble.

Pressed against him she gave herself up to pure enjoyment.

As promised, a feather-light touch circled her lips before invading her mouth with a searing intimacy. Arching her body towards him she allowed him full access, kissing him back with the same intensity and passion.

Eventually Jensen tore his lips away breathing heavily. "I only meant to kiss you goodnight! Sorry I lost control." Large hands wrapped around her upper arms, giving her seemingly boneless body, support. He stepped back with evident unwillingness. Abby stared at him in disbelief, passion still holding sway.

"No sweetheart," he cautioned. "I cannot take anymore without going beyond my point of no return."

Abby tried to take in what he was saying. She'd past her point of no return some time ago.

What was wrong with him?

"I don't want to spoil things. I can wait. You are on my boat with a lot of strange men – remember?" Smiling gently he moved one hand, placing it under her chin, forcing her to look at him. "When you are more comfortable with your environment, and we know each other a little better – then, well then, I hope there will be no stopping either of us."

"I'm feeling very comfortable." *Did she really say that?*

"Damn you woman, don't do this, I've been fighting for control all night trying not to think how good we would be together. Your perfume still tantalises my nostrils. You have no idea how much I want you."

Feathering a kiss on her forehead, he reluctantly released her.

Legs wobbling, lips throbbing and disappointment humming, Abby retired to her bed – alone.

Sitting on her bed, dressed in the same outfit she'd worn the day before, her packed suitcase at her feet, Abby thought about what had happened the night before. If Jensen hadn't been such a gentleman she could have been waking up in his bed this morning. Most of her was glad she'd awoken in her own room, but a small part, a part he must never know about, mourned not having made love with him.

By the time Mark knocked on her door to tell her breakfast was ready, she'd regained her common sense and was looking forward to finding some other accommodation and getting on with her holiday – Jensen free. Lying awake in the long dark night hours she'd come to the conclusion that she'd been given a reprieve, best to go now before she ended up being really hurt.

Finding the stateroom empty Abby sat down at the large table in the seat she was becoming to think of as hers. Two places had been set but there was no sign of her host. Mark re-appeared at her side carrying a silver jug.

"Coffee Miss?"

"Oh yes please. Where is Mr Stone this morning?"

"He said to tell you, he will be along shortly Miss." He poured expertly. "Do you wish to wait for Mr Stone or would you prefer to be served breakfast now?"

"I'll wait thank you."

Having played with all of her cutlery, fiddled with the cruet set and arranged her serviette into several lumpy, unidentifiable shapes, Abby was about to summon Mark when Jensen finally appeared.

"Hi beautiful," he greeted her with a smile which loosened those fluttery, butterfly things in her stomach again, "I should have been here to greet you. I'm sorry about the delay." He slid into the seat opposite her. "There's a problem with the housing for *Waverunner Two*. The control panel is playing up and the door won't close. I'm interested in computer technology and wanted to see what the problem was.

"Apparently the other day, as soon as I left with Willie and Parky, two crew members, Spen and Woody, took it into their heads to take her for a spin - allegedly to check her out! Bob and I have had to reprimand them for taking the launch without permission."

"Spen and Woody?" She frowned.

"Nick Spencer and Carl Woodward," he supplied. Shaking out his napkin, he placed it across his knees. "Have you ordered anything yet?"

"No, I thought I'd wait for you before I decided what I wanted."

Giving her a suggestive look he asked. "What do you fancy this morning?" He ran his tongue slowly over his bottom lip reminding her of how he'd done the same thing to her the night before.

OMG! Heat surfaced in her cheeks. *Did he really expect her to say - him?*

Clearing her, suddenly constricted, throat she managed, "Scrambled egg on toast if that's okay." Straightening her knife, she refused to look at him.

"You can have anything you - desire." Amusement tinged his words as he continued to tease her.

Laughter bubbled, Abby could not help herself. "You're incorrigible."

Assuming an innocent expression he raised his hands, palms upwards. "What? I don't know what you mean. I merely enquired what you wanted for breakfast."

"Of course you did," she mocked. "Anyway it tickled."

"What tickled?"

Smiling wickedly she flicked the tip of her tongue slowly around her lips.

"Oh that. I'm sure you'll get used to it." He ginned. "Although I'm not so certain I will, just the sight of you imitating my actions has sent blood rushing to places I'd rather it didn't - at least not while we're having breakfast."

Hot cheeked, she looked him in the eye. "You don't have to worry about coming over all un-necessary. I'm leaving today and I don't expect we will meet again." Despite her best intentions she could not keep disappointment out of her voice.

"We'll see," he commented, in his 'I'm the one calling the shots' tone.

Abby bit her tongue in an attempt not to show her annoyance.

Placing her empty coffee cup on its saucer, she leaned back, replete. "That was lovely. I thoroughly enjoyed it."

"Good." Jensen pushed his chair back. "We should be able to go ashore in about an hour if it's okay with you. I'll ring the car hire company and see if they can deliver something reasonable." Looking her levelly he asked. "Are you sure you want to leave?"

"Yes. I'm going to ring my apartment owner to see what other accommodation he has. Hopefully it will be something nearby as I want to be able to still use the little private beach."

"Okay, see you later."

"I'll be ready," she promised.

Bob Simms kindly took her case, leaving Abby time to check her rooms for any stray belongings. A distant, extremely alarmed masculine shout sent a fissure of fear darting through her. Forgetting her task she hesitated. Should she go and investigate? Maybe she would be in the way? While she dithered, the strident sounds of several angry voices teased her curiosity. *What was going on?* She simply had to know, spinning around she hurried towards the sound.

Reaching the main deck she almost tripped over her abandoned suitcase. A loud, heated argument ensued from the deck where the second launch was stationed. Abby made her way towards the shouting.

What she assumed to be the entire crew were assembled on the deck beside *Waverunner Two's* locker. Two men, one of whom she remembered seeing before, shouted abuse at one another while a plump, bald man examined the head of a soaking wet man lying in a pool of water on the deck like a newly landed fish. Blood seeped from the back of the prone man's head.

At his side knelt an equally drenched Jensen, applying rhythmic pressure to the man's chest as he attempted resuscitation? Abby stepped closer, alarmed to hear Jensen softly singing. Sea water dripped as he worked, drying quickly on the sun-warmed wood of the deck.

The prone man coughed, water spewed from his mouth.

"He's breathing." The bald man smiled with relief.

"Yes but he hasn't come around." Worry edged Jensen's words.

In the background the two men still argued.

"Quiet," Jensen commanded, loud enough to be heard over the row. "What the hell happened here?" he demanded rising to his feet. Abby thought he looked magnificent with his wet clothes clinging to his muscular body.

The only sound was a low croak from the injured man, followed almost immediately by everyone talking at once.

"One at a time," Jensen's voice sliced through the din. "Woody." He addressed the tall, gangly young man who had spoken up yesterday and was also one of those now arguing. "You appear to have a lot to say for yourself. Let's start with you."

Woody shuffled his feet seeming suddenly embarrassed at being the centre of attention. He cleared his throat. "I was having a fag on deck when I saw Moonie fall into the water, so I shouted for help because I can't swim."

"You could have thrown him a life-ring to hold onto you stupid, useless git," the other arguing young man shouted aggressively.

"Aye and if he'd done that, Moonie wouldn't be at death's door now," the bald man still kneeling beside the injured man butted in, his voice tight with anger.

"Well, if Woody had half a brain..."

"You'll get your say in a minute Spen," Jensen cut across before another argument could break out. "I have a feeling Moonie was unconscious when he hit the water, therefore quarrelling about what Woody may, or may not, have done is pointless."

"I think we need to get Moonie to a doctor, this is more than I can deal with. Looks like he's done something to his neck and I don't like the way the cut on his head is bleeding," the bald man spoke up again.

"Okay Bilbo. Let's get Moonie sorted first." Flicking open his phone, Jensen prepared to make a call.

"We shouted but no-one answered. I hope you do not mind that we came aboard." Appearing almost magically, like the shopkeeper in 'Mr Ben', the Greek policeman, who was fast becoming a familiar figure, walked towards the group accompanied by another officer. "Would you like to tell us what is going on here?"

Relief replaced the tension on Jensen's face. He addressed Captain Georgallis, "We have an injured man here who needs help fast."

The ambulance left with Moonie, AKA Graham Moon, accompanied by Bilbo, for a local hospital. Everyone else moved into the stateroom out of the sun's midmorning heat.

Jensen towelled his hair as he explained to the police that Moonie, who was the yacht's first engineer, had been attempting to fix the faulty door on the launch hatch and had somehow fallen into the sea.

"As the door wouldn't close, I can only assume he must have tried to shut it manually and lost his balance."

"And where were you Mr Stone?"

"Drinking coffee on the sundeck. When I heard Carl shout I dived from there and swam towards Graham. Unfortunately he'd disappeared under the surface and it took me a little while to locate him."

"A little too long by the look of him. A pity you did not rescue him sooner," Captain Georgallis commented with a touch of sarcasm.

Abby shivered, despite the high temperature, as suspicion reared its ugly head again. A strange sort of accident! It would be interesting to find out where everyone was when Moonie fell. Judging by the state of him, his injuries could well be serious - even life threatening.

CHAPTER NINE

Abby helped make sandwiches in the large, modern galley.

Bilbo had not, as yet, returned from the hospital so the boat was without its cook. Parky stood at her side, for once subdued, busy spreading the filling on the bread she'd already buttered.

"How long have you known Mr Stone?" Neil broke the silence.

"A couple of days." She deftly peeled another egg.

"So you didn't know him before...?" He shuddered. "Before Willie died?"

"No. Actually it was me who found Willie's body."

"It was?" He looked at her in amazement.

Abby picked up another egg, slamming it down on the counter harder than warranted, before rolling it between her palms to remove the shell. "Yes it was horrible. Jensen nearly scared me to death when he came out of the bathroom."

"Mr Stone was in your bathroom?"

"Yes." She added mayonnaise to the eggs and viciously beat them together. "Someone had knocked him out with a frying pan and his head was bleeding."

"Oh." He swallowed visibly. "Didn't you suspect him of being the murderer?"

"At first, yes."

"But not now?"

"No." Wiping her hands on a dishcloth she asked. "Do you think I've made enough filling?"

"I don't think anyone is hungry. The thought of poor Moonie half drowned is enough to put anyone off eating." Parky pursed his lips and exhaled, making a whooshing sound.

"Do you think it was an accident?" Abby probed. She needed to know what he thought.

"The police wouldn't be so interested if they thought he'd slipped by himself." Positioning the last slice of bread, he pushed down gently with the palm of his hand. "There, all done. Do you want to cut the sandwiches or do you trust me to wield the bread-knife?"

"I trust you." She realised that she did, and not just with the bread-knife. "So do you think someone caused his fall?"

Shrugging, Parky placed the cut sandwiches on a large platter. "Don't know really. Can't think of any reason why anyone would do that." He dusted the crumbs off his hands over the sink. "I don't think anybody had an axe to grind with Willie, he seemed to get on with everyone."

"What about Spen and Woody? They were in trouble for taking the launch without permission, could it have been Moonie who told on them?" Placing the lid on the butter carton, she held her breath waiting for his answer.

"Yeah, I suppose so. I didn't think of that."

He lifted the large serving plate. "I'll take these up and see if I can tempt anyone into eating them." Walking towards the door he called over his shoulder, "Coming?"

"In a moment." Taking a deep breath, she said softly, "Did you hear Jensen singing as he worked on Moonie?" This had been seriously worrying her, she could think of no reason why he should have been happy Moonie had drowned.

Swinging back to face her Parky chuckled showing his natural good humour for the first time that morning. "Apparently the song 'Staying Alive' is the same beat as the human heart. Singing the words helps to keep the correct rhythm." He grinned. "The whole crew had a course on life saving at the beginning of last summer. When I joined earlier this year Mr Stone insisted I learn too." His smile faded. "When it came to the crunch, only Mr Stone was brave enough to attempt to save Moonie."

Relief surged, it sounded such a silly way to save a life. "It worked though." Smiling happily, eyes shining she looked at Parky. "It actually worked! Moonie is alive!"

"Yeah, he's alive but not very good."

"No. Not good at all." Abby's face fell.

"I'm glad you haven't known Mr Stone long," he said shyly. "If you and he aren't... well you know... I could ask you out."

Cheeks flaming, she smiled. "That's very nice of you. I'm very flattered and if I was five years younger I might have taken you up on your offer."

"I'm not that much younger than you," he protested.

"Well I'm nearly twenty seven and you look..." She hesitated unsure whether to go on and maybe insult him.

"I'm twenty," he supplied, "and you only look to be in your early twenties."

"Well thank you for that."

Bloody hell!

He looked more embarrassed than she felt. She hadn't seen it coming, although she knew from his sidelong admiring glances that he liked her.

"Are you seeing Mr Stone?" he wanted to know.

Was she?

"No. No, not really. I will probably not see him again after today." She gave Parky a rueful smile. "We're not exactly from the same side of the tracks."

"You might be more like each other than you think," he replied cryptically.

"I doubt it."

"These sandwiches are starting to curl," Parky exaggerated looking down at the platter he held. "Are you ready now?"

"Yes." Wiping her hands on a nearby cloth, Abby picked up the butter tub and replaced it in the tall, pale green fridge.

Disturbing thoughts plagued her as she followed Parky up into the bright, sunlit stateroom. She'd been hoping he would dismiss her earlier suggestion that someone had caused Moonie to fall. It would seem she wasn't the only one who thought Moonie could be the killer's second victim.

Jensen had given Willie a dressing down, for something he didn't do, shortly before he died. This morning he'd reprimanded Spen and Woody because he'd discovered, somehow, that they'd taken the other launch out.

Yesterday Parky had been in trouble. There was an awful lot of telling off and accidents on this boat, perhaps there was a connection somewhere if only she could work out what it was.

Jensen stood to one side using his mobile phone. One of the policemen questioned Spen, who still looked agitated and upset. The other policeman happily munched on a sandwich while listening to what was being said. Abby looked for a seat so she could overhear Spen's conversation but could not find one near enough.

Instead she found she could hear Jensen harassing the car hire firm because his motor hadn't arrived. He was definitely Mr Bossy this morning, she was awfully glad she wasn't the person on the other end of the phone. It sounded like what the important, rich Mr Stone wanted, Mr Stone got!

Clicking his phone shut, Jensen moved to sit beside Abby on the large sofa she'd chosen because of its proximity to the big ceiling fan. "I'm going to visit Manolis and Agathi, the friends I was with the morning of Willie's death. I will have a car shortly so if you would still like a lift to your resort I will be happy to take you." Light fingers swiftly caressed her bare arm causing the fine hairs to stir. "Of course, I will be even happier if you decide to spend a few more days here with me."

Skin still quivering from his unexpected touch, Abby shook her head. "It would be better if I go. I've enjoyed the luxury very much but it wouldn't do to get used to it. I appreciate all you've done." Smiling up into his eyes was a mistake, her stomach somersaulted with longing. His striking good looks gave him an unfair advantage over her willpower.

"I rang the owner of the apartments earlier," glancing down she addressed the hands folded in her lap, "and there are a couple of vacant rooms a few doors away from where I should've been staying."

"What!" He looked at her in disbelief. "You're not thinking of staying in the same apartment block where you discovered a dead body? Have you taken leave of your senses?"

Looking up Abby almost laughed at the look of horror on his face. She gave him a determined look. "Why not? The body has been taken away, forensics are finished for now. I've been told my normal rooms are off limits until all investigations are complete. However, the other apartments are being rented out as usual. It's my favourite place to stay. I know the area and I am quite friendly with various locals and business owners. Why shouldn't I stay there?"

"You're forgetting they haven't caught the killer yet. What if he, or she, comes back and kills again. You cannot take that risk, please, please stay here with me."

His words were warm and persuasive. But then that's what he intended them to be.

Common sense and no nonsense were Abby's normal reaction to events, and even though this situation was the most bizarre she'd ever experienced, she was determined to stay true to her customary modus operandi. "Why on earth would anyone want to murder me? Most victims know their killers, and as I don't know the same people Willie did, I think I'm quite safe. Besides the perp could be, and probably is, miles away by now."

"Christ! What TV show are you quoting from now? What the hell is a perp?" His voice rose with barely suppressed irritation.

"A perp is the person who perpetrates the crime - the one who did it," she answered a tad smugly.

"Jesus H!" Jensen rose to his feet and leaned over her, filling her nostrils with the sharp, seductive smell of his expensive aftershave. "You forget you now know all the members of the crew. In other words you know the same people as Willie did," he hissed furiously in her ear.

Oh my God!

"Well I'm just saying..."

"Well I'm just telling," he clipped across her sentence, his ire apparent.

"Is everything alright Miss Grainger?" Captain Georgallis asked from behind Jensen.

Jensen swung on his heel taking a few angry strides before seeming to cool down. He spun back towards Abby again.

"Yes. Yes, thank you." Abby managed to answer the Captain, her mind awhirl with the implications of Jensen's words. It was true. If she stayed on the boat, and Willie's murderer was one of the crew, then she might be in danger. At the moment no-one had a motive to kill her, but if she were to discover who the culprit was! She had to get away from the boat now before she saw or heard something she shouldn't.

"Have any of my crew thrown any light on what happened to Graham?"

Jensen addressed the Captain.

"Not yet. It would appear that everyone was employed elsewhere. Someone from one of the other moored boats may have witnessed something. I will know more once I've spoken to their crews. Unfortunately as the Cassandra Rose is the last boat in line, and the accident happened on the seaward side, I'm not really expecting to have much luck. I'm hoping that the boats anchored further out in the deeper water might have seen what happened." He smiled grimly. "Don't worry; I intend to examine every avenue."

"Your car has arrived Sir," Bob Simms informed Jensen, handing him a set of keys.

Looking Abby in the eye, he spoke softly, almost daring her to defy him. "Have you definitely decided?"

"Yes. I'm coming with you thanks." Standing, she smiled across at him, her outer self calm, her insides shaking.

Jensen hissed a four letter word, his face tightened with annoyance, he nodded to Simms. "Ask Mark to collect Miss Grainger's case please Bob."

CHAPTER TEN

The light coloured Mercedes S500 glinted in the sunshine. Impressed, Abby's eyes widened. "Wow I didn't think it was possible to hire anything this posh!" Running her hand over the gleaming paintwork she sighed. "My sister, Jenny, and me normally run to a slightly battered, two door whatever, we hire locally for a discounted price because we know the guy who runs the firm."

Opening the door she sat on the pale leather seat and swung her long legs into the car. "I don't think Stefanos has anything like this on his books."

Seeming amused by her reaction to the Mercedes, Jensen's anger at her stubborn refusal to stay with him quickly evaporated.

"I'm glad that my choice of car meets with your approval."

"What made you choose this one?" She lowered the sun visor and checked her appearance in the mirror. She could see Jensen placing her suitcase in the boot.

"This car is similar to one I normally drive at home," he told her, sliding behind the steering wheel and adjusting the seat to his leg length.

Show off!

"You're sure about going back to those apartments?" Taking his gaze off the road momentarily, he looked at Abby intently. "Your decision doesn't have anything to do with me, does it?"

What!

"Not at all, why should you think that?"

"Because you find yourself attracted to me and it scares the living daylights out of you."

Conceited bastard!

"You don't scare me, and I'm not attracted to you." Resisting the urge to knock the smug look off his face she twisted her head away, staring unseeingly out of the side window.

"No?"

She could tell without looking at him that he was grinning.

"No," she confirmed.

"You were all over me like a rash last night." Humour apparent he continued, "If I remember rightly I had to prise you off me."

"That's not true. Anyway if you were a gentleman you wouldn't mention it. I'd simply drunk too much delicious wine. You know - beer goggles and all that." Really angry now, she spun back to glare at him. He was watching the road while making no effort to hide his mirth. Mortified she remembered that she had instigated the kiss on the deck and heavy petting session they'd indulged in later.

Crap!

"Well maybe I am a bit attracted to you," she allowed her inherent honesty surfacing.

"Don't worry," he soothed still sounding amused. "I loved it. You can tongue tango with me anytime you like."

The heat in her cheeks made her eyes water. Had she ever been this embarrassed? "Don't be crude," she mumbled.

"So are you determined to go back to those apartments?"

"Yes. Yes, of course I am. Don't keep asking me, I've made up my mind."

"There's plenty of time for you to change it. You could come back with me, or we could find you somewhere else, maybe a different village."

"Thanks but I'll be fine."

"Sure?"

"Very sure." Sick of his repeated attempts to change her mind, she didn't try to rein her temper in.

Abby worried her bottom lip with her teeth as they approached the small village where she was to stay. Jensen's continual onslaught about the danger of going back to the same place was undermining her confidence. Would she really be safer at the apartments?

All of the crew knew where the murder had occurred and by now they might also know she was returning to the same building. Perhaps she should have stayed on board? Mentally reviewing each member of the crew, could she honestly say that she trusted them? A searching look at Jensen, concentrating on the light, fast moving traffic, she speculated – could she even trust him?

Eyes once again on the scenery, a jolt of surprise coursed through her, they were leaving the village behind.

"Where are we going? You've missed the turn off to my apartments. What do you think you are playing at?"

"Relax. I thought I would introduce you to my friends."

Already stressed, she snapped. "It might have been nice to be asked if I wanted to meet your friends. What's the point? I have friends of my own who live quite close to the apartments." It wasn't strictly true as they lived in the main part of the village over a mile away, but he wasn't to know that.

Turning the car onto a narrow, dirt road, he smiled across at her. "Calm down. We're nearly there. They live down here. Their house is virtually on the beach, which is just around the headland from where you will be. A short scramble over the rocks, then a brief walk across the sand and you can be at their house in less than five minutes. I will feel happier about leaving you alone knowing they are within easy reach - should you need them." Swerving between stout wooden gates, he turned off the dirt track, which Abby could see ended a short distance away in a small car park on the very edge of the beach.

Sipping excellent coffee, Abby surveyed her surroundings. Surprised, at first, to find the swimming pool, around which they all sat, had been built into the first floor terrace, she could now appreciate the advantages. Relaxing in a roomy, white upholstered basket chair, she could see the entire sweep of the beach, complete with lines of blue and white striped umbrellas and loungers neatly laid out like a giant bar code in the sand. Because of the elevation, the terrace retained a moderate degree of privacy.

Manolis and his wife were eager for details of the murder and the attempt on Moonie. Listening, with half an ear, Abby heard Jensen relate the whole tale, including Spen and Woody taking *Waverunner 2* without his knowledge. He downplayed his own part in rescuing then resuscitating Moonie. He finished by explaining that he would appreciate it if they would keep an eye on Abby when he couldn't be around.

Say again!

Jerked to full attention by Jensen's last words she speculated as to how much time he intended to spend with her. She'd imagined herself alone for the rest of her holiday. That's how she wanted it. Last night she'd come dangerously close to sleeping with Jensen. She wanted to, oh how she wanted to, she'd never known attraction like this, but she didn't know him.

There was a killer running around free and she needed to divorce herself from the situation. How dare he think that she needed babysitting! Opening her mouth to give him a piece of her mind she suddenly thought better of it. She would wait until they were alone before giving vent to her feelings.

"Have you any idea who might have strangled Willie?" Manolis looked at Jensen.

"None whatsoever, although Miss Marple there," Jensen nodded towards Abby, "tells me that Willie is likely to have known his killer. That being the case, the police have confirmed that most of the crew were on the Cassandra Rose - apart from Parky. Woody and Spen could have been ashore, although they both deny it." He shrugged.

And you, you were definitely ashore and in the same apartment as the victim.

Dismissing the unsettling thought, she worried that apart from one single glimpse of the past, Jensen still suffered from amnesia - or so he maintained. Sighing, she concentrated on listening to the rest of the conversation.

"I don't need looking after," Abby insisted the moment Jensen drove back out onto the lane.

"Yes you do. Whether you like it or not I want to make sure you have someone to turn to if you feel threatened."

"The only threat I feel at the moment is you trying to suffocate me." She knew she was overreacting but couldn't help herself. The holiday she'd worked for all year had already been ruined. How could she relax and enjoy herself knowing a man had died and another was seriously ill in hospital? Add to that her inexplicable attraction to the man sitting beside her and there was no chance of unwinding anytime soon.

His finely defined jaw tightened in anger, the sight sent a fissure of sexual awareness coursing through her veins. She looked away disgusted with herself.

"I'm not trying to suffocate you. I'm trying to help. Damn you, why can't you see that?" he ground out.

"Sorry. I'm sorry. I'm not used to someone looking out for me. I know you're trying to help, but being around dead bodies and suspicious accidents is not normal for me."

"Me either." Jerking the car to a halt, he stormed out, marching around to the boot to retrieve Abby's suitcase.

"Please try to understand, I don't want to be involved in all of this. I want..." She slammed the car door behind her. "I don't know what I want. I wish I'd never come on holiday. I wish I'd never seen Willie's dead body, or met Bob, or Parky or..."

"Or me," Jensen finished for her.

Abby turned away not wanting to see his wounded expression. It would hurt her too if she wasn't able to see him again but it was the only way.

"I won't be a moment. I need to find out which apartment I've been allocated." She disappeared around the corner making for the caretaker's house. Returning a few minutes later, she was relieved to see Jensen didn't look quite so angry.

He carried Abby's case up to her new rooms, which just happened to be at the opposite end of the building. Like her original apartment, this one too had a semi private balcony at the rear.

"I'm sorry, I know this must be much worse for you, after all you know the people who are being harmed." She took his free hand. "Friends?"

His grip tightened around her hand, the rough pad of his thumb gently rubbing the soft skin at the base of her own.

"That will do for now," he sighed. Moving forward he turned the key and pushed the door open. "Want me to come in with you?" Jensen looked past her into the shady apartment.

"Yes please." Abby walked ahead, throwing back the curtains letting light and the early afternoon sunshine in while she checked the balcony area. Jensen made sure that no-one, either dead or alive, lurked in her rooms. This time she'd remembered to collect the control for the air conditioning. Jensen took it from her and adjusted the temperature to a comfortable 18 degrees.

Abby tried not to be too cross. *Typical man!* She was perfectly capable of setting her own temperature. Why did men always need to be in charge of any remote? Her father was exactly the same. *Boys and their toys!*

Turning from the air con unit, he looked her straight in the eye. "Would you like me to stay here with you?"

What?

Innards melting at the notion, she shook her head. Surely he hadn't said what she thought he'd said.

"You heard me," he answered her unspoken question with a cheeky grin. "I want you and I believe you want me. I can't think of a better way of knowing you are safe."

"No way!"

He took two steps towards her. His nearness suddenly overwhelming as his warm breath fanned her face, he whispered. "Sure about that?" Then he kissed her.

Startled she responded automatically, her arms clutching him for support. His hot mouth gentled, his hands moved to settle loosely on her hips, giving her the space to retreat. Traitorous body parts ached to move closer and continue the breathtaking kiss despite furious messages from her brain. Reluctantly she released him, her lips clinging until the last moment wanting to stay on his forever. He really was the most outstanding kisser she'd ever met. At last she tore her mouth away.

"I'm certain." Heart beat accelerated, cheeks flushed, she hoped he believed her.

Scanning her face, he nodded. "Okay." He appeared resigned to having to leave her. "According to Manolis there's a great restaurant not far from here. Apparently they do traditional Greek dishes with a twist, I can't wait. I thought we might try it tonight."

"No! No, it's okay. I plan to cook for myself tonight. It's been a hectic few days; I'd like to wind down and just simply relax." He still hadn't got the message even though she'd explained on the way over here that she did not expect him to look after her.

"Okay." Assuming a cheeky quizzical look, he looked around. "And your groceries are where?"

"I'm about to go shopping now." Taking her purse out of her handbag she attempted to wedge it into the pocket of her blue cut-offs, without success.

"I'll take you. We passed a large hypermarket on the way here. You should be able to get everything you need there, no problem." He grinned at her, daring her to disagree.

"Thank you. That would be very helpful." Aware that she did not sound very thankful, she managed a stilted smile.

"I could buy some condoms. Would you change your mind about me staying with you if I did?" He looked serious. "I wouldn't want you to worry about getting pregnant."

Bloody cheek! "I have a contraceptive implant." *Now why did she tell him that?*

Jensen appeared shocked. "So you have a boyfriend?"

"Not at the moment. I had the implant done nearly two years ago and I've simply left it in."

"Where is it?" He frowned as though this was something he wasn't familiar with.

"In my arm." She pointed.

"I can't see anything."

A large hand gently closed around her wrist as he lifted her arm for his examination.

"How do you know it's still working?" His puzzled blue eyes met hers.

"Because it lasts for three years and it affects my peri..." Realising she was about to give some very personal information she broke off. "Because I just do," she amended. "Can I have my arm back?"

"Yeah right, let's go."

* * *

Walking out of the apartment, Jensen headed towards the stairs. Halting, as a sense of deja-vu stole over him, he saw himself take the final few steps up to Abby's original room, his hand reached out to open the door, fear flickered, he knew something nasty was about to happen... Turning the handle he stepped into the tiny kitchen.

Temporarily blinded by sunlight pouring in from the balcony, his fear increased...

The thump of Abby colliding with his back scattered the fleeting vision.

"Oops, sorry! I didn't realise you'd stopped walking. I was looking to see if I'd brought enough money."

She made it sound as through it was his fault she wasn't looking where she was going. She must still be angry with him for wanting to look after her.

"It's okay. Come on."

Running lightly down the stairs the horrible feeling stayed with him. Aware that he should tell Abby he had started to remember, he pushed the thought aside. He didn't like the sensation that entering those rooms had given him. Perhaps it might be better if he never remembered.

CHAPTER ELEVEN

Opening sleepy eyes, Abby looked around at her strange surroundings. Recognising the furnishings, a sense of disorientation assailed her. It took a few moments before she realised the sensation was caused by the bed facing the wrong way. She'd forgotten this apartment was a mirror image of the one she normally rented. Also this one had a double bed instead of two singles. Smiling at her stupidity, she flung back the sheet and swung her feet to the cool, tiled floor.

Carrying a hot cup of tea out to the balcony, indignation flared. Riding at anchor out in the bay, like The Jolly Roger, was the Cassandra Rose. Well Captain Hook better watch out – she was no Tinkerbell.

Choosing the wicker chair facing the little harbour, she purposely placed her back to the Yacht. How dare he invade her holiday like this? What would it take to make him realise that she wanted to be left alone?

Pushing away the conflicting thoughts which didn't want Jensen anywhere but in her arms, she jabbed a custard cream viciously into her drink, breaking the biscuit in half. The soggy chunk floated for several seconds before disintegrating into several cloudy pieces. Abby stared in dismay.

Damn the blasted man!

If he didn't take the hint soon she could well end up falling in love with him - she was half way there already. How was it possible to have these feelings towards a man she hardly knew and didn't fully trust?

A fresh cup of tea, and half a dozen biscuits later, Abby accepted Jensen was not going to go away. A new strategy was required. Allowing him to escort her for a few days could be the answer. Once he saw she was in no danger he might leave her to her own devices. Quashing the small voice insisting her motive for spending time with him was questionable, she rinsed her cup out in the sink.

Someone banged on the door at ear level only a foot away from where she stood. An involuntary scream of pure fright escaped her lips.

"Abby! Abby for God's sake are you alright?" Jensen yelled his voice filled with panic, as his fist hit the door again.

"Yes!" Exasperated, she flung open the door before he could tear it from its hinges. "It just that I was standi..." Her words cut off by his fierce bear hug, she clung to him – she'd have fallen otherwise. Light kisses rained on her brow and hair.

Keeping a tight hold of Abby, Jensen used his foot to back-kick the door shut.

Held in place by the large, warm hands resting flat against her back she allowed him to continue hold her. Eventually, unable to resist the temptation, she turned her head meeting his lips with hers.

Desire surged. Pressing closer she revelled in the warmth of his embrace, the heat of his mouth. Groaning, she slid her arms around his waist loving the feel of his strong, well-muscled body. Opening passion drugged eyes, she studied the sun-kissed face only inches from her own. Fair tipped, dark lashes fanned his closed eyelids, small, lightly tanned creases radiated out from the corners. Captivated by a small mole peeping from under the lashes on his right eye, she did not notice his slight withdrawal.

Swept up into his arms some modicum of sanity returned. Being carried towards her bed by a lusty, hunky male was something dreams were made of. In the real world, Abby realised she was wearing the sweaty nightie she'd slept in, she needed a shower and the chance to remove the biscuit crumbs sure to be lurking between her teeth.

Deposited gently on the unmade, bed she rolled swiftly off the other side. Frowning, Jensen faced her, a knee resting on the edge of the bed, his fisted hands supporting his weight on the mattress.

"Sorry. I can see that I presumed too much." Pushing himself upright he stared at the rumpled bed.

"No. No, you didn't. It's my fault, I started it." Running her hands over her comfy pink and white, candy striped nightwear she gave him a shaky smile. "I..." Knowing she needed to be truthful she sought for the right words. "I want to, it's just I haven't done my ablutions yet." It sounded lame, should she elaborate?

Deep male laughter filled the room.

Oh! Feeling mocked, Abby's face tightened with anger. "I'm glad I amuse you." Snatching a scratchy, once white, bath towel off the dressing table stool she marched towards the bathroom.

"Abby!" Ignoring him, her back ramrod straight, she continued on. "Abby luv, I don't care if you have... abluted, or not, come back here."

Unable to look at him she spoke over her shoulder. "I don't think there is any such word as abluted," she reprimanded in her best secretarial telephone voice. Upset because he didn't seem to understand that the first time should be perfect, she'd sounded snooty and petty.

"Don't let's argue," he pleaded.

"I'm not arguing."

"So what's happening?"

"I'm going to take a shower first." Her voice dropped to almost a whisper, she could not look at him.

"So this is not a definite 'no' then?"

"It's not a definite anything."

"Okaaay?"

"Okay," she said softly before closing the bathroom door.

Abby showered quickly in the small cubicle. Would she, should she, actually go ahead and make love with Jensen? At the moment her blood sang with the need to be possessed by this gorgeous sexy man but would she still feel this way by the time she finished her wash? This was not her normal MO. She'd only slept with two other men and both times it had taken her weeks to get up the courage to do so.

Glancing towards her bedroom she imagined Jensen waiting for her. What was he doing? Was his ardour cooling? Fear curled around her heart, her stomach somersaulted at the thought he might have changed his mind - had she?

The bathroom was so tiny it was impossible not to soak the floor. Luckily there was a small drain to take away the excess water. Towel draped around her hips, Abby cleaned her teeth. The click of the door handle alerted her to Jensen's presence. He stood just outside the doorway which was directly behind her. *Oh no!* Her heart rate kicked into overdrive.

Spitting out the last of her mouthwash she wiped her mouth with the back of her hand. Stuck with the dilemma of pulling the towel over her breasts and possibly exposing her bottom or leaving her top half uncovered, she remained slightly bent over the sink.

"I thought you might need a hand to dry your hair." He tried, without success, to sound serious. "I'm getting a bit lonely out here."

Taking a swift peek in the mirror positioned over the basin, she noticed he carried a hand towel.

What now?

"Thanks." Reaching behind her she attempted to take it from him.

"It's okay, I'll do it for you," he offered, ginning.

Waving her hand up and down, she indicated she wanted him to hand her the towel. His low throaty laugh sent shivers of desire dancing along her nerves.

Oh she definitely wanted him.

"You have me at a disadvantage. If you haven't already noticed, I'm half dressed," she teased, amazed at how ragged her voice sounded. How could this man, whom she'd only met a few days ago, make her feel so uninhibited, so different from the buttoned up person she normally was?

There was a moment's rustling silence.

"Now you have me at a disadvantage. I'm fully undressed."

"What!" Forgetting her bare breasts she swung around to face him. "You're cheating." Her half laughing, half breathless accusation was filled with need. Jensen held the hand towel loosely at his waist, suspended by a fist on each hip. It covered him to his knees.

"I would say we were even." His sexy smile faltered as his hot gaze moved to her breasts then back to her face. He groaned a low animal growl deep in his throat. Dark, passion-glazed blue eyes stared into hers. "I think we're overdressed for what I have in mind." Nodding towards her towel, "You first luv," he whispered, in a rough husky voice.

Feeling incredibly brave, Abby took a step forward, she yanked the hand-towel from his unresisting fingers and swiftly wrapped it around her wet hair. "No please, after you," she taunted, attempting to squeeze by him to leave the room.

He blocked her, moving into the bathroom and trapping her up against the hand-basin. "Now you have the advantage." He sounded jagged, needy and very un-Jensen like.

Hmmm this was nice! It appeared that, in this department, she might have some power over him.

Still busy with her hair, she could not immediately respond as his hands pulled the towel from her waist. It soon lay trampled underfoot, soaked and un-noticed by the two people entwined in each others arms.

Abby returned his mind drugging kisses, when his tongue invaded her mouth and she sucked gently, Jensen's groan vibrated along her nerve ends. Pulling away slightly, his voice gruff, he whispered. "There's not enough room in here for what I want to do to you."

Oh Wow!

Quivering at his words, Abby allowed him to lead her by the hand back into the bedroom.

The cold draught from the air conditioning wafted over her naked body as she lay on the bed, the sensation cooling her overheated skin whilst heightening her pleasure, Jensen's lovemaking taking her to unknown heights as his warm lips curled around her nipple, teasing the tip gently with his teeth. Winding her hands in his hair, she held him to her while glorying in the sensation he unleashed.

Then his lips were on her mouth, his tongue stroking hers. Warm weight spread over her body as he moved to cover her, she adjusted to accommodate his body. If she wanted to change her mind, this was the time to say so. *Not likely!* If he didn't take her soon she would die of frustration. There was no way on earth she was stopping him now.

Coming down from her second climax, which they'd shared, she wondered where he'd gained his experience. The thought made her sad as she didn't like to think of him with other women.

Gasping for air, Jensen rolled away from her. "Woman you've got me worn out," he growled.

Stretching catlike, she laughed. "That's strange, I feel great."

"Well it's a delightful sort of worn out," he amended. Turning onto his side, he nuzzled her neck. "Roll over and let me hold you until I get my breath back."

With Jensen curled warm and naked against her bare back, his body-hair tickling slightly, she fell asleep.

"What time is it?" Abby rolled onto her stomach to reach her mobile phone, lying on the bedside cabinet.

"Does it matter?" Jensen pulled her back into his arms.

"My stomach tells me I've missed lunch." Kissing his neck, she gloried in his smell.

"What, you expect love making and lunch?" Rolling her onto her back he took one of her nipples into his mouth.

Groaning, Abby pulled at his hair. "Don't, I'm not sure I can take any more at the moment."

"I'm positive one more time won't hurt – too much." His hand crept downwards.

Stretching languidly, she whispered. "I'm not so sure. Why don't you try and persuade me?"

"With pleasure luv."

Standing nude, Jensen took his time covering a half dressed Abby with suntan lotion. Teased beyond endurance, she snatched at the bottle. "Here, let me have that before we never get out of this apartment and end up starving to death."

"Whatever do you mean?" He gave her a sexy grin.

"You know fine well what I mean." She pulled the bottle out of his hands. "And if you want me to put any lotion on you, you'd better put your boxer shorts on first."

"What a nag," he sighed, reaching for his clothes.

Stepping into a short pink dress Abby asked, "How is Moonie? Have you heard anything?"

Jensen stilled. "I was hoping you wouldn't ask," he said finally, zipping his pants.

"Why?" Heart racing, she held her breath.

Had he died?

"Because I didn't want to worry you." He buttoned his shirt.

"Is he…? He's not…?"

"No he's still alive but hasn't come around yet." He shrugged. "You might as well know the latest. Apparently the marks on his neck were caused by someone trying to strangle him."

"Like Willie!" Legs suddenly weak, she sank onto the side of the bed.

"Just like Willie. The police suspect it was probably the same person. They came aboard last night and took away all likely objects for analysis. They even took items of clothing which might have been used to try and murder him."

"When do the doctors think Moonie might come around? He should throw some light on what happened to him."

"They aren't sure. Apparently, some people react to a traumatic situation by staying in a coma to avoid accepting what's happened to them. As the time spent in a coma is different with each individual, we can only wait and see." He pushed his feet into dark grey Crocs.

"He must know who tried to kill him."

"Not necessarily. It appears he was attacked from behind so he might not have seen his assailant."

"So the police might not be any nearer finding the killer." Abby stepped into her own shoes.

"Let's hope that's not the case." Jensen ran his fingers through his hair. "I remembered something earlier just after I stepped through the beach gates," he admitted.

Abby's hands stilled. "About what happened to Willie?"

"About what happened to Willie," he confirmed.

"Tell me." Her eyes pleaded with him to share his memory.

"I was coming up from the beach. I watched you leave your balcony and disappear into your rooms. I couldn't wait to see you again." He smiled at her. "I looked towards the other end of the building and thought I saw Willie standing on the balcony of your original apartment. He was waving frantically as though something was wrong."

"That's great. It shows your memory is coming back."

"Yes, I guess another piece of the puzzle has dropped into place." He sat beside her on the bed.

"Do you remember anything else?"

Closing his eyes he seemed to be willing the memory to continue. "I can only recall seeing Willie on the balcony of your apartment trying to catch my attention." He shrugged, looking frustrated. "The memory was so fleeting that..." Eyes widening in shock he exclaimed. "Someone was behind him, partly concealed so I could only see the top of their shoulders." Jumping to his feet, his eyes alive with excitement, he almost shouted. "Now I'm getting somewhere."

"What else do you remember? What were they wearing?" Abby fired the question at him.

Looking astonished he replied. "It was another crew member. Both of them were wearing identical coloured tops." Sitting heavily on the bed again, he said in amazement. "You know I've tried all ways to summon up more details. All it took was someone to ask the question and the answer popped into my head."

"Did you see his face or the colour of his hair?"

Jensen shook his head. "No, I don't think so. The memory was so fleeting that there wasn't time to notice specific details."

"Why didn't you tell me you'd started to remember when you first arrived?" she glared at him, exasperated.

"This is the first chance I've had. You were so desperate to have your wicked way with me I couldn't think of anything else," he grinned.

"Oh you!" Laughing she concentrated on finishing dressing.

"Actually I recalled something yesterday but at the time you were mad at me so I didn't say anything." Quickly he recounted the strange visions he'd experienced just before they'd gone shopping.

"Did you notice anybody when you opened the door?"

Jensen thought about it for a moment. "No, looks like I'll have to wait for another revelation." Standing, he walked towards Abby. Gathering her into his arms he placed a gentle kiss on her lips. "Come on, you can ask me some more questions later, who knows what I might remember." Pulling her gently towards the door he went on, "We've had an absolutely wonderful day so far. Don't let's spoil it by dwelling on this now."

Half amused, Abby could not help teasing. "An absolutely wonderful day! Well, I suppose that's one way of describing the last few hours." Inside she glowed.

Hair gently stirred by the overhead ceiling fan, Abby leaned her elbows on pristine white cloth partly covering the blue painted table and gazed out over the sea. Outside, in the sunshine, the cicadas made their usual racket.

Everything looked and sounded the same as it always did. This time she was different, sights, sounds, smells and tastes were magnified. Had she ever felt this happy? Glancing at Jensen, a small shiver of pleasure travelled along her nerve ends at the hungry look he gave her. Blushing, she looked quickly away. It wasn't hard to guess what he was thinking about.

Each time she chanced another glance at him she caught him studying her, their eyes locking for a few seconds before one or the other tore their gaze away. How quickly things could change. Only hours ago she'd planned to spend a few days with him before she moved on. One kiss and her plans not to get too involved had flown out of the window. What an idiot! Not only had she'd fallen for a man she'd only known a few days, she'd slept with him. Erotic memories of the last few hours invaded her mind sending scalding lust scorching through her body.

The taverna sat on a slightly elevated position reached by a short flight of broad, white steps. Abby sipped her cold beer, served in a tall, ice frosted glass. Looking around the pretty interior she made an effort to distract her thoughts from the man sitting beside her. It wouldn't do to jump each others bones in public.

Could this be the same taverna Parky and Willie had come to? There didn't appear to be an English waitress, but then it could be her day off.

"Penny for your thoughts," Jensen interrupted her musing.

Unwilling to bring up the subject of murder once again, she searched for something to say. "I'm simply soaking up the atmosphere while debating which bikini to wear when I go down to the beach later," she lied.

"I'm disappointed." Pursing his lips he gave her a hurt look. "You could at least pretend you were thinking about me."

Laughing, she reached across and patted his hand. "There, there. It may make you feel a bit better to know that I'm doing my best not to think about you."

Adopting a comical leer, he leaned forwards. "And why would that be?"

"Because I need to eat to keep my strength up and if I allow my thoughts to stray in your direction I might drag you back to my bed," she whispered.

Pleased, he gave her a wicked look. "We could always eat quickly."

"We need to get served first. This is Greece, remember? They're so laid back they're almost horizontal." She grinned at him, "You'll just have to control yourself."

"I'm not sure I can. You look so delectable I'd rather have you for lunch."

"Did you bring the launch yourself today?"

"You're just trying to change the subject," he accused, flashing her that, oh so sexy smile which made her body hum.

"Yep, one of us needs to."

"Woody brought me. I left him lying on that little beach. He intends to spend the day swimming and reading." Noticing the guilt on Abby's face, he went on. "Don't worry about him. He's got a big bottle of water and a couple of Bilbo's meat pies. He'll be fine, he intended to enjoy himself."

The warmth of Jensen's hand wrapped around hers made her heart race as they made the short walk back to her apartment. His gently caressing thumb heightened her anticipation of what was to come.

"Would you like to know what I have planned once we close your apartment door?" Jensen whispered into her ear, the tip of his tongue traced the delicate whorls, the heat from his mouth igniting tremors of excitement.

"What do you have in mind?" Her breathy request for more information was scarcely audible.

He kissed her ear and resumed walking. "Well first I'm going to get you naked then... What the hell do they want now?"

The police car parked outside the building, looking like a large ink blot on the white gravel, spoiled the mood.

"I hope nothing has happened to Moonie," she voiced her first thought.

"Me too." Gently letting go of her hand, he strode towards the vehicle as Captain Georgallis and another policeman exited the car.

"Ah Mr Stone! We understood you were visiting Miss Grainger."

"What's happened?" Concern rimmed Jensen's words.

"Our forensic team have discovered what caused the abrasions on Mr Moon's neck." He allowed himself a small smile.

"That's great," Abby acknowledged, joining them. "What is it?"

Looking at Jensen, the policeman replied. "A man's silk tie."

Surprised, Abby queried. "A tie? Why would anyone need to bring a tie on holiday on board a yacht?"

"I have ties together with a selection of business dress shirts, suits etc.," Jensen admitted.

What!

"Why would you need them?" She couldn't get her head around it.

Jensen smiled at her naivety. "I often use the boat for business as well as pleasure. Plus if I have a meeting abroad I sometimes sail and sleep on board rather than fly and book an hotel."

Horrified by his admission, she gasped. "So the tie might be yours?"

"Very easily, however the crew are also required to wear a shirt, tie and jacket when I'm entertaining clients."

"Then the tie could belong to one of them." Relief laced Abby's words.

Captain Georgallis turned to her. "It was found in Mr Stone's suite. We will of course confirm who owns it by taking DNA samples from Mr Stone and the rest of the crew."

CHAPTER TWELVE

Leaning on the balcony wall, the sun warming the back of her head, Abby watched '*Waverunner two*' skimming across the sparkling sea heading for the 'Cassandra Rose'. She could make out Jensen at the controls with Woody at his side, the two policemen, their caps removed, sat in the back.

Jensen promised to return in the evening so they could have dinner together at the restaurant he'd suggested the previous evening. Alone with her thoughts, she attempted to sort the facts, plus what she'd learned today, into some sort of order.

First Moonie - when he was attacked Bob Simms had been helping her with her luggage, every other person onboard, including Jensen, had been on their own.

Woody had been on deck smoking, Parky on his way to the staff restroom, both Spen and Jensen were drinking coffee, the first in the staffroom and the other on the sun deck. Bilbo maintained that he'd been writing up menus in the galley and Mark busy tidying Jensen's stateroom. All of them had the opportunity - but who had the motive?

A slapping noise made her swing around in surprise expecting to find someone standing behind her. A lone curtain flapped in the doorway caught by a sudden gust of wind. As she watched, it snagged on the clothes dryer, sending it crashing onto the concrete floor of the small platform. Her way inside blocked, Abby stood the dryer upright again, weighing the legs down with the large rock intended for the purpose.

Handling the clothes lines reminded her of how Willie had been killed. Had the murderer been about to untie the rope when Jensen saw him? She mentally ran through the members of the crew who'd had the opportunity to strangle Willie. Jensen and Parky were the prime suspects. Knowing them both, as she did, she was disinclined to believe it could be either of them.

That left Woody and Spen. Neither would admit to having put ashore when they, 'borrowed', *'Waverunner two'* but that didn't mean that they weren't covering for each other. Again there was no apparent motive for either of them to murder Willie. It was a puzzle which led around in circles.

Try as she might she could not put the thought of someone using a necktie to attempt to strangle Moonie out of her mind. Was it the same person who had strangled Willie? Why would anyone do such a thing? - No answers presented themselves. Feeling the need to relax, she went in search of a bikini.

Book in hand, Abby lay on the beach attempting to read. The words refused to register, they might as well have been written in Swahili for all the sense they made. Sighing, she laid her novel face down on the hot sand. There was no escape from the questions buzzing around in her head like angry wasps. Perhaps when the owner of the tie had been identified she might find some answers.

The thrum of an approaching engine drew her attention, the launch was returning. Spen gave her a wave as he deftly manoeuvred the craft into the small harbour entrance. The only other people aboard were the two policemen returning to collect their car. Disappointment flooded, she'd been so sure Jensen would come back to her as soon as he could.

Pushing to her feet, she walked over to the narrow pathway which led around the giant, limestone boulders separating the beach from the manmade anchorage.

"What happens now?" she addressed Captain Georgallis as soon as he gained dry land.

"Now we wait until we have the results of the DNA tests, although they may not be very helpful. Mr Stone has already admitted that the tie is his."

Bloody hell!

Abby gasped with shock. Had he made up the stories of his returning memories?

Wearing a look of sympathy he continued. "The steward, Mark McDonald, handles all of Mr Stone's clothes so we are expecting to find evidence of this. In fact all of the crew had the opportunity to take the tie as it is some time since it was last worn." He walked towards the tall wrought iron gates leading up to the apartments. "Don't worry, we will catch this killer but until we do I would suggest you don't trust anybody - and I mean anybody."

Rusting, brine encrusted hinges squealed. The Captain stepped through the gap. The other policeman gave Abby a half embarrassed, half apologetic, look before following his superior through the gates. Pivoting away she watched Spen, negotiating the narrow channel leading out to sea, through the blur of her tears. Would Jensen take her to dinner tonight? Did she even want him to?

Applying her lipstick at the bathroom mirror she listened for the sound of Jensen's car, not entirely sure she'd hear it over the racket the cicadas were making. She'd persuaded herself he would, indeed, turn up. She dressed with care, her body a quiver of anticipation. Having given what she knew of him a lot of thought, she looked forward to seeing him, convinced that he was not a murderer.

The Cassandra Rose had upped anchor several hours ago so presumably it had gone back to the harbour where Jensen's hire car was parked. He would need the car to take them to the restaurant as it was in a little village up in the hills.

A vehicle pulled up outside, a car door clicked shut. Abby had already unlocked her door to allow Jensen to enter. Giving her hair a final fluff before spraying it lightly, she picked up her lipstick and walked into the bedroom to collect her handbag from the bed. Turning, her breath caught.

Oh wow!

Jensen lounged casually up against the door-jam, arms and feet crossed. He wore cut off jeans and a pale blue shirt open at the neck, he looked relaxed, tanned and very, very sexy. Any remaining doubts Abby might be harbouring melted like snowflakes on warm skin.

"You look lovely." He sounded gruff, aroused.

"You're not bad yourself." Walking up to him she pressed the palm of her hand against his firm chest and offered her lips for his kiss.

He groaned against her mouth. "Do we have to go out immediately?" he begged.

Laughing at her power over him, she pushed him gently away. "Yes, come on. What happened to the man dying to try the menu in this new restaurant?"

"I'm finding you addictive. You seem to be replacing my need for food." He reached for her.

Deftly she avoided his hands. "Later. The sooner we go the sooner we will return, and then…" Tapping her bottom lip with her fingernails she pretended to consider. "Well then we can indulge ourselves to our hearts content. You're not the only one with cravings." She gave him a naughty look. Nipping out of the door she ran down the steps before Jensen realised what was happening, leaving him to secure her apartment before he could join her.

Waiting until the waiter finished placing their drinks, Abby leaned across the table. "Captain Georgallis told me that the tie used to try and strangle Moonie belongs to you."

Oh God please let him say the right thing. Under the cover of the table cloth she crossed the fingers on both hands.

"Yes I recognised it instantly." Shaking his head slowly, he sighed. "You don't believe I'm the killer do you?" He looked so anxious, so defenceless.

"No. No of course I don't." She relaxed her fingers. She didn't need luck, she trusted him. "I wouldn't be here if I did, would I?"

His relief was palpable. Smiling he shook out his napkin and placed it across his lap. "No I suppose not. But I wouldn't blame you if you had some doubts."

"I had. I'll admit that. However the more I get to know you the more improbable it seems that you would be capable of killing anyone." Reaching across, she took hold of his hand, rubbing her thumb over the top in a gesture of comfort.

"Thanks." Flipping his hand over, he grasped hers. "I appreciate your trust in me." Bright blue eyes studied her face earnestly. "I couldn't bear it if you doubted me." He pressed a soft sexy kiss into her palm.

Hot lust licked her innards. *Oh wow!* "Of course I trust you," Abby confirmed huskily. "But someone is guilty. Have you any idea who it could be?"

"Not really. It's more complicated than I first thought. It appears Mark was with Spen and Woody on the day that Willie was murdered - they allowed him to pilot Waverunner. They didn't want to say anything before as Mark was supposed to be on duty and has not been taught how to handle the launch. He had no business being anywhere near it." Jensen's lips tightened in anger.

"How did you find out?" A plate of steaming food appeared in front of her. "Thank you." Glancing up she automatically smiled at the young waiter.

The man placed Jensen's meal before him. "Thank you that looks great." Picking up his knife and fork he stabbed a piece of marinated lamb. "That's not all, they did go ashore." Popping the meat into his mouth he chewed with appreciation.

"What?" Shocked, she stared at him her own meal forgotten. "Where?"

"That's the thing, they're not sure." Deftly cutting another piece of meat he shrugged. "Mark pointed in the direction of your apartments. The others disagreed with him."

"They were at the village!" Aware her voice had risen sharply, she looked around to see if anyone had heard.

"Not necessarily. According to Mark they used a small pier at the end of a long narrow beach to disembark. It could have been anywhere."

"No. No, it couldn't. I know this area, apart from the beach where your friends live, the only other long stretch of sand for miles is the main one around the headland from my apartments. If they came ashore on either one, they could walk into the village in a matter of minutes." Taking a long drink of her wine she mentally added Mark to her list of suspects.

Pushing all thoughts of murder from her mind, she picked up her cutlery determined to enjoy this evening. After all this was technically their first date, an event to remember forever. She wasn't stupid - there could be no future for them. Northern girls, who'd skimped and scraped to be able to afford their annual sunshine holiday, only dreamed of meeting a millionaire who'd sweep them off their feet. The thought of Jensen in her mother's tiny, cluttered living room eating Mr Kipling cakes and drinking coffee from cheap, chunky mugs made her smile.

"What's the joke?" Jensen frowned across the table.

"Nothing. Just thinking how lovely this food looks."

"Try eating it. It's heavenly, best I've had in a while." Grinning, he warned, "Don't tell Bilbo I said so."

"Bilbo's cooking is great. I wouldn't dream of upsetting him, your secret is safe with me – for a price." She gave him a saucy look.

"What sort of payment do you have in mind?" Food temporarily forgotten, he looked interested. "Do you know how lovely you are?"

Pleasure surged at his words. "Oh some sort of sexual favour, I'm sure I'll think of something – later," she teased.

"If only luv! I can't stay at your apartment tonight." He sighed, "I'm sorry."

"Why?" Disappointment apparent, she stared at him. "I don't understand." Did he consider her rooms to be too down market and shabby for him now he'd had time to see them better?

"I'm still under suspicion until the police can totally discount me as the murderer. We've all been instructed to spend from ten at night to eight in the morning aboard the Cassandra Rose until further notice. Also the yacht is not to be taken out again. There is to be an overnight police guard at the end of the pier. They've confiscated all of our passports, apart from Neil's, as he seems to have mislaid it."

Gosh! "How long do you think it will take for them to realise that you didn't kill Willie or attack Moonie?"

"How long is a piece of string?" Shrugging he went on. "There's nothing to stop you coming back with me."

"I'll think about it," she promised.

Darkness pressed around the car, Abby peered out of the side window. Confused, she still hadn't decided what to do. Sleeping with Jensen in her own apartment meant she'd some sort of control over the situation. On the boat she'd be on his territory.

"I don't think you should come back with me," Jensen spoke suddenly, interrupting her thoughts. "If someone on board is a killer, I don't want to expose you to any more danger. You will be safer on your own."

"I was just thinking the same thing." Giving a shaky laugh, she went on. "What about you? Who will keep you safe?"

"I don't have any choice, I have to be there, but I promise to lock my door."

Abby smiled into the darkness. "See that you do."

The lights of the village soon surrounded them.

"Drop me off on the main street. There are a couple of people I'd like to catch up with and it's early yet."

"How will you get home, it's quite a walk from here?" He pulled up to the kerb.

"I've walked loads of times. Don't worry, apart from the last couple of hundred yards, there will be plenty of people about, and I have a torch in my bag. If I get sloshed I'll take a taxi."

"Do you need any money for the taxi?"

"Don't be silly, it's only a couple of euros. Thanks anyway."

Leaning across he took her in his arms and his lips captured hers. Heat coursed, she melted against him. He tasted of the honey and spices the lamb had been cooked in. She wanted to go on kissing him forever. Eventually she wrenched her mouth away.

"You need to go."

"I need to make love to you." He cupped her chin and dropped a quick hot kiss on her lips. "I feel like a teenager with a curfew." Releasing her he muttered, "Go on then, go visit your friends."

Pete and Brenda were thrilled to see her. Brenda wouldn't allow Abby to pay for her drinks. Sitting in the bar they reminisced, the couple taking it in turns to get up and serve their other customers. The English couple had owned the taverna for five years. Abby and her sister, Jenny, had helped them arrange the furniture and stock up when they first bought the place and they'd been friends ever since.

Within an hour of Abby's arrival, the bar became busy and they could no longer talk. It was either sit on her lonesome or have an early night. Yawning, she made her decision.

Slipping off the bar stool she raised her voice. "I'll catch up with you guys another time." Quick nods were the only answers she got. Outside the warm night air engulfed her. She breathed deeply, loving the familiar smells and sounds of this lovely Greek Island.

The taxi rank along the road beckoned. Yawning again, Abby opened her handbag to retrieve her purse. Dismayed she remembered she'd decided not to bring it with her tonight. A large crowd pushed past, going into the bar. Her friends were too busy to be interrupted simply to borrow a few euros. The taxi driver would probably wait for her to retrieve the money from her room but the thought made her uneasy, vulnerable. There was only one other solution.

The lights of the last hotel faded behind her. Switching on her torch she shone it on the badly rutted road ahead. She'd always hated this stretch of road with its twists and bends. To each side loomed bushes, waist high walls and a half built house. Daunting, even when her sister was with her, alone it was downright scary. She quickened her pace.

Momentarily the road ahead was pierced by another flashlight. Abby looked back to see a small, wavering beam of light flickering between the shrubs, as she watched, it disappeared then reappeared again as the person holding the torch turned a corner. It wasn't unusual for other people to be using this road. She had to pass a couple of houses before reaching the apartment gates. Also she wasn't the only one staying there.

Continuing, she quickened her pace. She didn't know who was following her and this dark, quiet road was not somewhere she wanted to be found alone. A stitch gathered on the left side of her waist, pain lanced when she hurried. Slowing, she leaned to the right and massaged the ache. Footsteps sounded, spinning around she expected to see the torch bearer. Nothing but inky blackness met her gaze.

To her left a large shrub thrashed making her jump, cats screeched. A large dirty, black and white cat ran out from under the bush followed hotly by a ginger tom she recognised as belonging to the owner of her apartments.

Heart hammering from shock, she pressed her hand against her painful side and almost ran towards the apartments large wrought iron gates, illuminated by the lights shining from the building. Switching off her torch, she stepped into the relative safety of the apartment grounds. Standing with her hand on her chest, she waited for her breathing to return to normal.

Footsteps again, becoming nearer. No sound of voices. Fear rocked once more. *Oh bloody hell!* Fright gave her the extra speed needed as she hurried towards the steps leading to her floor, desperate to gain the sanctuary of her rooms as soon as possible.

"Meow, wow, wow." The ginger tom, Theo, ran to greet her at the top of the stairs. Maybe he'd recognised her earlier and remembered that she often fed him.

Relief flooded, she was no longer alone. "Well hello Theo." Looking back towards the road she tried to detect some sign of light, nothing but darkness met her eyes. She'd been stupid, imagining things. No wonder, with all the awful things which had been happening lately. Reaching down she carefully scratched Theo behind his ears. "It's been a while since I last saw you. What are you after?"

"Meow, wow."

"Yes, lucky for you I bought a tin of sardines yesterday in case you were still around. Wait until I get my key."

Cat twisting around her ankles meowing loudly, Abby fished in her handbag trying to find her key with the aid of the small light above her door. At last it was in her hand. Jamming it in the lock she repeatedly attempted to open the door without success.

Theo growled and ran off. Without the distraction of the cat she could hear someone behind her, feel their breath on her neck. Before she could turn a man's hand covered hers. A voice she didn't know spoke in her ear.

"Need some help with that?"

Filled with terror, Abby screamed.

CHAPTER THIRTEEN

Abby's scream echoed around the small platform.

With a grunt of surprise the man leapt away as though scared half to death.

Spinning around, she was confronted with the sight of a middle aged man holding his hands in the air as though he was expecting to be shot. A plump blonde woman stared over his shoulder, her eyes wide with shock.

"What did you do to her Bobby?" puzzlement laced the woman's words.

"Nothing. I didn't do a thing, I promise. I only wanted to help." Slowly he brought his arms down to his sides. "Why did you scream?" he addressed Abby, still amazed by her reaction.

"Sorry," Abby gasped, in need of some air. "I'm sorry. You startled me I didn't hear you approaching."

"It's these shoes," he explained pointing to his feet which were encased in soft, white loafers with thick soles. "We followed you down from the village so we knew you were on your own. Our torch battery ran out otherwise we would have caught up with you sooner. When we were crossing the lawn we could see you struggling with your lock. I thought I might be able to help." He shrugged. "Sorry to have frightened you. I should have called out first."

So she had heard footsteps, at least she wasn't imagining things. It must have been the woman's steps she'd heard.

"No harm done." She accepted his apology.

"Would you like me to see what I can do?" he offered.

Sighing with relief, she meekly handed over the key. "Yes please."

"Bobby's good with locks and things." The woman boasted giving Abby an encouraging smile.

Minutes later, Bobby shook his head in bewilderment. "Are you sure this is the right key?"

"Yes I've been using it for a couple of days."

"Well that's odd; it doesn't feel right in this lock." He tried again to get it to turn.

Fear dried her mouth. Had someone been trying to get into her rooms while she'd been out? Who would want to get in? An opportunist thief or, *please God no*, the Cassandra Rose crew member responsible for Willie's murder and the attempt on Moonie?

"Could someone have tampered with it?"

Bobby scratched his greying head. "It's possible of course, but this feels more like trying to fit a round peg in a square hole."

Remembering, she hadn't been the last one to lock up, dismay filled her. What if Jensen had taken her key with him? But then – where had the key in Bobby's hand come from? Enlightenment dawned. Of course! It belonged to her original apartment. The police had not asked her for it and she'd forgotten to give it back. What now?

"I think that might be the wrong key," she admitted, searching her handbag again. Relief flooded when her fingers closed around a long piece of metal - another key. Jensen must have slipped it into her bag without her seeing. "Here, try this one."

Door open, Abby thanked the couple for their help. Desperate to activate the air con and cool the rooms before going to bed, she declined their kind offer of a cuppa in their apartment. A little later Theo returned for his promised treat. Abby fed him outside her door before locking up for the night.

Lying on her bed staring into the darkness, she wondered if Jensen was thinking about her and missing her as much as she missed him. At least his bed would not remind him of their lovemaking as hers did. Every thought of what they'd done in this bed sent exquisite thrills shooting through her body causing her stomach to tighten with longing.

So much for not getting involved with him, she was about to get her heart broken one way or another. What was a rich man doing getting romantically involved with the likes of her? Was she being taken for a fool? What did it matter anyway? It wasn't as though she'd see him again after her holiday. Why not just enjoy it while it lasted? *Carpe diem Abby. Seize the day*. Thumping her pillow with frustration, she wiggled into a more comfortable position, closing her eyes she willed sleep to come. Eventually, imagining Jensen's strong arms around her, sweet oblivion claimed her.

Hunger gnawed. Sitting up on the sun lounger, Abby looked out to sea. She'd promised herself to wait until the glass bottomed boat returned at one o clock before going up to her rooms to have lunch on the balcony. No sign of it yet, or the Cassandra Rose, which was noticeable by its absence. What was Jensen doing? She'd half expected to find him on her doorstep first thing this morning. Disappointment still lingered.

Barely cool water lapped around her legs as she waded into the sea, feeling only slightly cooler when it reached her thighs. Relaxing into the turquoise depths she floated for a while before swimming around to the next bay. Treading water she looked towards the villa which belonged to Jensen's friends. It was impossible to see if anyone was sitting around their pool. If Jensen was with them she couldn't tell. Disappointed, she made her way back to the little beach.

The glass bottom boat still hadn't returned. Having left her watch in her rooms she'd no idea of the time. Deciding she was too hungry to wait until one, Abby picked up her beach bag and made her way to the shower located just inside the gates.

Soaking hair dripping, feet slipping wetly inside her pink crocs, beach-wrap clinging to every curve, she rounded the corner of the building in time to see Jensen exiting his hire car wearing stone coloured slacks with a cream shirt.

Oh wow! Her breath hitched, he looked delectable, fresh, well-groomed and oh so sexy.

"Good morning beautiful," he greeted her. "You're looking rather," he hesitated, "wet!" His hot appraisal indicated he liked her that way.

"Thanks." Heart racing with pleasure at the sight of him, she managed to sound pert. "I consider this to be one of my best looks." Placing her beach bag on the ground, she struck a few poses.

"I agree." He took his time looking her up and down. "You've taken the wet tee-shirt look to a whole new level."

Wiggling her hips she sashayed towards him. "Would you like a little cuddle?"

Backing away he waved his hands in front of him. "I'll pass until your dry thanks."

Reaching him she pouted as she took his hand and hung her head. "That's not very friendly," she complained swinging their joined hands.

Just as she'd hoped, he curled the finger of his free hand beneath her chin and tilted her head up. Dropping his other hand she flung her arms around him and pressed her wet body against his chest.

"Oh you sneaky…" The rest of his words cut off as her mouth met his.

With reluctance she withdrew her lips after a few moments, her purpose now achieved, she stepped back to survey the damage. "You're a bit damp." She grinned. "Why don't you come up to my rooms and we can hang your clothes on the balcony until they're dry."

"Sounds like a plan to me." He laughed, not bothered in the slightest about what she'd done. "I hadn't intended wearing them once we got inside anyway."

Jensen wandered in from the balcony clad in a pair of pale blue, cotton boxer shorts. "If you rinse your bikini through I'll hang it out for you," he offered.

"You're just trying to get me naked," Abby teased, loving the easy domestic familiarity they'd automatically fallen into.

"That's the idea." He wiggled his eyebrows at her. "Need any help undressing?"

How could one man make her nerve ends quiver yet at the same time be so easy to make love to? Everything was new and wonderful but without the normal restraints and embarrassment. It was as though they'd been lovers forever.

The soft bed supporting her back, Abby gasped with pleasure as his questing fingers found her most sensitive spot, her own hands reached to grasp him. His mouth covered hers as he kissed her deeply, their bodies arching against each other as they sought relief.

Leaving her lips, his mouth trailed hot kisses down her neck, between her breasts and across her stomach, making slow but steady progress down to where she squirmed against his busy fingers. "Please. Oh please," she begged.

Jensen looked up briefly, his blue eyes blazing with passion. "Don't worry luv, I'm getting there," he told her, his voice hoarse with need.

She loved the way he said 'luv' in that posh voice of his, it always made her quiver. This word added to his sexual onslaught was too much. Abby arched her back and gave herself up to pure sensation.

Later Jensen's lips nuzzled her ear lobe, his hot breath stirring the sensitive whorls. "You're wearing me out, woman," he whispered, his words a sexual promise of more to come.

"That's easily solved." Wanting to tease, she made as though to get out of bed, loving it when he began to pull her back into his arms.

"You're not getting away from me that easily."

Twisting, she picked up her pillow and hit him soundly on his naked hip and thigh.

Chuckling he sat up, and collecting his own pillow, whacked her on the arm. A huge fight ensued, grunts, shouts and yells mingled with joyous laughter. Standing by the bed arms raised above his head, Jensen prepared to take advantage of his position to strike Abby who knelt in the middle of the bed. "Yield," he demanded grinning from ear to ear.

Abby flung her missile with all her strength hitting him squarely on the chin and upper chest. Dropping his own pillow, he staggered back a few steps before regaining his balance. Picking a pillow from the floor he approached her with a feral gleam in his bright eyes. "I've thought of another use for this," he told her softly. "Why don't you lie down luv?" He almost purred. She followed his instruction without question. Lifting her buttocks he slid the soft fabric underneath.

Oh wow and double wow!

Ages later, Abby slid off the bed and made for the bathroom, hot and sweaty she desperately needed a shower.

"Where are you going?" Jensen's sleep drugged voice followed her.

"For a wash. I'd ask you to join me but there's only room for one at a time."

"I'll have one later," he murmured.

Stepping into some dry bikini bottoms, she gazed at his sleeping form. He looked good even while relaxed, not a sag to be seen anywhere. The sight of his flat stomach caused answering flutters within her own. The part of him that was quintessentially male, twitched, alerting Abby to the fact he was no longer sleeping.

"Fancy a cheese and tomato sarnie?" she squeaked, entranced by the spectacle, yet determined to put some space between them if even for a short while. She needed their relationship to be more than just sex.

"Is that all you have to offer?" He opened dark blue eyes filled with lust.

"What would you prefer?" Ignoring his come hither look, she pulled a pair of green shorts over the swimwear and donned a matching sun-top.

"You, followed by you, followed by…" He stroked the invisible beard on his chin, "Oh yes – you."

"When did you last eat?" she accused.

"I had brunch," he consulted his watch, the only thing he was wearing. "About three hours ago."

"I had breakfast around seven and I'm starving." Making her way to the kitchen she prepared her lunch.

"Want a beer?"

"Better not, I'm driving, a glass of cold water will do." Wearing a towel around his lean hips he sauntered over to her, pulling her back into is arms so that her bottom fitted against his sex. He kissed, and lightly bit, her neck.

Mmmmm.

"Since it looks as though you're not going to play nicely I might as well have my shower." He didn't sound too upset. With a final kiss to the nape of her neck he let her go. While he showered she tided up her clothes and put some to one side to wash later.

Picking up her plate and drink, she took them out onto the balcony.

Jensen followed her wearing his boxer shorts.

"Poor restaurant this, I'm sure I ordered a glass of water."

"Oh sorry! I'll get it now sir."

He swatted her backside as she squeezed by him.

"See that you do."

Sprawled in one of the two basket weave chairs, Jensen looked good enough to eat. Her stomach somersaulted with longing. *Maybe later?*

"Thanks luv." He lifted the glass she offered and took a long drink.

Watching his strong brown throat contract with each swallow only heightened her returning desire. With reluctance she looked away. Eyes alighting on her plate she smiled.

"Mice living out here, are there?"

"I'm sure I don't know what you mean?" Failing to keep his face straight, his mouth turned up at the corners.

Pulling up her chair, she picked up one half of her sandwich, pretending to examine the large bite-sized hole. "Rather a big mouse I would think. In fact if I didn't know better I would suspect a rather sexy man who said he wasn't hungry."

"I'm not. I simply wanted to make sure that it was just right for you."

Pointing to the untouched half, she arched an eyebrow. "Would you like to test the other bit?"

"The only thing I want to sample is you. Unfortunately I don't have time." Pushing his chair back, he stood up. "My clothes have had more than enough time to dry. I'm going to get dressed while you finish your lunch. Otherwise I might become distracted and be late for my appointment with the Greek authorities this afternoon."

"You're leaving?"

Please no. The bread in her mouth turned dry and stale.

"Yes, but I'd planned to take you with me."

Relief flooded. She was coming to hate being separated from his man.

CHAPTER FOURTEEN

Abby roamed around the old town while Jensen attended the meeting to try and lift the order which banned him from taking the Cassandra Rose out of the harbour in which it was moored. Whilst he could understand why the Hellenic Police would want to keep him and his crew under surveillance – none of them had been arrested or charged.

Hearing someone call her name, Abby turned to see a few crew members sitting around a large, wooden table outside a pretty taverna. Sitting in the cool shade cast by the building behind them and with tiny bunches of grapes dangling from the vine covered trellis above their heads, they looked relaxed and happy.

"Come and have a drink with us," Parky offered, getting to his feet. Having been taught good manners, Abby appreciated his gentlemanly gesture.

"You're more than welcome," Spen chipped in, exposing a set of teeth which would not have looked out of place on a mule.

Smiling her thanks, Abby dropped into the spare chair which Woody quickly retrieved from an empty table. "That would be lovely. I'd love a diet coke."

"I wouldn't recommend the food," Bilbo confided in a low voice. The others laughed.

"Bilbo doesn't trust foreign food," Spen said through his mirth. "He always warns us off. We think he just says it's awful so that we will eat everything he serves up later."

"I do not." Indignant, Bilbo tugged the peak of the bright blue baseball cap he wore to protect his bald head from the sun.

Everyone laughed at the huffy look he gave Spen. Abby could feel the companionship within the group, they were part of a team and Bilbo was obviously a respected member. How could any of these men be capable of murder?

The waiter placed a tall frosted glass in front of her. "How is Moonie?" Abby directed her question to Bilbo hoping to lure him out of his sudden bad mood. Ice cubes tinkled softly against the side of her glass as she took a deep drink.

"Oh! He is a little better. Thank you for asking. He came around this morning while I was visiting him."

"You never said," Woody accused.

"You never asked." The sulky look was back.

Abby suddenly realised that Bilbo was gay. How hadn't she seen it before?

"Did he say who attacked him?" Spen wanted to know, his gaze intent upon Bilbo.

"Not yet. His throat is damaged and it's still too sore for him to speak." Bilbo wrapped his hand around his own neck to demonstrate. "The cut on his head is healing well, though."

"What caused the head injury, does anybody know?" Abby inquired.

"The doctors think he struck the side of the boat on the way down. He has a number of other bruises that bear out that theory." Bilbo shook his head. "He's fortunate to be alive. I for one can't wait until he is able to tell the police what happened."

Parky mumbled his agreement.

"Who could have done it? Anyone got any ideas," Parky wanted to know.

"I've got my suspicions." Bilbo nodded sagely. "But I can't bring myself to believe that this person could have tried to strangle Moonie, never mind murder Willie." Taking a drink of his beer he wiped his mouth with the back of his hand before going on. "Therefore, I'm saying nothing and praying that I'm wrong."

Abby noticed that during his whole conversation he'd kept his eyes down, purposely looking at no-one in particular.

"You don't know any of us," Woody who'd had nothing to say so far, addressed Abby. He leaned back in his seat so that it balanced precariously on two legs. He looked relaxed and slightly bored. "As an outsider, who do you think the culprit is?"

"Who knows?" This was a tricky question, best to confess that she hadn't a clue. "Apart from Bilbo, everyone sitting here is in the frame for poor Willie and, apart from Bob Simms, anybody on board could have attacked Moonie."

"Sound's like you've given this some thought." Woody gave her a curious look, chair legs clattered to the floor as he leant forward, his eyes narrowing with suspicion.

"Yeah," Spen added, "I heard Mr Stone tell that police Captain Feller that you're a bit of an amateur detective."

Oops!

"Not at all, that was straight off the top of my head," she lied. *Change of subject required.* "I don't even know what jobs you all do." Plastering an interested smile on her face, she prepared for a longwinded explanation of their various roles.

"I'm the cook," Bilbo offered. "Spen is the second engineer, although I suppose he is the first at the moment what with Moonie in hospital. Woody and Parky are both lowly deckhands." He made a face in their direction.

"Hey, not so lowly," Woody complained. "We keep the exterior of the yacht clean and maintained, that's pretty important. Apart from that we're often called upon to fill in for you lot when you cannot cope." He folded his arms across his chest, his face tight.

Bilbo ignored him, continuing as though there had been no interruption. "Bob's the captain, Willie was first officer, that's just below captain, and Mark's the steward."

"Talking about me again, I hope you're not telling tales." Mark stepped behind Bilbo, one hand holding a selection of colourful carrier bags; the other gently caressed the cook's shoulder. "I've bought you a lovely purple shirt." Dumping the shopping on Bilbo's lap, he looked around. "I'll just get myself a chair."

Struggling to keep her astonishment from showing, Abby got to her feet. "Here, you can have mine. I'm meeting Jensen soon and I need to find my way back to where I said I'd see him."

"I'll walk with you," Parky offered. "It's quite steep around here and those little cobbles can get very slippery.

Abby smiled. She liked his company - why not? "Thanks, I'd enjoy that."

Spen smirked. "Hands off, Parky, she's too old for you. She'd have you for breakfast."

"What a delicious thought." Parky grinned.

"That's if the Boss didn't get you first," Woody joined in, laughing.

Parky brushed his wayward hair out of his eyes. "You're all jealous," he teased.

"Yep," Spen confirmed with a big toothy grin.

"Thank you for the coke." Face flushing, Abby felt she had to say something to break the banter up.

"You're welcome," several voices chorused.

Parky altered his pace to match Abby's. "So what do you think of our little crew?"

"I'm a bit surprised Mark is Bilbo's partner. He looks straight. Although I remember the day after the murder he looked as though he'd been crying."

"Yeah, he's always been a sensitive sort. He's been very cut up about Willie and Moonie."

A thought struck. "Was Willie gay?"

"No." Parky laughed. "Not to my knowledge. He seemed to like the ladies just as much as the rest of us."

"And Moonie?" Stopping, Abby wiped sweat from her brow. This road really was quite steep.

"I don't think so. You never can tell." He grinned. "You should see me in my frock."

Abby laughed out loud at the thought. "I'm sure you look very fetching." She started walking again.

Parky caught up. "But seriously. Do you have any idea who is going around harming people?"

"As I said before, it could be anyone. Let's face it you and Jensen are the prime suspects."

Parky looked taken aback. "You don't believe it was one of us. Do you?"

"Of course not." They'd reached the top of the hill, Abby glanced around. "This is where I was supposed to meet Jensen but he's not here yet."

"I'll go and see if I can find him," Parky offered. "He's in that big building over there – right?"

"Yes. The main door is just around the corner."

"Okay. If I see him I'll send him to you and go back to the lads. If not I'll come and tell you." He looked down at her earnestly as though he wanted to say more. "See you later," he managed eventually.

Abby was left with the feeling that the lads hadn't been far wrong, Parky obviously still fancied her.

Could this holiday get any more complicated?

Half an hour later Jensen returned, hurrying across the square looking hot and bothered. Abby rose from the stone seat, situated beneath the shade of a large mulberry tree, and went to meet him.

"Sorry luv."

Her lower body tensed in sexual response at the sound of her favourite word.

Jensen kissed her hair, then her lips. "God I've missed you. Bloody officials kept me waiting for over an hour then refused to listen to what I had to say. Apparently the police are within their rights and I have to wait for the ban to be lifted before I can up anchor. What a waste of time."

"There's a café over there, you look as though you could do with a drink." All she wanted was him.

"Certainly could. What have you been doing with yourself?" He stopped at the first table and pulled a seat out for her. Parky wasn't the only one who knew how to treat a girl.

"Having drinks with the crew."

"What!" Dropping into his own chair, he picked up a plastic covered menu and fanned his hot face.

"Yes, they're all here apart from Bob."

Jensen's pocket buzzed, followed immediately by Katie Perry singing 'Firework'. Fishing out his phone, he glanced at the display before smiling apologetically at Abby. "It's Captain Georgallis. Let's hope he has some news."

Watching the colour leech from his face, coldness settled around Abby's heart. *Oh God what now?* What could have happened to make him look that way?

"What? What is it?" she whispered as he clicked his mobile shut.

"It's Bilbo."

"Bilbo?"

"Yes." He took a deep shuddering breath, "Seems he's fallen down a cliff."

"What! Is he dead?"

"They don't know. He's lying on a ledge above the sea and the rescue services are attempting to get to him."

CHAPTER FIFTEEN

A large area at the top of the cliff was cordoned off. To one side the crew stood in a loose knot, their faces tight with concern. Hot air swirled around blowing Abby's short, dark hair busily around her face. A heavy vibrating noise made it impossible to talk.

Within a few minutes of their arrival a helicopter materialised over the top of the cliff, a stretcher bearing Bilbo, attached to its underbelly like a large bird carrying newly caught prey. Abby shivered at the thought despite the wave of heat pushed down by the rotating blades.

Sun-top billowing, shorts flapping around her thighs and momentarily deafened, Abby watched as it flew out to sea gaining height, before heading inland, presumably for the hospital.

"Did you notice the yellow head and neck brace?" she yelled in Jensen's direction.

"Yes. Its good news of a sort, at least he's still alive."

"What happens now?"

"It depends what Captain Georgallis has to say on the matter." Jensen gestured sideways using only his eyes.

Without moving her head Abby followed his example. The policeman headed purposefully in their direction.

"I'd rather get to the hospital to find out first hand how Bilbo is before speaking to the Captain," Jensen told her.

"What Captain?" Abby said innocently. "Do you think he saw us looking at him?"

"I don't believe he did." He grabbed her hand. "Shall we?" Still holding hands they ran towards where Jensen had left his car.

By the time Jensen found a space in the hospital car-park, Bilbo was already receiving treatment. The doctor on duty refused to give any details until she'd seen the x-rays and had the results of all the tests. They were told he was being made comfortable and more information would be available later.

Plain whitewashed walls, unadorned apart from a couple of unexciting floral prints, which would have looked at home in a hotel bedroom, surrounded them. There was nothing to look at in the visitor waiting room except each other. Having caught Jensen studying her with a hungry look several times, Abby could no longer bear the building sexual tension. This was neither the time nor the place to give in to their feelings.

"Is Moonie in this hospital?"

"Yes he's in ward 18. Would you like to see how he is doing luv?" Jensen looked relieved to have an excuse to get out of the sterile looking room and be doing something.

Apart from a bandage at his throat, Moonie looked to be doing well. Still in bed, he lay propped up reading a James Patterson novel that looked to have seen better days. A faint, but noticeable, smell of disinfectant lingered.

"How you doing?" Jensen greeted him.

Smiling with pleasure Moonie placed the dog-eared book on the bedspread and picked a notebook and pen off his bedside table.

FINE. BEEN TOLD NOT TO TRY TO TALK YET, he wrote.

"You know Miss Grainger." Jensen inclined his head towards Abby.

Moonie gave a slight nod accompanied by a wince. He picked up his pen and wrote. THANKS FOR SAVING MY LIFE.

Jensen stepped up to the bed and they shook hands. "My pleasure," he smiled. "Although I don't want to make a habit of it, I was absolutely terrified it wouldn't work."

They spent over an hour talking to Moonie who wrote, he had no idea who'd attacked him, as he'd already informed the police. He'd been looking up to see if there was something stopping the door from closing when someone came up behind him and slipped a noose around his neck. He'd no idea of the height of his assailant. There had been no telltale smell of aftershave and, apart from a few grunts, the person had not spoken.

Mark and Spen were sitting drinking coffee from white polystyrene cups when Jensen and Abby returned to the waiting room.

"Any news?" Jensen wanted to know.

"Nothing yet." Mark looked as though he'd been crying again.

"Any idea what happened?"

Rising from one of several pale blue, vinyl covered chairs, Spen answered. "We decided to walk back to the boat across the cliff top. Being cooped up on board we all felt like stretching our legs."

"Wish we'd got a couple of taxis like we'd planned," Mark whispered, crushing his cup. Leftover coffee ran through his fingers, dripping in fat brown splodges onto the white tiled floor between his feet.

"Yeah well we didn't." Sympathy warmed Spen's words. Looking at Jensen, he continued. "We were all messing around teasing Bilbo like we normally do. Everyone was laughing, nudging and jostling each other like. Then suddenly Bilbo was too near the edge. A few of us grabbed for him but he went over." Shaking his head, he studied his shoes for a few seconds before going on. "I felt his tee-shirt slip through my fingers - I thought I had him." He sighed. "It all happened so quickly."

"Mr Stone." The young female doctor they'd spoken to previously, stood in the doorway.

"Yes."

"Mr Bowman's results are back. I'm pleased to be able to tell you there are no serious injuries. Apart from a badly broken leg, he suffered only cuts and bruising. Some of the cuts are deep and required stitching. We are keeping him in overnight just to keep an eye on him. If you would like to see him, he can have two visitors at a time."

Mark and Spen went first. They stayed for twenty minutes or so before Spen took himself off to inform the rest of the crew that Bilbo wasn't in any danger. Mark retreated to the waiting room to allow Jensen and Abby to visit. He intended to stay at Bilbo's side for as long as the hospital staff would permit.

Bilbo looked as though he'd been beaten up. Patches of puce, purple and blackish blue bruises covered arms which stood out violently against the white sheet on which they lay. Peering at them out of the eye which wasn't swollen shut he managed a small smile.

"Sorry boss you'll have to make your own supper tonight," he joked.

"How did this happen?" Jensen wanted to know.

"Bloody clumsy I guess. I didn't realise how close to the edge we were."
He sighed. "A few of the lads tried to grab me, I could feel their hands on
my clothes but I still went over. Spen recons I was weighed down with all
the pies I've eaten."

"You could have been killed. Look at the state of you." Jensen failed to
keep his concern from showing.

"I'd have been a hell of a lot worse if I hadn't landed on that shelf. The
fall knocked me out for a bit. If I'd gone into the sea I'd probably have
drowned."

"Thank God you didn't. In retrospect it must be your lucky day."

"Guess my luck hasn't changed much then." Bilbo winced as he moved
a bruised arm slightly.

Abby closed the door of her apartment and switched the kettle on. "Do
you want coffee or something stronger?"

"Have you got any tea?" Jensen ran a hand through his caramel
coloured hair, causing long curls to spring between his fingers.

"Yes. Go on the balcony and I'll bring it out."

"Just milk please."

"Okay."

Jensen's phone rang. "I'll take this outside." He moved away.

The mugs rattled together as she lifted them from the shelf. Today had
shaken her more than she cared to admit. Bilbo had admitted, he thought
he knew who the killer was and less than an hour later he was lying on a
ledge on a cliff face, too much of a coincidence for it have been an accident
as far as she was concerned.

The only good thing to come out of it was that Jensen hadn't been
involved. With great relief she mentally drew a second black line through
his name, well and truly crossing him off the list of suspects.

Jensen's face looked as tight as a drum skin. Sipping his tea, he stared
out to sea obviously deep in thought.

"What are you thinking about?"

He answered without taking his eyes off the view. "I can't get my head
around all the incidents. Why is this happening to my crew? Who's next?"

Sitting next to him, Abby took one of his large hands into her own and gave it gentle tug, forcing his attention to her. "Do you believe that Bilbo's fall was an accident?"

Frowning, Jensen shook his head. "No. No I don't." He took a sip of his tea. "For one thing Bilbo was far too cheerful for having had a near miss with death."

"Yes I thought that too. Although I don't know him as well as you do."

"He's been known to make the odd funny comment and make the crew laugh, but doesn't normally make fun of himself. It was out of character, too forced. I have the horrible feeling he was covering something up."

"He mentioned having a good idea who the murderer is."

"What? When?" Startled, Jensen jerked upright causing the small table to rock.

"When I had drinks with them this afternoon. He said he couldn't believe that this person was capable of killing so he wouldn't say who his suspect was.

"If the culprit was there he could have manipulated Bilbo's fall. It would be interesting to find out whose idea it was to walk back to the yacht."

"That was Georgallis on the phone before. He says they are treating the Bilbo incident as purely accidental. You're going to have to tell them about the conversation in the taverna if we're going to get to the bottom of this." He checked his watch. "I'd rather be with you when you speak to him. I have to be back onboard in a few hours and we need to eat first, so no time tonight. I'll pick you up in the morning and we'll go together."

Enjoying dinner at a local taverna, Abby remembered Jensen's earlier flash of memory. "Have you remembered anything else about Willie's murder?" Keeping her tone casual she speared a carrot and lifted it towards her lips.

"No, nothing." Frowning, he eyed her fork. "Lucky carrot," he deftly changed the subject, "wish I was heading for that luscious mouth of yours."

"I have an idea," she continued ignoring his attempt to divert her.

"Oh! So have I." His wicked grin made her smile.

"Tomorrow morning, before going to the police, we could go to my original apartment and see if anything jogs your memory." She held her breath waiting for his reply.

"Is that what you would like to do?" Jensen had given up any pretence at eating.

"It might supply some answers." Popping the food into her mouth she chewed.

"Okay," he said slowly. "How will we get in? It's bound to be locked."

"I expect it will be. However, I have a key." She took another bite of food.

"How?" Jensen resumed his meal.

"I must have automatically popped the key in my handbag when we left. I wasn't thinking straight and probably did it without thinking. I found it the other night." She didn't tell him how. "If the door's locked they probably used the maid's key." Opening her handbag she retrieved the key from an inner zipped pocket and handed it to him. "I meant to return it today but then forgot all about it."

Jensen turned the key over in his hand unable to believe its existence. He slipped it thoughtfully into his pocket. Abby was right. It was time to face his demons.

Later they walked back to Abby's apartment. Long lingering kisses almost undermined Jensen's willpower, only the thought of being locked up for disobeying the orders issued by Captain Georgallis got him to the doorway.

"I wish you didn't have to go." Abby nibbled his throat.

Jensen groaned. "Not as much as I do, beautiful. Stop torturing me." He pulled her closer. "See what you do to me?"

Wriggling against his arousal, Abby turned her attention to his earlobe.

"Stop! Stop! I'm going now." Reaching behind him he jerked the door open. Disentangling himself, he gave her a quick peck on the lips and darted outside. "Lock the door straight away," he ordered as he disappeared around the corner into the dusk. Abby waited until she heard his car door close before she went inside and turned the key.

Within minutes there was a soft knock at the door. "What have you forgotten?" Throwing the door open she imagined he'd returned for a few more kisses.

A figure stood under the doorway's meagre light dressed totally in black, his head covered by a black ski mask, a gun glinted faintly in his hand. He looked like an armed Cadbury's milk tray man who'd forgotten the chocolates.

"Get your coat; we're going for a little ride," a harsh voice said. His free hand shoved hard on her shoulder.

Abby stumbled backwards into the apartment.

CHAPTER SIXTEEN

Too shocked to think straight, Abby said the first thing which came into her head. "It's too hot to wear a coat!"

The masked man pushed her through the kitchen into the bedroom. He gestured towards the blue, hand painted wardrobe with his gun. Hands shaking, Abby found it difficult to pull the small, round handle, it slid through her fingers and the door banged shut. Her second attempt met with more success.

More scared than she'd ever been in her life, she thought she might throw up. Finding poor Willie dead hadn't been as terrifying as this. Sweat beaded her brow and coated her skin. Harsh rapid breathing quickly dried her mouth. Even to her own ears she sounded terrified.

Draping Abby's cream coloured jacket over his arm to hide the weapon, the masked man forced Abby to walk ahead of him. On quaking legs she staggered down the steps and across the lawn. The warm darkness cloaked their passage. Cicadas made their nightly racket, a cat screeched and music played softly from one of the apartments. No-one appeared to rescue her.

A prod from the gun steered her towards a dark coloured hire car parked deep in the shadow of the trees growing around the walls. Once in the car he quickly cable tied her trembling hands so that they rested palm to palm in her lap. He then bound her ankles together and secured a series of linked ties between them and her wrists, the full skirt of her blue sundress somewhat hampering his movements. Her feet and hands were now attached.

Away from town lights, he pulled the car over. Taking a woman's silky, red scarf from his pocket he wound it around her eyes so she could no longer see. Already traumatised by her abduction, Abby fainted clean away.

Clammy cheek stuck to what felt like glass, eyebrow painfully resting on a narrow ridge and hair whipping around her head, Abby came to. Fighting nausea she attempted to work out where she was. The gentle hum of an engine and the supporting shape of the seat convinced her that she was still in the car.

Cautiously moving her head, waves of pain penetrated her skull. Taking a deep breath she sat upright. Air from the partly open window she'd obviously been lying against, fanned her face, drying the sweat and making her feel marginally better.

"Where are we going?" She sounded as though she'd been eating gravel.

Stupid question, if he'd wanted her to know their destination he wouldn't have blindfolded her.

No answer. Come to think of it, the only time he'd spoken was when she'd first opened her apartment door. Did this mean that he was afraid she would recognise his voice? - *Of course it did!*

If her abductor was linked to the attacks on the Cassandra Rose crew, then it could only be Spen, Woody or Parky. Bob had been in her cabin when Moonie fell. She discounted Mark as, having thought about it; she deemed it unlikely he would have pushed his lover, Bilbo, over the cliff. Jensen had been with her at the time, and even if that wasn't the case, she knew in her heart that he could never harm anyone.

The rhythm of the wheels changed, they had moved onto different terrain - a side road perhaps? Before long the car rocked and bounced as the ground roughened. Unable to hang on, Abby was tossed around, her head pounding at every jolt. Twisting around, she groped for the elbow rest protruding from the door. Wrapping both hands around the hard plastic surface she held on tight.

An age later the car stopped. The driver's door clicked open, footsteps crunched on gravel. Fear spiked. Had he brought her here to die? Her door opened suddenly, still holding onto the elbow rest, she fell out onto pebbly ground scraping both her knees. Tears gathered abruptly.

Hauled to her hobbled feet, a rough hand on her elbow, her bent over form was dragged along.

"Steps," the harsh, disguised voice warned.

Manoeuvred up a couple of steps and through what felt like a doorway, the ground under her feet suddenly felt marginally smoother. Had they entered some sort of building? Brushing against another doorframe she realised they must have entered an inner room. He turned her around and she stumbled backwards. A coarse surface pressed against the back of her knees forcing her to sit down. A thin mattress gave slightly, cushioning her bottom.

Swiftly her ankles were freed, then her wrists. The thud of a weighty door closing, followed by the loud rattle of a heavy metal bolt, told her that she was alone. Tearing the scarf from her eyes she looked around. Nothing, she couldn't see a thing, only uninterrupted blackness everywhere she looked.

Oh God! A sob of pure terror escaped her lips.

Shortly, she heard the muted sound of a car door closing. Abby held her breath listening intently. An engine roared to life, the subsequent noise becoming steadily fainter until there was nothing but the haunting quiet of utter remoteness with only the song of the cicadas to relieve the pressing silence.

"Noooooo…!" Abby screamed. Scared stiff, locked up and alone in the dark, she realised the fear of instant death was marginally better than the thought of being left to slowly die in a strange place with no hope of rescue.

After a while she gingerly felt around, her head filled with images of fleas, spiders, cockroaches, rats and snakes, her heart racing faster at each new thought. When her questing hand touched a cold wet object she thought she'd pass out. Common sense prevailed; reaching out again she tentatively explored the object. Almost laughing with relief, she realised it was one of three large bottles of water lying on top of her jacket.

Curled on the fairly wide bed, her head cushioned on the lining of her jacket, she eventually fell asleep. Awake at first light, the first thing she noticed was the sun shining through a large hole in the corner of the roof on the opposite side of the room, far too high up to be a way out. The second was a blue plastic bucket accompanied by a roll of toilet paper.

After using the bucket and taking a long drink of water she explored her prison. An average sized room which showed signs of having been recently swept. Jagged cracks radiated from the damaged roof down to the floor like forked lightening. A dusty, broken stone sink stood where the wall with the door met the fractured wall. Closer inspection showed a glimmer of daylight at the bottom of the ancient drainage system. At least she had somewhere to empty the bucket which could become very unsavoury in this heat.

Her, not quite double sized, bed was made of solid concrete built into one of the walls. A large cardboard box sealed with strong tape stood beside the bed.

Ripping open the box she discovered several packages containing pre-packed food together with some fruit and more bottles of water. Sitting back on her heels she burst into tears. Her relief at finding the food – proof that he didn't intend to kill her - was outweighed by the knowledge that her captor obviously planned to leave her here for some time.

Sitting on her bed, she pulled the wrapping from a chocolate croissant and ate it slowly, making sure she did not drop any crumbs. At present the room seemed to be clear of insects and rodents, however, one sniff of food and the place would be crawling with uninvited diners.

Pondering who her kidnapper could be gave her something to do. Convinced that it was one of the crew she thought about the voice. By the time she'd finished eating she was no further forward. Switching her thoughts to his build she imagined him standing in her kitchen doorway. He'd seemed tall, taller than Jensen. Woody was the tallest of the crew with Parky not far behind, but then Spen and Mark were not exactly short either. It was no good. She had no clue as to who her captor could be.

The thought of being trapped in this room all day was terrifying! From the amount of food and water in the cardboard box she wouldn't be surprised if she was to be left alone tonight as well. What did he want with her? Why hadn't he just killed her like he had Willie? He'd had plenty of opportunity to do a thorough job, unlike his bungled attempts on Moony and Bilbo, so why was she still alive?

Once Jensen noticed she was missing, he would raise the hue and cry. Her swift elation at this thought was soon dampened by the realisation that no-one would know where to look. There were always a number of hire cars parked in the apartment grounds, how would the police know which one had carried her here?

Hopelessness stole over her. Exhausted by fear, a virtually sleepless night and the steadily building heat, she curled up on her bed and closed her eyes. Tears seeped from under her lids, spiking her lashes before pooling on the meagre mattress as she drifted off to sleep.

CHAPTER SEVENTEEN

Jensen parked outside Abby's apartment. Having risen early he'd been ready to leave the yacht as soon as he was allowed. Having discovered that it had been Mark's idea to walk back across the headland, he couldn't wait to speak to the police. Once Abby repeated Bilbo's admission that he knew who the murderer was the police would be able to make an arrest.

Drumming his fingers lightly on the steering wheel, he went over the facts. Mark had been on shore when Willie was murdered and this had been kept hidden. Mark said that he'd been alone in Jensen's room when Moonie was attacked so he had no alibi. Plus he had access to all Jensen's clothes – including his ties. Finally, when Bilbo said he couldn't believe who the killer was, Mark would've known his partner was protecting him.

Slamming the flat of his hand against the dashboard, Jensen swore out loud. Bilbo wasn't the only one who found it hard to believe Mark was the culprit. Jensen had known him for over four years and in that time he always appeared to be a friendly, meek mannered man. How wrong could he be!

At the top of the apartment stairs Jensen halted, looking along to where it had all started. If only he could remember more about what happened. Warm fur tickled his shins. Looking down at the ginger tom weaving around his legs, he smiled. "Hello, I guess your Theo. I've heard all about you. Come on; let's see if your friend Abby is awake yet."

Knocking again, Jensen called out softly. "Come on sleepyhead let me in." Theo added his voice to the appeal. Jensen tried the handle, surprised when it turned in his hand. Everything looked the same as when he'd left the previous night. The light on, curtains drawn and the bedspread rumpled from where they'd lain earlier yesterday. Even their tea cups still sat on the bench unwashed. The bathroom door stood open, he could see at a glance that Abby wasn't in the apartment.

"Meow," Theo commented.

"Yes I agree, very strange." Where could she be? Should he be alarmed or was there a rational explanation? Theo mewed again. Opening the fridge, Jensen took out a saucer holding a large sardine covered in cling film. Swiftly uncovering the fish he placed the saucer outside the door. "Here you are boy. Enjoy."

Pulling out his phone he called Abby, once he discovered where she was everything would be alright. Abba's Mamma Mia sounded behind him. Swinging around he saw Abby's mobile lying on the bedside cabinet. Picking it up he checked the caller id and recognised the photo of himself sprawled on her bed – naked, which she'd taken the previous day. "Damn it." Worry gnawed at him. Where was she? He speed dialled Captain Georgallis.

The Captain stood in Abby's apartment, his sharp eyes looking for signs of a struggle. "Wherever she's gone it looks as though she went of her own accord." A long sigh escaped his lips. "Sorry Mr Stone I don't know what you expect me to do."

Frantic, Jensen appealed to the policeman. "Don't you see? We were about to come and see you this morning with some important information. Apparently yesterday Bilbo admitted to Abby, and the other members of the crew, that he knew who the killer was. He was the victim of an accident an hour later and now Abby has disappeared. There has to be some connection."

"Seems to have disappeared," the policeman reasoned.

"What?"

"Miss Grainger *seems* to have disappeared," he repeated. "I'm sorry. Even if there is a link between the two events, where would we start looking? Your crew are the main suspects. All the members, apart from those who are still in hospital, were logged by one of my men when they boarded the yacht last night and again when some of them left this morning." He spread his hands in defeat. "No-one could have smuggled Miss Grainger aboard without my men noticing."

"She has to be somewhere." Jensen ran a hand over his worried face. "What about a local search in case... In case..."

Looking sad, the Captain finished the sentence. "In case her body is lying nearby."

Sinking onto the bed, his body hunched forward, Jensen whispered.

"God I couldn't bear that." How could he live without her? The few days they'd know each other were enough to convince him that Abby was important to him.

"Unfortunately without a body or some sort of proof that there has been some foul play, I cannot proceed."

"What am I supposed to do now?" Anger vibrating through his system Jensen surged to his feet. "Without your help I don't know where to start looking for her." His raised voice startled Theo, who had sneaked into the kitchen looking for more sardines.

"Just because my hands are officially tied, it does not mean I cannot give you some pointers," The Captain offered. Pinching the bridge of his nose he looked down at his shoes. "First we need to establish what time she went missing. What time did you leave last night?"

"I remember looking at my watch at about nine and saying that I had to go. I probably left about five or ten minutes later."

"Well according to Andreas, the policeman who logged you all aboard, every crew member got back before ten last night. You and, 'our friend' Mark were the first to leave this morning, which doesn't give a lot of time to hide Miss Grainger." He pulled at his bottom lip. "It might be worth looking into whether any of the crew hired a car recently. If so, you'll have to widen your search."

"You say Mark has left the yacht?"

"Yes. Both Mr Moon and Mr Bowman are being discharged this morning. I believe Mr McDonald has gone to collect them in a taxi." He pulled out his phone to make a call.

Jensen's frustration mounted as he stood listening to the one-sided, rapid Greek conversation without being able to understand one word. Georgallis had hardly finished speaking before Jensen begged again for help.

"When will you 'officially' be able to help me look?" He ploughed his fingers through his already tousled hair.

"As soon as you can confirm that she has been missing for twenty-four hours, or you find proof that there has been some sort of foul play. I've instructed my officer to pick up Mr MacDonald for further questioning. Perhaps we can persuade him to tell us where she is," he comforted, putting his mobile phone away.

"I still cannot get my head around Mark being the killer." Jensen shook his head. "All the evidence points that way, but something still doesn't ring true."

"It's rarely the person who you would normally suspect," Captain Georgallis confirmed.

"It's hard to suspect anyone. Until this week I trusted them all implicitly." Sadness and puzzlement tinged his words.

"Look, there's a small travel agents in the village, they find accommodation for tourists, do local trips and hire out cars. It might be a good place to start your investigations. I'm sure they will be able to supply you with details of other car hire places if they can't help."

By mid afternoon Jensen was no further forward. Abby was still missing and, as far as he could tell, none of his crew had hired a car. He'd spent most of the day trawling around the mostly deserted lanes, his heart in his mouth as he peered over walls and behind bushes. He'd even searched the partly built house further along the road from the apartments. All he'd got for his trouble was being spat at by an angry female cat defending her litter of kittens.

Sitting outside Abby's apartment, his fingers, once again, tattooing the steering wheel, Jensen wracked his brains for inspiration.

"Hello." A middle aged woman stood beside his elbow, which jutted out of the open window.

"Hi. Can I help you?" He could do without a pointless, polite chat.

"Are you waiting for your friend?"

Straightening, suddenly alert, Jensen revised his opinion of the possible conversation. "Have you seen her?"

"Not today." She shook her head.

Heart plummeting as disappointment washed over him, Jensen almost stopped listening.

"I saw her go out with a strange man last night though," the woman continued. "Me, and my Bobby thought it funny because he was wearing a balaclava on such a hot night."

"A balaclava?"

"Yes, you know, one of those black knitted things which cover the head and neck," she explained patiently.

"Yes I know what they look like." Sounding short, he gentled his tone. "Where did you see them? What were they doing?"

"Oh! Well the reason I noticed them was because he was dressed all in black and carrying a light coloured coat over his arm. That looks odd, I thought. I just came out to throw a cup of water over the damn cat you see. Your friend was leading the way and they were nearly at the car when I saw them." She nodded to herself as if to confirm she had her facts right.

"What time did you see them?"

"Oh it must have been about quarter past nine or thereabouts."

So almost immediately after he'd left!

"Did Abby look as though she was being forced to go?" Heart hammering, Jensen waited for her answer.

Looking surprised by the question, the woman slowly shook her head. "Couldn't say, they had their backs to me you see." She nodded again.

"Did you see the car?"

Please, please say that you did.

"Oh yes."

Thank God!

"What type was it?"

"Dark, yes it was dark coloured. Don't know much about makes but it was fairly small and either dark blue or maybe even black." She gave a little laugh. "It was parked over there." She pointed to a spot not far from the gates but deep in foliage. "Truth to tell it could have been any colour, it's hard to say. Now if my Bobby had seen it, then he would have been able to say what kind it was. He's good at that sort of thing is my Bobby."

"I'm sure he is. Thank you for your help."

"Oh! No problem. I'd better get going or he'll be wondering what's happened to me."

"Thanks again."

As soon as the woman was out of sight, Jensen rang Captain Georgallis. After relaying what he'd learned, the Captain promised to get a search organised without delay.

Retrieving the courtesy map from the glove compartment, he calculated how far a car could travel and still get back to the yacht in time for curfew. Drawing a rough circle on the map he pondered where to start.

Manolis insisted Jensen drink a cup of tea and eat the sandwich Agathi had made for him. He studied the map Jensen had handed him while his friend ate.

"Well?" Jensen demanded around a mouth full of ham and tomato.

"Give me a chance." Manolis scratched the short bristles on his cheek absently, as though reminding himself that he needed a shave. "There are a couple of places where I would search first." He flattened the map on the kitchen table so Jensen could see where he pointed. "The first is these hills here. There are a number of small caves which could be used to keep a prisoner in and..." He glanced at his friend, "a number of crevasses where a body could be hidden."

Viably shuddering at the thought, Jensen marked the area with a large X. "Where's the second?"

Manolis ran his finger a short distance from the X to what looked like a flat area near the bottom of the hills. "This used to be a village but it was badly damaged in an earthquake during the nineteen fifties. I haven't been there since I was a boy and there wasn't much left then. But I do remember exploring the larger ruins and some of them still had rooms and roof parts."

Jensen drew another X.

"What about old Aristotle's place?" Agathi suggested.

"Aristotle?" Jensen was intrigued.

"Yes, he was an old farmer who died about seven years ago. He had no family so his house has fallen into disrepair. It's here." Agathi leaned forward and tapped the map.

Flooded with excitement Jensen exclaimed, "That's not far from the harbour where the yacht is moored!"

After speaking to Captain Georgallis, who confirmed he would send a car to Aristotle's farm to look for signs of Abby, Jensen turned his attention back to the map.

"How about we check out the caves and then take a look at the ruined village?"

"Great! Let's go." Jensen washed the last of his sandwich down with the now cold tea.

"We'll take my four by four; it's more suitable to the terrain." Manolis picked up his keys. "Come on, the day's getting shorter by the minute."

The caves were spaced far apart. Frustrated by the time it took to climb up the shale covered slopes to the individual caverns, followed by the time needed to search the larger ones, Jensen's stress levels were at an all time high. Emerging into the sunlight again, he wiped the sweat out of his eyes.

"What's that down there?" He pointed to a ruined village way down at the bottom of the next slope, maybe a mile away. "Is that where the earthquake was in the fifties?"

"Yes that's it. Quite a mess isn't it? Just shows you what Mother Nature can do."

"Some of the houses still seem fairly whole," he mused. "Would you mind if I left you to look at the rest of the caves?"

"No, not at all. We're almost finished here. There aren't too many more caves to see. What are you thinking?"

"I thought I'd go and look through the village. There's more to it than I thought. I have a feeling..."

"Okay, go for it." Manolis shaded his eyes. "You might strike lucky. I'll finish off here."

"Will you pick me up at the village?"

"Of course, but remember we've come quite a distance. It will take me a while to get back to the car and then I have to drive almost back to the main road before I can turn off for the village. I'll call you if I find anything."

"Great, I'll wait for you. See you later."

"Right," Manolis said to his friend's retreating back.

Jensen had almost reached ground level when he saw the small, dark blue car heading for the village. Alarm sent adrenaline spiralling, giving him the extra speed needed to race through long abandoned fields towards the nearest ruined house.

CHAPTER EIGHTEEN

Restless and bored, hands dirty, nails ragged, Abby used a torn flap from the cardboard box to fan her hot face. Earlier she'd spent an exhausting ten minutes rattling the door in an attempt to loosen the bolt to no avail. After clearing the debris out of the old broken sink with her bare hands, the larger hole she'd created would allow a rabbit-sized animal to squeeze out but not a grown woman. With defeat, she accepted she knew every inch of the room and there was no way out.

Carefully opening a wrapped, wilting, spinach and cheese pie, she sat on the bed to enjoy her meal. Grimacing at the state of her hands she wished for spare water to clean the grime off them. Unfortunately she'd used nearly a full bottle to have a thorough wash after lunch. If her kidnapper didn't bring some supplies in the morning, she would soon run out. Licking crumbs off her lips she tried not to think about surviving another hot day without anything to drink.

Folding the wrapping carefully into a tight roll, she placed it back in the box. Bored and therefore hungry, she rummaged around for something else to eat – there was nothing else to do. The dwindling tepid water, unappetizing food, hard bed and exhausting heat were bad enough. But by far the worst thing to endure was the crashing boredom. Lying back on the bed, her stomach pleasantly full, she listened to the incessant sound of cicadas, possibly the only other living things for miles.

The damage to the roof caught her attention. If only she could reach that she might be able to escape. Following the ceiling line to directly above her head, a sudden thought struck. Maybe, just maybe, the whole roof was rotten. Standing on her bed she reached up. Elation flooded through her as her fingertips brushed the underside of the roof.

Scrambling down, she ran to retrieve a triangular shaped piece of concrete she'd unearthed from the old sink. Resuming her standing position on the bed, she repeatedly struck the ceiling with the makeshift tool. Old plaster rained down like a heavy snowstorm, the large flakes temporarily blinding her. Wiping her watering eyes with the hem of her dress, she continued her task.

Later, plaster, bits of snapped, rotten wood, cracked and broken tiles littered the bed on which she sat and rested. A dead cricket lay crumpled at her feet, a victim of her crusade to escape. Sobbing with a mixture of elation and exhaustion Abby knew it would not take much longer before she had made a large enough hole to wriggle through.

A distant noise made her sit straighter.

Oh no!

The sound of a car engine sounded louder. Someone was coming, but was it friend or foe? If her kidnapper had returned he would see the mess. Leaping to her feet, she upended the cardboard container spilling the pathetically few items of food onto the floor. Using the flap of cardboard she'd used earlier to fan her face, she swept the rubble into the box. Quickly shaking bits of plaster from her coat, she flung it over the remaining dust on the bed just as the vehicle stopped outside the building.

Abby stood behind the door, heart beating erratically, her hand curled around the, much reduced, piece of concrete, waiting for her chance to strike. She intended to hit the kidnapper hard, and while he was down, escape from the room and bolt it behind her.

A car door clicked open, Abby heard the unmistakable sound of gravel scrunching underfoot but no-one entered. Her arm, tired from all her hard work, drooped, almost causing the temporary weapon to drop from her hand. Almost deafened by her own frightened, ragged breaths, she struggled to hear what was going on outside. Only the song of the insects met her ears. Either he was standing still or he'd walked away. Her overactive imagination visualised the scenario of a tall, black clad, masked man standing looking into the boot of the car.

It seemed like forever before she heard the sounds of movement again. A dragging noise accompanied by heavy breathing and the occasional grunt of exertion made her hair stand on end. What was going on? Not knowing what he had planned for her was terrifying. Breathing deeply she fought down her fear. Perhaps he'd simply brought a large supply of food? Of course – what other explanation could there be?

Relief made her light-headed. With his hands full she'd find it easier to clobber him. Poised to strike, she clutched what was left of her bashed and battered chunk of concrete, high above her head. The dragging noise stopped outside her door. Taking another deep breath she readied herself.

"Keep away from the door," the brusque, heavily disguised, voice advised. "I'm going to kick it open."

Oh!

Dropping the weapon-cum-tool, Abby jumped out of harm's way.

The door crashed open, cement dust billowed as the handle clipped the wall. A large object was hauled into the room and almost thrown at her feet.

"Jensen! Oh God! Jensen!" She dropped to her knees beside him. "Are you alright?" *Idiot! How could he answer her - he was unconscious.*

The door clashed shut. A few moments later it opened again and a cardboard box, similar to the one she already possessed, was shoved into the room. The bolt slammed into place and a few moments later the unmistakable sound of a car engine faded into the distance. This time she wasn't afraid, she was no longer alone. Although she'd have been a lot happier if it had been the kidnapper lying out cold at her feet.

Using some of the precious water, and the hem of her grubby dress, Abby bathed Jensen brow. The half healed injury on the back of his head seeped blood, but hadn't totally split open again and didn't look as serious as it had the last time he was knocked out. Already he was showing signs of recovery.

Sitting up, he put a hand to his head and groaned. "Hello beautiful, I guess he got me again."

"Oh! Jensen!" Abby gathered him close, kissing him gently. "I'm so pleased to see you."

"I'm overjoyed to see you too luv. I thought you were…" Hesitating, he appeared unable to speak the words aloud. "Well let's just say I've been very worried."

"Have you got your phone?" Hope flooded. They could soon be out of this mess.

A groggy Jensen patted his pockets. "Sorry luv. Guess your, 'perp', already thought of that." He gave her a somewhat shaky smile to show he was teasing, but couldn't quite hide the fact that the effort hurt his head.

Ignoring his attempt to mock her amateur forensic and police lingo knowledge, Abby helped him to his feet. "Come and sit down on the bed. I want you to tell me how you're here. Did you see who hit you?"

"No. I saw the car and ran into the village."

"I'm in a village?"

Giving a whooshing sort of sigh Jensen tottered towards the bed. "Yes, it was abandoned in the nineteen-fifties after a large earthquake." Lifting the almost empty bottle off the mattress he sat down. Unscrewing the cap he drained the last of the water. "Anyway he must have seen me coming and lain in wait. Just like last time he hit me from behind."

Coward!

"Did you walk here? What happened to your car?"

"Manolis brought me. I left him searching some caves, he'll be here shortly." Distractedly he picked at the label on the empty bottle with his thumbnail. "Got any more water?"

"I'll see." Relieved to find the new box held several small bottles of water, she opened one and handed it to Jensen.

"Thanks." He drank. "What I don't understand is why are we both still alive?" He seemed a little better.

"What do you mean?"

"Well he killed Willie and if I hadn't dived in to rescue Moonie, he'd be dead too."

"Bilbo's still alive," Abby reminded him.

"Yes but that could have been a genuine accident." He considered. "On the other hand if it hadn't been for that cliff ledge he'd be dead too. Didn't someone once say, it's not the fall which kills you, it's landing that's the problem?"

"Maybe the killer likes us," Abby offered, disregarding his attempt at humour.

Touching the back of his head, Jensen looked pointedly at their surroundings. "Yeah I'm feeling the love."

Taking his face between her hands, she kissed him soundly. "At least we have each other."

He returned her kiss, clinging to her when she tried to pull away. "No, come lie with me. I need to feel you in my arms to reassure myself that you're really here and relatively safe. I'm afraid I'm not up to anything else at the moment." He gave her a rueful smile. "I really do have a headache."

Lying in his arms, Abby remembered what she'd been doing before his sudden arrival. "I know a way out and now you're here my problem of how to make myself taller is answered." She pointed to the ceiling above the bed. "You could lift me up."

"I don't need to, Manolis will be here soon. He said he would pick me up. As soon as we hear his car we can shout for help."

While they waited, Jensen told Abby how he'd found her. Abby laughed when she heard how her neighbour had helped. One dose of Bobby and his ditsy wife had been enough for her. Since the key incident she'd managed to avoid them. Now she'd make sure she thanked them properly for being instrumental in freeing her.

"So have you any idea who the perp is?" She grinned, having used the word on purpose. Lying on her side, her head propped on her elbow, she searched his face for answers.

"Well, Mark was arrested this morning so it's obviously not him," he mused.

"They could have let him go, or he could have escaped."

"Perhaps, I think it's more likely to be Woody or Spen. They both lied about coming ashore." His long fingers raked though his hair, a sure sign of his aggravation.

"I've had a long time to think about it and I've more or less discounted Mark anyway."

"What made you come to that decision?"

"Because I don't think he would have harmed Bilbo. Did you see his face at the hospital? I'm sure it was genuine concern," she argued.

"Maybe... Yes, thinking about it, you could be right."

"What about Parky?" She hated saying it, but he was still on her suspect list.

"No. His alibi for Willie's murder checked out." He raked his hair again, wincing as his fingernail scraped his new injury.

"Not really."

"What do you mean?" He furrowed his brow. "Ouch!"

"Well he saw you going towards my apartment. We have to assume that was only moments before you were attacked."

"I suppose. But if he was outside the apartments he couldn't have been the person who hit me. Plus the police didn't find any of his fingerprints inside your original apartment."

"That's true." Secretly she was relieved. She liked Parky. Everything about him was so open. It was hard to believe he could be capable of killing anyone. However, appearances could be deceptive, she was not about to cross him off her mental list – yet.

"Of course the other thing is that it might not be a member of the crew at all," Jensen mused.

"How so?"

"Well, Willie was murdered onshore and we were moored up when Moonie fell. If you remember the police came aboard while I was resuscitating him."

"That's right. All this time we have assumed that the murderer had to be someone from the Cassandra Rose, but that's now obviously not the case. It could be anybody, anybody at all!" Abby's grin was pure happiness.

Later they sat on the edge of the bed sharing some of the new food supplies. Jensen felt much better. His headache now a dull ache, his stomach demanded his attention. Outside the sun began to set.

"Something's happened. Manolis should have been here hours ago." Jensen rose, brushing crumbs from his trousers onto the dirt floor. He paced the small room like a caged lion. "Whoever the culprit is, he might slip off the boat and come back here to finish us off. I think we'd better revert to Plan A and attempt to get out of this room. Maybe we can climb back up the cliff to see if we can spot where Manolis has got to."

Jensen made short work of making the hole in the roof large enough to accommodate Abby's slight form. Stripping off the hampering dress, she scrambled out of Jensen's supporting arms and through the gap out into the warm, gathering dusk. Taking a moment to appreciate being out of the stifling room, she took in the sight of the ruined houses and the surrounding countryside. It was hard to believe these desolated buildings had once been populated by families, the fields tended by busy hands.

"Everything alright out there luv?" Jensen called out to her.

"Yes. Yes fine. I'm just taking a minute to appreciate my freedom."

"We haven't got time for you to do that," he warned.

"I'm just saying..."

"And I'm just telling," he growled.

God she hated it when he said that.

Crawling along the roof she looked for a place where she could climb down. Finding a section of wall covered part way up with rubble, she leapt down. Loose stones cascaded down the slope, her left foot slipped. Slithering, she slid down the slope ending in an ungainly heap at the bottom.

Hobbling around the building, she found the gaping doorway. The broken, rotting, discarded front door lay on its side propped up against the far wall of the inner room. The large new bolt on the door of her former prison gleamed in the failing light.

"Are you alright?" Jensen handed over her dress. "It sounded as though you had a bit of trouble out there."

"I slipped on some stones. I'm fine." She pulled the garment over her head.

"Here." He pushed her jacket into her arms. "Put it on, it's easier than carrying it," he advised. "There's a bottle of water in each pocket."

Bare-chested, Jensen gathered up his shirt into a bulging bundle which he carried with one hand.

"What have you got in there?"

"The rest of the water and the food."

"Great." She shook the skirt of her grubby, creased dress so the folds dropped into place. "I'm ready."

"Let's go." He strode off.

Scratched and bruised, her ankle aching where she'd slightly twisted it jumping down from the roof, Abby followed Jensen out of the deserted, broken village and across the long disused fields towards the hills.

The light faded completely before they'd climbed very far. The moon was waning and didn't give much illumination. Jensen thought he might have seen the outline of a parked car in the distance before the last of the sun's rays disappeared over the horizon, but he couldn't be sure.

Feet slipping in the shale, her sore ankle protesting at the further abuse, Abby knew she could not go much further. "It's too dark to go on," she grumbled. "One of us will end up breaking a leg."

"Not much further. Try to hang on. I can make out a dark shape a little way up to the right. See?" He pointed. "Think you can make it there?"

"Yes, I suppose I'll have to. Is it a cave?"

"I hope so. I certainly hope so."

The floor was cold and hard, various shaped pebbles pressed into her soft flesh. Cuddled against Jensen, their heads pillowed on her folded jacket, Abby tried to sleep.

"It's not very comfortable is it?" Jensen's voice sounded disembodied in the total blackness pressing down on them.

"No, but at least I'm free and not alone any more."

His arms tightened, his lips found hers in a long slow kiss.

Breaking contact Abby whispered, "How's the headache?"

"What headache?" His warm mouth returned, covering her smile.

Desperate for the safe feeling being with Jensen gave her, Abby kissed him back with a hunger which bordered on desperation. The relief of being released from her prison, together with the absolute darkness, gave her a newfound boldness. With great daring she pushed him down onto his back and straddled him.

Lifting her arms above her head, Abby pulled off her bedraggled dress, followed by her bra. Leaning forward until her freed breasts brushed his bare chest, she whispered, "Now it's my turn to show you a good time. Just lie back and think of England." His deep groan of pleasure assured her of his submission. It was all the encouragement she needed.

Fingers of sunlight crept slowly over the horizon by the time they finally fell asleep, the night's dark hours having been spent alternatively talking and making love. At one point he'd teased her about not being able to ablute. Abby was past caring, yesterday she'd thought she might never see him again - simply being in his arms was wonderful.

Abby awoke as Jensen eased his left arm from under her neck. Feigning sleep she watched him from under her lashes. After massaging his arm, he stretched and rolled away from her. Picking up a bottle of water he strolled out of the cave mouth, if he'd been any taller he would've had to stoop the ceiling was so low.

Within a matter of minutes she followed Jensen outside, blinking at the brightness after the semidarkness of the cave. "Good morning camper," she called, setting off in the opposite direction to answer her own call of nature.

"Morning beautiful how was your night?" he called after her.

"Wonderful. What's for breakfast?" she joked.

It only took a few moments of being in the hot sunlight to realise that it was much later in the day than she'd first thought. Judging by the position of the sun, it appeared to be late morning.

Returning to the cave mouth, she found Jensen standing outside sipping from the water bottle as he surveyed the hills and countryside.

"Penny for them?" Taking the bottle he offered, she finished off the drink.

"I'm looking for any signs of Manolis. See there's the vehicle I thought I spotted last night."

Abby followed his pointing finger. "It looks to be a burnt out wreck."

"Yeah. No help there then."

"No." The word came out as a long sigh.

"We were lucky to find shelter this low down. Most of the caves are much higher." He made to re-enter. "I believe madam required breakfast."

Turning, she examined the cliff face. He was right, they'd been very lucky indeed to find shelter this far down. The nearest cave was a long way further up. There was no way she could have climbed so far in the dark.

Jensen reappeared. "Here you are. I'm sorry but this is the best I can do." He handed her a bent, badly crushed chocolate croissant. They ate in companionable silence while looking admiring at the beautiful countryside stretched before them.

"Jeez! Look over there." Shocked surprise held him immobile, the last bite of his own pastry halfway to his mouth.

Abby followed his gaze to the ruined village. A ray of sunshine gleamed off a portion of blue metal peeping out from behind the building near where she'd been held. If it hadn't been for the tell tale glint, she would never have seen it.

"I think we have company."

As she watched there was a sudden flash of fire accompanied by a hollow thud. Immediately a large chunk of ground, a few metres away from where they stood, exploded, throwing stones, grit and earth in every direction.

Bloody hell!

CHAPTER NINETEEN

Jensen flung his arm around Abby's shoulders, soil and small stones rained on their unprotected heads as he propelled her towards the sanctuary of their cave.

"What the hell was that?" she demanded, shaking grit and earth out of her hair onto the cave floor. She couldn't keep the shock out of her voice.

Jensen sighed. "My worst fears have been well and truly confirmed. It would appear the murderer come kidnapper, could be a member of my crew after all. That looked like a flare gun."

"A flare gun?" Abby glanced at him, a puzzled expression puckering her brow.

"Yep, you know, they're used to signal for help if you have a problem at sea. They're not something which can be picked up anywhere so I suspect it belonged to the Cassandra Rose."

"Can it be used more than once?" Abby's practical side kicked in, she needed the facts.

"No, they're not like a normal gun they look like a large stick of dynamite with a ring pull on the bottom. Once it's been used it can't be used again."

"Sounds like a party popper."

"Similar, but much larger and full of explosives instead of ribbons of paper."

"Great. So if it can't be used again, we're safe."

"No, unluckily, I have four."

Oh God!

"So potentially he might be armed with another three?"

"I'm afraid so." He kicked a small rock, causing it to skitter and bounce across the floor. "The yacht normally carries only two but I have two that are nearing their sell by date, they have to be returned to the firework factory to be disposed of and I haven't had time. I bought a couple of new ones before I came away." He used a popular four letter word and ran his fingers through his untidy hair. Another unoffending stone ricocheted off the wall as it was viciously toed.

"What are we going to do?" Her voice rose, threaded with fear. *Stay calm.* 'He hasn't hurt us so far why should he start now?"

It sounded like a reasonable question so why did she tremble so?

"Flare guns aren't made to be accurate. The idea is that you fire them up in the air to attract attention. The fact he could strike the rocks so close to where we were standing, indicates that he didn't care if he hit us or..."

A distant hollow boom followed, almost immediately, by an explosion drowning out the rest of Jensen's words. A crack appeared above their heads as various shaped boulders showered down in front of the cave mouth.

Abby screamed, leaping into the shelter of Jensen's arms.

Rocks, rubble and dust billowed inwards forcing them towards the back of the cave. The noise echoed around them, the small space intensifying the sounds which seemed to go on forever. Terrified, she huddled closer to the solid wall of Jensen's chest. The steady beat of his heart pounding against her ear felt strangely comforting.

"You okay?" Jensen's lips brushed her brow.

"Yes – you?"

"Yeah."

The cave entrance was filled with rubble from the floor up to about two foot from the roof. Through the swirling rock dust, Abby could see the bright blue sky through the upside down, smiley mouth shaped gap at the top of the blockage. Small pieces of stone and little pebbles fell intermittently, making plinking sounds as they bounced and slithered to the floor.

Relief flooded. "We can climb over that, right?" Coughing she wiped tears from her stinging eyes as they both backed further towards the clearer air at the back of the cave.

"Only if you want your head blown off." Jensen dragged a hand through his unruly curls before using the back of it to swipe his suddenly runny nose. "We have to assume he has the other two flares, not to mention the gun he used to force you to get into his car. That means we need to try to find another way out, or a least find somewhere to shelter if he climbs up to the cave." Ruffling her hair, he continued. "This is when you are supposed to produce your torch." He attempted to lighten the mood.

Oh crap!

"It's in my handbag back at the apartment."

"That's what I thought."

It took a moment or two before she realised he'd been joking.

"What now?" Wiping the sweat off her brow with the hem of her ruined dress, Abby tried not to cry as the events of the last few days finally caught up with her. Having escaped and found relatively safety with Jensen, it seemed they were now in more danger than ever. To cap it all, she'd lost half of her breakfast, the chocolate croissant lay somewhere under all the rubble.

Taking her hand Jensen pulled her in the direction of a tapering recess set into the rock wall near where they stood. "I have no clue what to do, but I don't intend to stay here and wait until the killer climbs up and fires the next flare directly into the cave mouth."

Oh God! Oh God! Abby hadn't thought about that. She'd seen firsthand the damage one of those damn things could cause. The idea of one being fired into this confined space did not bear thinking about. Holding tightly to Jensen's hand she followed him deeper into the darkness.

"Be careful," he warned as she tripped against him.

"I can hardly see the bloody floor. The ground's not exactly level in here," she complained as he disappeared into a seemingly deep, narrow fissure.

Oh holy crap! Abby's fear resurfaced. Stepping in after him, cool stone walls brushed against her arms. Now she could no longer see anything her imagination went into freefall, there could be anything lurking underfoot – including a bloody big hole in the floor. "Put your free hand on the wall to feel your way, and keep your head down the roof seems to slope a bit here." A warm thumb rubbed over the top of her hand in a gesture of comfort.

They stumbled along in complete blackness, Jensen cursing whenever his battered head grazed the rough ceiling which became progressively lower as they advanced. Only the scuffling of feet and the ragged sound of breathing accompanied them on the pitch dark, nightmarish journey.

Please, please, please don't let us get trapped in here.

Almost bent double, they turned a corner. "Can you see that luv?" Jensen's voice rose with excitement.

Abby angled her head so she could see around him. "Yes! Yes it's becoming lighter. Is there a way out up ahead?" Optimism bloomed.

"Not sure but there's definitely a bit more air in here."

He'd no sooner said the words than her wispy fringe stirred against her hot forehead. "Oh that's lovely." Lifting her chin she allowed the draft to play over her sweat dampened face.

A few moments later Jensen stood up, Abby soon joined him. Crushed together at the bottom of a tall, narrow chimney she looked up in dismay. A patch of sun-washed, blue sky peeked at her through a hole which, from where she stood, looked about the size of a child's beach ball.

"It's a dead end," Abby wailed, wiping her nose and face with the hem of her dress, before carefully stretching the kinks out of her cramped limbs in the small space provided.

"We should be able to climb out," he grinned, sounding pleased at the thought.

Typical man!

Even the danger they were in couldn't dampen his obvious excitement at the thought of a physical challenge.

"Oh no, I can't possibly! I've never, ever, climbed anything! There is no way in hell I'm going up there." Eyes stinging as the previously threatened tears spilt over onto her cheeks, Abby hung her head so he wouldn't see the terror she felt.

Jensen wrapped his arms around her, his lips moving gently over her hair before moving down her face to briefly capture hers. The kiss tasted of her salty tears.

"You can do this," he told her softly. "It's just a matter of walking up one wall while easing your back up the other, as long as you keep your back pressed tight against the rock, you'll be fine. I'll go up a little way to show you how it's done, then I'll come back and you can go first so I can help you if you get stuck."

Crap! "Stuck?"

Visions of being unable to move either up or down closed her throat making her voice come out as a squeak.

"I didn't mean that sort of stuck – silly. I meant if you weren't sure where to put your feet next." He glanced up the high vent. "Hell, I know it's wide enough for me so you should have no problem."

"Sure?"

"I'm sure." He hugged her. "There really is nowhere else we can go. We can't go back – you know that don't you?"

Abby shuddered at the thought of going back along the narrow tunnel and what possibly awaited them there. "I know," she whispered.

"Ready?"

Nodding, she swallowed, attempting to hide her fear, she hated heights.

Legs wobbling with the effort of bracing her body across the tight aperture, Abby expected to fall at any moment. It would have been difficult enough with her legs stiff but the narrowness of the chimney forced her to keep her knees bent. Rough stone rubbed against her shoulders, the skirt of her dress continually snagged, threatening to drag her downwards - she really should have removed it before making the climb as it seriously hampered her progress.

"I need to rest," she panted, tugging the trapped material until it bunched around her waist.

"Not yet. Keep going, you don't have time to stop."

"I can hardly move for this stupid dress." Tears threatened again.

"Too late to worry about it now, we are nearly two thirds of the way there." Jensen thrust his hand against her bottom in an effort to hurry her. "Nice view by the way," he joked.

Blinking away her tears, Abby pushed against the rock with one leg while she slid the other into the next position. Wiggling she manoeuvred her back another ten inches upwards. With a sigh of relief, she leaned her head back to gain a moments respite, cool air swirling through her sweat soaked hair. *Oh crap!* Fear rocketed. "There's nothing supporting my shoulders!" Panic made her voice shrill.

"Keep calm," Jensen's unruffled command intruded into the scalding alarm racing through her. "What do you mean there's nothing supporting your shoulders?"

"There seems to be a gap behind me. I can feel a breeze!" Tears of fright choked her throat.

"Okay! It's probably a small recess. Move up a little more and see if you can feel what it is while I support you."

Eyes squeezed shut, Abby did as he suggested. What would happen if she could no longer keep the tension in her legs? Would she fall back down the shaft taking Jensen with her? Trusting in his instincts she cautiously moved first one foot and then the other. When it came to sliding upwards, she placed the palms of her hands level with her hips to give the extra push required. Jensen's firm hand settled under her bottom while she explored with tentative fingers.

"It feels like a wide ledge."

"Good. Is it deep enough to sit on?"

"I think so."

"Right, after I count to three I will give you a shove up. I want you to rest your cute little bum on that shelf for a few moments. Okay luv?"

"Yes okay."

The momentum of Jensen's push sent her sprawling onto the ledge. The top of the aperture brushed briefly against the hair on her crown as she rolled backwards into the small tunnel, her arms shooting into the darkness beyond.

"Oh!" Gasping with shock she wiggled around amazed at the amount of space there suddenly seemed to be.

"Hey. Watch it." Jensen complained as one of her feet hit him on the head.

Propped on her elbows, Abby looked along her legs, which ended at her bent knees, jutting out of the opening of the short tunnel; the rest of her appeared to be in yet another cave. Lifting her feet, she scrambled back until she could stand. The small amount of light filtering in from the chimney showed a good sized cavern with large stalagmites and stalactites forming huge pillars.

"Jensen you've got to see this," her voice echoed softly - an awed whisper in the semidarkness.

A few moments later he crawled in on his stomach. Rising to his feet he laid his index finger on her mouth to indicate silence. Abby strained her ears trying to hear what had spooked him. Finally she heard the faint sounds of someone approaching the bottom of the chimney.

Bending slowly, Jensen picked up some fist-sized stones from the cavern floor, placing them quietly on the wide edge at the entrance to the cave to make it look as though the tunnel hadn't been disturbed. He finished by placing a larger boulder in the opening to the new cave.

Abby could imagine that from the chimney it might look as though the aperture was a dead end. Jensen's hand closed around hers as he pulled her to one side so they couldn't be seen. Heart hammering, Abby stood in the almost total darkness, the tension in Jensen's body a sure indication that he was ready to attack the killer should he try to follow them into this new cave.

Scraping sounds, muttered curses and grunts could be heard coming ever nearer. Shaking with fear, her mouth dry, she listened with growing horror as their pursuer started making his slow climb up the chimney towards them.

CHAPTER TWENTY

Abby hardly dared breathe, the approaching killer could be armed with a further two flare guns as well as a normal handgun. She could hear him clearly now as he neared the entrance to their hiding place. Crouching in the darkness, she likened them to a pair of mice waiting for a particularly nasty cat to discover their mouse hole.

A shout of surprise accompanied by the rattle of falling stones sounded loudly. The clunk of a small rock hitting the much larger one, partially covering their hiding place, caused Abby to jump. She bit down on her bottom lip to stop herself from crying out. It didn't take much working out to realise that their pursuer had climbed with his back to the opposite wall to the one she and Jensen had used. The killer's foot must have slipped into the tunnel and dislodged some of Jensen's carefully placed stones.

A grunt or two accompanied by some scuffling followed. Tears of fright spiked her eyelashes when a second or two later a small beam of torchlight played over the boulder partially blocking the end of the passageway.

Oh holy crap!

Abby squeezed Jensen's hand tightly, her heart beating so fast and loud she felt sure it must be audible.

The light suddenly disappeared, something metal bounced against rock several times. A string of four letter words softly spoken told their own story – he'd dropped the torch. After a seemingly never-ending moment the sound of climbing resumed, appearing to go on for ever before there was silence once again.

"He's gone," Jensen whispered. "Bloody Hell, I don't believe it! We fooled him."

"What now?" Abby's relief was short lived as she realised she would need to climb either up or back down the narrow chimney.

"I'm going to see if I can get that torch." Dropping to his knees he rolled the large rock away from the tunnel.

"We don't need the torch to climb up and you can simply collect it if we go down." Confused she wondered what Jensen had in mind.

"Sorry sweetheart we can't go either way. I would imagine from up there," he pointed towards the top of the chimney, "he will be able to see for miles. It won't take him long to realise we didn't go that way. I don't want to go back the way we came as we could be seen leaving the cave and I don't want to get shot at."

"What the hell else can we do?" Anxiety made her voice sharp.

"This cave seems like our best bet. A lot of underground caves are linked to each other, with a torch we should be able to either discover a way out or find somewhere to hide until night." He disappeared into the tunnel feet first.

"Be careful," she whispered.

"I will. I won't be long luv," his words just above a murmur as he slipped away.

He appeared, grinning, a short time later. "It didn't fall all the way down and best of all it still works." Pressing the button he shone the light gleefully around the large cave.

"Wow, it's beautiful," Abby breathed. "I feel as though I'm standing in a huge, science fiction kind of cathedral."

"Yeah it's something else - almost magical." The torch beam gleamed off giant stalagmites and stalactites which must have taken eons to form. The multicoloured structures shone with moisture, while small pools reflected their magnificence, giving the impression that they were fathoms deep.

"This is much larger than I thought. I can't see any other walls apart from the one behind us - we might get lost," her voice wavered.

"All the more places to hide and maybe get a jump on the bastard if he comes looking for us." Taking her hand Jensen walked between the massive pillars. "Come on, we don't have time to sightsee."

"It's so spooky." Pain bloomed from a stubbed toe, Abby stumbled.

"Watch where you're placing you feet, the floor is very uneven."

"Yes I got that." Looking down she stepped more carefully. "I keep expecting some mythical creature to appear."

He grunted a laugh. "Like fairies or elves?"

"More like goblins and things that go bump in the night."

"Don't worry I'll protect you. I can hit them over the head with my trusty torch."

"My hero! If we are in here for any length of time it will be a rusty torch."

Jensen chuckled.

Sweat beaded Abby's forehead, they'd been walking for a long time – maybe even an hour or more. Her hand slipped from Jensen's grasp. "I need to stop." Sitting down on the cold floor she scooped water from a nearby pool, splashing it over her hot face before cooling her wrists. "God, it's so humid in here."

Following her example, Jensen used the small pool to cool down. "There's a wall up ahead which looks as though it curves around to the right."

"Great! What now?"

"We follow it for a while looking for a way out. If we have no luck after say – quarter of an hour - we can turn around and search the other way. I'm hoping to find an opening either to another cave or, if we're really lucky, a way out of the cave system altogether."

"That would be nice, I'm starving."

"Me too. Ready to go?"

"Um-hmm can't wait." Sarcasm laced her words. Placing her hand in his once again she allowed him to help her to her feet.

Staggering around in semidarkness wasn't Abby's idea of fun. At first the size and beauty of the cave kept her going, now an uneven, undulating, cool wall scraped her palm as she felt her way along in Jensen's wake. For the last few minutes she'd experienced the awful feeling of being enclosed. Reaching out to one side with her free hand, her finger tips encountered cold, damp stone.

"We're in a tunnel!" she accused.

"Yep for some time now and it's becoming steadily narrower. I'm hoping we don't have to turn around." Jensen sounded worried and that wasn't a good sign.

Biting her tongue against an angry retort at literally being kept in the dark, she continued moving while holding a cautionary hand above her head to check the ceiling height.

Sick of the sound of shuffling footsteps and the occasional crunch of loose stone, Abby longed to be outside in the fresh air. A distant drumming noise finally penetrated her misery.

"Can you hear that?"

"Yeah what do you think it is?" Jensen stopped suddenly.

"Oops sorry," Abby stepped on the back of his shoe accidentally scraping his heel. "It sounds like someone striking a large gong."

"Maybe it's a supernatural being doing a bit of mining?" Jensen grinned.

"Of course – that's it. Dwarves are known for carving out miles of tunnels under the earth and carrying magical hammers." Being flippant hid her fear.

"I think we've both read too much Tolkien. Come on beautiful, there's only one way to find out."

Boom, boom, boom the sound echoed eerily around, becoming louder with every step Abby took. Was it her imagination or could she see better – yes it was definitely becoming progressively lighter. Rounding a bend she entered another huge cavern. Coming to stand beside Jensen, she gawked in amazement.

Deep, crystal clear water filled the floor of the cave reflecting the sky and a few wispy clouds. Above this amazing sight Abby could see a large gaping hole where the roof had fallen in. More surprising still was the sight of a boat filled with tourists. A heavily bearded man stood in the prow between two massive oars, wielding them so they both hit the water at the same time, the resulting boom was even louder here than it had been in the tunnel.

"Guess we found the way out," Jensen commented.

"Yup." Abby eyed the massive expanse of the chilly looking underground lake. "Hope you can swim."

The surreal day became even more unbelievable as she sat in the boat with Jensen listening to the boatman giving his spiel about the depth of the water and how nothing lived in the pure depths. After having finished with previous tourists the boatman had returned to the small jetty to pick up his next party, leaving two seats free so he could collect the, unexpected and scruffy, individuals who'd suddenly appeared on the far bank of his lake.

Advised that they would be expected to pay on the way out, then forced to undergo the full experience with the rest of the holidaymakers, Abby felt hysteria building. Giggling, she hid her face in Jensen's shoulder, fighting for control which continued to elude her.

Helped from the boat, scalding tears of mirth still blurring her eyes, Abby eventually calmed down. All they needed to do was to follow the other tourists out of the cave system, then enlist someone's help to get back to civilization.

"You okay?" Jensen bent to whisper in her ear.

"Yes." Drying her face on her dress hem she ignored the shocked looks of the people to whom she'd just flashed her grubby knickers. Past caring about the niceties of polite behaviour, all she wanted was to feel safe, clean and fed.

The heat of the sun hit Abby like a hammer blow as she emerged from the entrance to the underground lake. Blinking, she took in her surroundings. The small fenced-in area thronged with tourists who'd already bought tickets from the booth at the gate. A tiny shed-like building sold souvenirs and post-cards. Beyond the enclosure she could see a large car park where a multicoloured van did a roaring trade selling drinks and ice-creams. Her mouth watered.

"Have you any money?"

Jensen shook his head sadly. "Yes loads, unfortunately I haven't got any of it with me."

"How are we going to pay to get out?"

"We aren't. Come on let's go." Placing a hand under her elbow he steered her out through the gateway.

Halfway across the car-park, Jensen halted. "Look who just got served."

Holy hell!

Abby noted that Parky nearly dropped his ice-lolly as a look of pure amazement crossed his face followed by a huge smile. "Hi," he shouted, waving his free hand at them.

"Should we trust him?" Abby dropped behind Jensen using his body as a shield.

"At this point we have no reason not to." He moved toward his smiling crewmember. "Hi yourself. What are you doing here?" Jensen greeted him.

"The same as you I would imagine." Parky drew level with them. "Is it worth seven Euros?"

"Of course. We had the full tour."

"You're in so much trouble sir." Parky bit into his ice and crunched loudly.

"Oh! Why's that?"

"When you didn't come back last night that Greek policeman, with the funny name, went ape. He was talking about search parties and the like. We all sort of guessed you would be with Abby, err, Miss Grainger." He took another bite of his, fast melting, lollipop.

Abby licked dry lips, nodding towards his hand. "I don't suppose you would buy us one of those?"

Parky glanced at Jensen, who shrugged.

"Yes, of course, no problem."

"Actually Parky, we've had a bit of trouble, we need something to drink and a lift back to Abby's apartment," Jensen admitted.

"A lift?" He gave them a puzzled look. "How did you get here?"

"We came by taxi, my car wouldn't start and we didn't want to miss out on seeing the caves."

Bloody hell that was one whopper of a lie!

They certainly hadn't missed the caves, in Abby's opinion they'd seen far too much of the damn things.

"Do you have a car?" Jensen's tone indicated he'd switched to his 'I'm in charge of the situation' head.

"Yes sir, I hired one this morning." He dug some keys out of his pocket and tossed them to Jensen. "It's the white Ford Fiesta over there next to that dark green van." He smiled at Abby. "Go and get yourselves settled while I get you both something cold to drink – and a couple of ice-pops."

"You weren't very friendly," Abby hissed as they made their way to Parky's car.

"What do you expect, he's my employee and I'm paying him for all the time off he's enjoying. His habit of being a bit too familiar, especially with you, annoys the hell out of me. Besides, we aren't absolutely sure we can rule him out as a suspect."

"Well, I'm just saying."

"And I'm just telling." He ended the conversation.

Jensen drove. Abby realised that he wasn't taking any chances. Parky, who'd had no option but to take the passenger seat, hung onto the door handle as the car careered around another sharp corner at speed.

"So what happened to you both, sir?" Parky tried to disguise his nervousness by making conversation.

Abby answered, leaving Jensen free to concentrate on his driving. "We wandered off from the main party and got lost in the caves for a while. Jensen dropped his wallet down a crevasse and we couldn't reach it." This was the story they had concocted whilst sitting in the car waiting for Parky to bring their ice pops.

"I wondered why neither of you looked like your normal immaculate selves." He gave a half laugh, his eyes still on the road. "I didn't like to ask too many questions." Turning slightly, he wiggled his eyebrows at Abby, who was sitting behind Jensen.

Forcing a smile in return she went on. "Those underground caves are larger than you'd think; it doesn't take much to get lost."

"Yes, I imagine they are. I'll probably go to see them another time. I've had enough excitement for today." He jerked his head towards Jensen indicating that being driven at high speed was not something he enjoyed.

Jensen slowed as they reached a village.

"What made you hire a car today?" he questioned Parky in a tone laced with accusation.

"I was going stir crazy. There are only so many times you can look around the local shops and visit the same tavernas."

"What about the others - has anyone else hired a car?"

Parky shrugged, "Not that I know of. Most of us get off the boat during the day but we don't always stick together. The harbour is always packed with vehicles at night and most of them are hire cars, so I suppose it's possible. Why?"

"No reason." Jensen lapsed into silence for the rest of the drive.

With a look of relief, Parky took the keys from Jensen and slid into the driving seat. "Are you sure you don't need anything else?" he asked out of the open window.

"No. Thanks for your help," Jensen replied.

"No problem." He waved and drove off.

Abby mounted the stairs to her rooms. All she wanted now was a shower, a change of clothing, something to eat and a hot cup of tea. Surprised to find the door unlocked, she walked tiredly into the apartment and turned on the air con. Hearing the door close behind her, she turned to see Jensen stripping off his clothes.

"Not now Josephine," she told him.

"You should be so lucky. Anyway, you're not Napoleon and the only thing I'm interested in is getting in the shower before you, because you take ages." Naked he walked into the tiny bathroom.

By the time he emerged, a nude Abby stood beating eggs in a bowl, bread lay on a nearby plate waiting to be toasted.

"Next," he told her, swatting her bottom as he passed on the way to dress. "I'll finish the cooking in a sec."

Clean and dressed in lavender shorts and sun-top, the simple meal felt like the best she'd ever tasted. Replete, she sat on her balcony with Jensen, a cup of tea cradled between her palms. Beyond the pink, blue and white blossoms of the Oleander trees, which framed the apartments' garden, the sun sparkled on the azure waters of the bay. Everything looked so normal, so peaceful, the events of the previous days seemed like a crazy dream.

Unfortunately, her subconscious nudged the momentary enjoyment to one side, reminding Abby that this calm was just a small hiatus. Across the table Jensen half sat, half sprawled in a patio chair, shirtless, jean clad legs angled apart, head thrown back, eyes closed, his finger-linked hands clasping his chest.

"Are you asleep?"

"Hmm not really luv - just thinking."

"What now?"

"Now I borrow your mobile and ask Manolis to bring my car around and maybe one of his shirts." He ran a hand over his bare chest, "I've put the other one in the bin along with your ruined dress."

"I like what you're *not* wearing," Abby interjected.

"Then I'll bring Captain Georgallis up to speed." Jensen ignored her innuendo.

Sighing, Abby inwardly acknowledged that they were still no nearer discovering who the murderer-cum-kidnapper was.

"I'm not sure where I left my phone."

"It's beside your bed."

"Oh."

"Yeah and I don't appreciate my caller id."

Her heart lurched at the stern look he gave her.

Smiling wickedly, she attempted to lighten his mood. "You looked so cute lying there fast asleep in your birthday suit and I couldn't resist."

A half smile tugged at his lips. "Just wait until I get myself a new mobile, the picture I take of you will be triple X rated," he warned.

Oh wow!

She grinned - at least he intended to stay around.

Jensen returned a few minutes later. "I've updated the Captain and he says we are to wait here until he sends a car. I couldn't get an answer from Manolis so I'll try again later."

A strange expression crossed his face.

"What?"

"I'm not sure you'll like what I suggest we do now."

"I'm sure I will." Standing, she placed the palms of her hands against his finely muscled chest before sliding them upwards and around his neck. "In fact I can't wait," she whispered into his mouth before covering it with her own.

Coming up for breath, he whispered. "Yes, that too, but there's something I need to do first."

Hiding her disappointment, Abby stepped back. "More important than making love to me?" she teased.

"Sweetheart you know having you in my arms means the world to me. The things you do to me are like nothing I've ever experienced before.

You're unique and I find you madly addictive."

"I feel the same about you," she whispered, thrilled at his words.

Gently he placed his forehead against hers, his hands framed her face. "There is something I need to do before the police arrive."

Intrigued she waited for him to continue.

Raising his head he stared into her eyes. "I still have the key for the apartment where Willie was killed." He looked sick at the thought. "I have to do this Abby."

"Of course you do. It will be alright, you'll see," she encouraged. "This could answer all our questions."

"God I hope so. I've spent days trying to remember, with little success. This is my last hope."

The first cool shadows of late afternoon cloaked the small, private, back balcony. As they rounded the corner the police incident ribbon, taped across the door like one half of an X, fluttered as though attempting to escape its confines. White powder clung to the numerous fingerprints on and around the door handle.

Using one of the tissues Abby insisted they bring with them, Jensen opened the door and flung it wide. Stagnant air wafted out of the gloom, carrying the faint stench of death. The rooms held the secret of what had happened here. To Abby they appeared to be waiting silently for them to enter. A violent shudder suddenly ripped though her body.

CHAPTER TWENTY-ONE

Jensen staggered against Abby momentarily. "This isn't right," he muttered. Beads of sweat appeared on his brow and top lip. Leaning forward, he pulled the door closed.

"What! Why not? I thought we'd agreed that you would try this." Shocked, and slightly relieved, Abby could only stare at him.

"Yes and I intend to. But not like this."

"What's wrong?"

"I've remembered how I originally opened the door."

"Oh!"

"In fact I remember everything. Talk about total recall. I entered slowly, unsure whether I had the right apartment or not." Placing his hand on the door he gently opened it again and peered inside. "The balcony door was open and the curtain flung back." Ducking under the police tape he stepped into the kitchen continuing to speak aloud. "I remember thinking I would have some explaining to do if I'd got my bearings wrong and some poor holidaymaker thought I'd come to rob them.

"I stood here for a second wondering where Willie had gone, then I heard a sound to my left and turned towards it." He fitted his words with actions, pivoting until he faced the sink area. "It was this." He twisted the metal ring holding a pale green tea-towel, making it squeak. "I'd left the door open. The breeze blew while I looked for the cause of the noise, the towel billowed and the ring squealed again." He demonstrated again for Abby's benefit.

His face serious, he continued. "I heard the bathroom door swing open and thought it was another trick of the wind so I ignored it." He shook his head. "As I turned towards the bedroom I glimpsed a bare, upraised arm coming from my right just before everything went black." Raking his hand through his hair, he appeared distraught.

Eyes clenched shut, fists curled tightly at his sides, Jensen radiated anger. "All this time trying to remember what happened - and for what? I'm no nearer knowing who hit me than I was half an hour ago. It's not as though I can identify someone from a momentary glimpse of an arm."

Abby placed a comforting hand on his back. "Come on let's go, the police could arrive at any moment and we're not supposed to be in here."

Jensen allowed her to lead him outside and watched as she used a tissue to close and lock the door before pocketing the key.

"Did the arm belong to a man?" Abby queried as they walked along the open sided corridor which ran behind the upstairs apartments.

"Yes, definitely a man's arm."

"How do you know? Was it hairy?"

"No not particularly, but it seemed very muscular."

"So the arm was bare?" The last time she'd used this quick fire question routine Jensen had remembered more than he'd first thought. They turned onto her back balcony.

Grinning, he gave her cheek a swift kiss. "You're not only beautiful but brilliant too," he told her. "Yes, the arm was bare and he was tall, taller than me."

"That's great! Did you see what he wore?"

Squeezing his eyes shut, Jensen concentrated. "Yes I recall a flash of blue material."

"Like the ones your crew wear?"

"Exactly like that."

"What about jewellery - a watch, wristband or something?"

His answer was a long time coming. "There was something, a flash of silver I'm sure of it. I just can't remember exactly what I saw."

Stepping into her apartment Abby extracted two beers from the fridge. "Want one?" She rattled the bottles together to attract his attention.

"Yeah thanks."

Expertly flipping off the caps, she handed Jensen his drink. "What's up? You've got a face like a wet weekend."

"Thanks." Raising the bottle to his mouth he took a long drink before replying. "You do realise we are no further forward?"

"How's that?" She sipped her own beer while drinking him in with her eyes.

With a faded blue-jean covered hip casually balanced against the door jamb he managed to look relaxed despite the strain of the last few days. Soft light brown hair grew between his flat, penny-like, man nipples, tapered over his flat stomach and disappeared into his low slung waistband. The wild toffee coloured curls framing his handsome face were out of control and definitely in need of a trim.

God, he looked gorgeous.

Abby's breath caught in her throat as she waited for his answer. Doubts suddenly assailed her, what was such a fabulous man doing with an ordinary girl like her? He often referred to her as beautiful, but it was only a term of endearment – wasn't it?

"I've only confirmed all the things we already knew."

Tearing her thoughts back to the present, she attempted to concentrate on his words.

"Such as?"

"That the killer is a tall member of my crew and that he knocked me out either before, or after, murdering Willie." He drained the last of the beer before thumping the empty bottle down on the bench. "We knew all this before today's excursion. I could have saved us both the pleasure of revisiting the horrors of Willie's death."

"Don't. Please don't think that way. Going back to my old rooms was something you had to do. A piece of your life was missing and you needed to find it – no matter how painful the experience." She wrapped her arms around him.

Warm breath fanned her neck as he buried his face against her shoulder. Strong arms pulled her close. Desire sizzled as she responded to the sudden contact with his naked torso. Lips nuzzled her neck and she trembled as a low growl vibrated through his body. Temper over, his tail had stopped lashing and her, very own, tawny tomcat was ready to play again.

"The only good thing to come out of this damn mess is you," he whispered fiercely before capturing her lips with his.

His kiss held tenderness, desperation, passion and anger in equal measures. In her entire life she'd never known a man who kissed with such emotion. As the warmth of his mouth moved over hers, she responded with equal fervour. His arms tightened, gathering her even closer against his hard, male body.

Abba's Mamma Mia rudely interrupted their ardour.

Abby sighed against his lips before breaking contact. "I'd better get that. I expect it will be my sister, we text each other most days and I haven't been in contact since I was kidnapped." Stepping out of his embrace, she picked up her phone.

"Hi Sis." Abby walked to the far side of her bed and plonked down so that she looked out over the balcony to the sea beyond. In her ear, Jenny complained about how concerned their parents were that Abby hadn't bothered to get in touch and how thoughtless she'd been, considering she was alone in a strange country on her own.

Abby detected envy, after all she was here in the sunshine supposedly enjoying the holiday on her own while Jenny was stuck at home, in the flat they shared, with her leg in plaster.

"I've been a bit busy," she began.

"Busy!" Jenny hissed in disbelief. "It only takes a minute to send a couple of lines of text to confirm you're okay. What on earth have you been doing?" Her voice turned petulant. "We normally spend most of our time on the beach," her tone plainly stating that Abby had no right to do something different just because she was on her own.

"I've been sailing, visiting caves, looking around ruins - you know the sort of thing." *Jenny would never guess what those excursions entailed.*

Her tirade over, Jenny calmed down a little. "You've met a man, haven't you?" she now accused.

The bed dipped and rocked as, the man in question, shuffled across until he sat directly behind Abby his legs either side of hers. "I might have," she tried, without success, to hide the fact she was grinning.

"So this new bloke is more important than your family? Well, that's just great."

Jensen wrapped his arms around her waist and pulled her against him, her bottom tight against his maleness.

Oh God!

How could she think what to answer when he was so close?

"No of course not," *Or was he?* "I've been on a trip for a couple of days and forgot to take my mobile, that's all."

"Is he rich and handsome?" Her sister persisted, her tone changing from irritation to interest.

Jensen gently coaxed her legs apart and lightly ran the fingers of both hands back and forwards up the insides from knees to groin.

"Oh yes," Abby murmured not sure who she was talking to.

"Have I interrupted something?" Jenny sounded annoyed again.

Abby stilled Jensen's hands with her free one, surprised at how astute her sister was, or maybe she'd heard a moan.

"No, it's just he's sitting beside me so it's difficult to talk about him."

Jensen's hot mouth nibbled the side of her neck causing her to squirm with pleasure.

"Mmmmm," he murmured with appreciation.

Someone banged on the open apartment door. Abby jumped up spinning towards the noise, her phone still at her ear. A young policeman stood in the doorway, his face bright red.

"I've got company. Must go. Will text you later."

"No don't go. You haven't answered my question."

"Bye. Love you. Love to the wrinklies." Abby hung up.

The phone immediately rang again. Seeing Jenny's smiling face on the caller id, Abby switched her mobile off.

Giving Jensen a few moments to pull himself together, Abby joined the policeman. "Hello. Sorry we didn't hear you arrive, we were a bit preoccupied."

Oops - wrong thing to say. The poor man flushed beetroot again.

Clearing his throat he managed to convey that he was to take them to the police station.

"Great." Picking up her handbag, Abby made for the door.

"What about you sir?" the young Greek addressed Jensen. "Don't you need your shirt?"

"No I'm afraid it is no longer wearable and I don't have anything else."

Taking the key from the worktop, he locked up.

"We can stop off at a supermarket if you like," the policeman offered.

"Yeah, great thanks. I can grab a tee-shirt." Jensen looked at Abby, "Got any money on you?"

"Yes. I haven't had time to spend much yet."

They pulled up outside a colourful little shop a short while later. Jensen's face when he saw the gaudy souvenirs displayed in the window and entrance made Abby laugh out loud.

"Want me to go in and pick something out for you?" she offered.

"Yes please. Not too bright."

"I don't think there will be much choice, I'm afraid."

"Okay, go for it."

Returning to the police car she handed Jensen a white tee-shirt with small Greek characters picked out in blue across the chest.

"Not bad." He pulled it over his head.

Abby liked the way it showed off the powerful muscles of his torso.

"What does it say?" he peered down at his chest.

"According to the shopkeeper it says, 'I love Greece,' but really it could say anything."

"Like 'I'm a plonker?'"

"'Like you're a plonker'," Abby laughed. "But hey, what the hell, just live a little.

The young policeman eyed the shirt. "I can assure you that the shopkeeper was correct," he confirmed with a straight face.

Captain Georgallis listened to their story intently, unfazed by the broken slat on the air conditioning unit which clattered in the background like a demented rattlesnake.

Folding his hands over the slight rise of his stomach, he looked Jensen in the eye. "Sounds like you were lucky to escape with your lives," he commented. "It appears the killer is no longer reluctant to kill either of you, his plans seem to have changed.

"From what you've just told me I can now concentrate on investigating your crew members, all the evidence plus the return of your memory points their way." He made a face. "I'm asking myself why Miss Grainger is now involved. Why would Mr Thomas's murderer stop attempting to harm other members of the crew and turn his attention to kidnapping her? The other thing which confuses me is why he keeps knocking you out?" He looked pointedly at Jensen.

"I don't have any answers. We have discussed this at some length." He indicated Abby. "Neither of us can figure out what he's up to."

"Well we had better catch him soon then I can have the pleasure of asking him myself." The Captain gave a pained smile. "But first I'd like to have our doctor take a look at your head." He picked up the telephone.

The elderly doctor examined Jensen's injury while Abby looked on.

"You have a slight swelling to the left of the original injury but luckily this time the skin has not been broken." After taking Jensen's blood pressure and asking a few questions about nausea and headaches, he announced, no permanent damage had been done and no further treatment was required. The doctor handed Jensen a small bottle of tablets. "Take these painkillers when required." He packed his bag and left.

Turning from his contemplation of the view beyond the window, the Captain announced, "I should tell you, your friend Manolis is in hospital having his burns treated."

Jensen's face drained of colour. "Burns? What happened?"

"Apparently, after he checked the rest of the caves he returned to his vehicle. As he approached his car, it exploded and he was hit by burning debris. After hearing your story, I suspect it was hit by one of your flares."

"Is he badly hurt?" Jensen looked sick.

"No, he was very lucky. He could end up with one or two scars on his arms as he threw them up to shield his face but, all in all, he got off very lightly. A few moments later and it could've been very serious indeed."

"Thank goodness it wasn't. He was only trying to help me find Abby, he didn't deserve this. If I'd realised that I was putting him in danger, I wouldn't have accepted his offer of assistance." Jensen turned to Abby. "Poor Manolis, now we know why I couldn't contact him earlier. It also explains the burnt out motor we saw and why Manolis didn't come to collect us at the village."

The list of crimes to lay at the killer's door grew day by day. No-one appeared to be safe, he didn't seem to care who got hurt. Abby wanted more details. The thought of Manolis lying injured in the middle of nowhere with no transport did not bear thinking about.

"How did he get home? Did he call for help?"

The Captain sighed and shook his head. "His phone had no signal because of all the hills. He managed to walk to the main road before he collapsed. Unfortunately it isn't a major road so he wasn't spotted by a passing vehicle until early this morning. The driver took him straight to the hospital."

"Poor man!"

"If you're finished with us I'd like to go to the hospital now. I feel responsible as I was the one who dragged Manolis into this mess." Jensen rose to his feet, ready to depart.

"Constable Kouris will take you via the Cassandra Rose, your man, Mark McDonald, has packed some of your clothes for collection – you will not be allowed to leave the car. Afterwards he will run you to the hospital."

"I don't understand. Why can't I lea…" Jensen started to say.

Abby cut across him. "Mark is on board?" her suddenly loud voice was full of accusation.

"Yes. We only held him for a few hours, with no concrete evidence we decided to allow him to go. We'd hoped that if he was the kidnapper he might lead us to you, however, he returned to the boat and we didn't see him leave again."

What! "You didn't *see* him leave!" Jumping to her feet, she prepared to do battle. "That's ridiculous! He could have left without your knowledge. I would feel a whole lot happier if you could confirm that he *did not* leave."

Jensen quickly butted in. "Thank you; we would appreciate a lift to the hospital. I really need to check how Manolis is doing."

A large hand grasped Abby's upper arm, she shot Jensen a look of surprise. His amazing blue eyes warned her to calm down as did the cautionary shake of his head.

Although fuming at Jensen's attempt to change the subject, she had enough sense to realise he was only trying to help. It wouldn't achieve anything to anger the policeman and perhaps get herself locked up. Cooling her temper, she allowed him to take over.

"If we go straight to the hospital your officer wouldn't need to wait for us, as we could get a taxi to the yacht afterwards. I think we've taken up enough of your resources for one day."

"I'm afraid you don't understand. Clothes have been packed for a few days. You won't be going back to the yacht after visiting your friend - it isn't safe anymore. I would like you both to stay at a hotel of my choice so we can keep an eye on you. We need to catch the guilty party and I, for one, would feel much happier if I knew where the pair of you were."

"What about my clothes?" Abby asked.

Georgallis scratched his head thoughtfully. "Kouris or another officer can sort that out later." Standing, the Captain nodded towards the door. The interview was over.

They met up with Manolis in the hospital car park. Agathi was busy helping him into her car as Kouris pulled up. Jensen jumped out of the vehicle before it came to a complete halt.

"Manolis I'm so sorry for what happened. How are you doing?"

Manolis gave his friend a reassuring smile. "Not too bad. I'm sure I'll be right as rain after a good sleep." He waved his heavily bandaged arms at Jensen. "This is worse that it looks. I've partial thickness burns on both arms so cream should fix it. I have to come back in a couple of days to get the dressings changed and then again a few days later. Hopefully I should heal quite quickly."

"That's great news!" Jensen gave a heavy sigh. "After learning about the explosion I didn't know what to think. I'm so relieved to see you looking so well. God, when I think what might have happened!"

Manolis smiled. "Don't worry about me, I'll mend. I'm relieved to see you both safe and sound." He looked from his friend to Abby, who'd joined them. "At one point we thought we might never see you again," he told her. "Jensen was going crazy worrying about what had happened to you."

"Thank you for your help in trying to find me," she smiled. "I'm only sorry that it turned out so badly for you." She indicated his swathed arms.

"No problem." He smiled back at her. "But how did you get here? Did Jensen find you?"

Jensen interjected. "It's too long a story to tell you now. Go and get some rest, we can catch up later."

After goodbyes all round, and an open dinner invitation from Agathi, Abby and Jensen returned to the police car.

The hotel they were taken to was some distance away from where the yacht was moored. The young constable assured them that only the police knew about the hotel so they would be perfectly safe.

"It's lovely." Twirling with glee, Abby took in the large living area of the top floor suite.

Blushing, Kouris opened one of the two flanking doors. "This is an ensuite bedroom." He indicated the opposite door with his head. "There is another over there." He looked uncomfortable; his expression conveying that he suspected only one of the two rooms would be used. "I'm sure you will be very secure here."

Jensen took pity on him. "It's great. Don't worry about us," he smiled.

"Are we going to collect my things now?" Abby couldn't wait to change into her favourite bikini and make use of the massive swimming pool she'd seen on her way in.

"One of my colleagues is on their way to your apartment to collect them."

Crap! Taken aback, her tone tart, she snapped, "I would rather have chosen what to bring."

"I believe all of your things are to be packed." Kouris reddened again.

Oh! Not sure what she thought of that, Abby found she had nothing to say.

"I haven't been to this part of the island before. Are there any decent restaurants nearby?" Jensen wanted to know.

An expression of surprise flickered across the young policeman's face. "I thought you understood Sir. You are not allowed to leave these rooms until Captain Georgallis deems it safe."

Great!

CHAPTER TWENTY-TWO

Elbows propped on the bedroom windowsill, Abby looked out over an extremely large, elaborately shaped swimming pool spanned by a couple of wooden bridges with pretty white decorative trim. At the far end a thatched pool bar allowed customers to sit on high stools up to their waists in the sparking waters while being served a selection of brightly coloured cocktails by waiters dressed in lightweight white suits. Beyond the pool a long stretch of golden sand fringed the gently lapping, glittering turquoise sea.

Another prison! This time there were gorgeous views, large, beautifully appointed accommodation and every comfort provided, there was also Jensen – but this was a prison nevertheless. It might take days before it was deemed safe for them to leave. Turning from the window, her eyes misting with tears, she lay down on the king sized bed and gave in to her misery.

In the distance she could hear water running as Jensen showered in the en-suite off the other bedroom. She'd needed to get away so that he wouldn't see her unhappiness at being forced to stay indoors once again. They weren't even allowed to venture out onto the long balcony which ran the length of their rooms and was accessed by the wide double doors in the living area.

"What are you doing in here luv?" Jensen spoke from the doorway a little while later.

Dashing away the last of her tears, Abby struggled to sit up. "Feeling sorry for myself," she gave him a wan smile. A cream towel rode low on his lean hips, water droplets gleamed on his upper-body and in his chest hair. He took her breath away.

Oh boy, how would she ever live without this amazing man?

The thought that she would shortly be losing Jensen made her cry harder.

"Come on beautiful; feel free to have a moan. You're certainly due one."

Taking a shuddering sigh, Abby said. "I'm due to fly home in less than a week and at this rate I won't even have a tan to show off." It was the least of her concerns but somehow, in her present state of mind, it had taken on gigantic proportions.

His deep musical laughter didn't make her feel any better.

"Yes, I know that with everything going on I'm being petty and pathetic but I look forward to this annual dose of sunshine all year." She sniffed loudly, "Sorry I'm being stupid."

"No you're not." He sat beside her, wrapping a damp arm around her shoulders. "You're being very brave. Sorry I laughed, it's just that wasn't what I expected you to say."

Oh! "What did you think I was going to say?"

"That you were frightened – after all someone is trying to kill, or at the very least, injure us. Any other girl would be hiding under the bed by now."

Sniffing back her tears, she giggled at the thought of trying to squash under this low level bed.

"Over the past few days you've been kidnapped at gun point, locked up, nearly blown up, conquered you're fear of heights by climbing an extremely high chimney and done some cave exploring that most people would have balked at. I think your one courageous lady and I…" He stopped as though having second thoughts about his next words, "and I'm proud to know you," he finished lamely.

Was he going to say he loved me?

Did she even want to hear those words? Slipping out from under his arm she got to her feet.

"I wish we'd met in different circumstances - then we might know how we really feel about each other." *Did she actually just say those words?* Walking away she wondered if she'd revealed too much.

Jensen followed her into the living area. "What do you mean? Are you trying to say we don't know how we feel?"

Selecting a plump peach from a bowl of fruit, Abby turned it between her hands, inspecting the velvet-like skin for blemishes. "How can we?" she murmured over her shoulder. "Things haven't exactly been normal since we met."

"What are you saying?" his voice sounded raw.

Surprised by Jenson's reaction to her statement, she spun around to face him. Softening her voice she said. "You have to admit that we are in the middle of a whirlwind romance, one that's been liberally spiced with intrigue and danger."

"So our lovemaking is based on nothing more than the circumstances we find ourselves in." Hurt and underlying anger laced his words.

Oh Hells Bells!

"You have to agree that the way we met and everything that's happened since is what most romantic stories are based on."

"So now that we are locked safely in this hotel and away from danger, you no longer want me?" his unsteady voice held incredulity.

"I'm only saying, we shouldn't read too much into how we feel."

He closed the gap between them. "Do you still want me?"

She avoided his pain-filled eyes, her tense fingers pressed into the ripe fruit breaking the soft skin. The sweet smell of bruised peach filled the air. "Of course I do."

How could any woman not want him?

"Good, because you might be confused but I sure as hell know what I want." He pulled her into his arms.

"I was only saying…" she began.

"And I'm only telling," he growled, placing his mouth on hers, expertly stopping her from saying anything further.

Mr Bossy had returned with a vengeance.

Jensen switched off the television. It was the second morning they'd spent trapped on the top floor of the hotel. Meals were delivered regularly, breakfast having been served a couple of hours ago.

"I'll go mad if I have to stay here much longer." Jensen stretched and started to pace.

Lifting her nose from her Kindle, Abby had to agree.

"I'm only pleased I'm not here on my own." Feet tucked up she reclined on the sofa.

"So am I." He gave her a lavish look. "We've had fun haven't we?"

Hot faced she glanced away. "Fun?" she queried his choice of word.

"You know what I mean. Of all the girls to be locked away with I wouldn't wish for anyone else but you."

"You wouldn't?" Turning, she searched his face for the truth.

"Don't you know how beautiful you are?"

"I am?" Unconsciously she ran a tidying hand over her tan and green flowered playsuit.

Smiling he shook his head. "Every time I look into your amazing green eyes I'm lost, and each time I touch your silky black hair or your soft skin I want to bury myself in you."

Oh wow!

"You do?"

"Of course I do." Coming towards her he dropped a light kiss on her lips. "What about you?"

Her face reddened again. "I can't stop looking at you, I watch you sleep," she confessed.

A large grin lit his face. "I watch you sleep too," he admitted.

Oh! She gulped, hoping she hadn't been drooling.

"Want a coke?" Jensen made his way to the small fridge.

"Yeah, go on, might as well."

"Can you hear that?"

Jumping to her feet Abby ran into their bedroom. "It's my mobile, that's the noise it makes when I receive a text."

Frowning, she walked back to Jensen. "I don't recognise the number."

"Let me see."

She handed him the phone.

"It's for me," he advised a little while later.

"On my mobile? Who knows that we are together and how did they get my number?"

"It's from Bob, Bob Simms - my Captain. I gave him your number ages ago in case he needed to contact me. I thought it would be better if he had both our numbers."

"What does it say?"

"Apparently the police have arrested Spen."

Oh God!

"Spen?"

"Appears he's confessed. Anyway one of the crew will be along later to collect us. He suggests that we get packed and ready."

"Yippee." Abby leapt off the sofa and jumped around the room like a small child while Jensen laughed at her antics.

"Do you think I have time to use the lovely pool first?" Jensen swatted her bottom as she danced past him. "I doubt it. Come on, stop celebrating or I'll start to think you're glad to be rid of my constant company."

"Oh don't think that – I already said I would never have got through the last few days without you."

"Good." He kissed her briefly. "Now let's go."

Sobering, she asked, "How do you feel about the killer being Spen?"

"Not great, but it had to be someone and no matter who it was I'd have been just as surprised."

"Me too!"

Parky knocked at the door about half an hour later. He insisted on carrying Abby's case down to the hire car.

"Where to?" he joked when they both got into the back seat as though he was a taxi.

"I think I'd like to see how Manolis is doing before going back to the yacht," Jensen decided. "I can pick up my own hire car while I'm there."

"And I can go back to my apartment for a couple of days," Abby added.

"Your wishes are my command," Parky confirmed.

"Don't you want to spend some time with me on the yacht now that the danger has been removed?" Jensen tried, and failed, not to sound wounded.

"Maybe on my last day. At the moment I wouldn't mind a little time alone."

"Fine by me," his tone suggested that it was anything but.

Oh no!

They'd spent so much time together Abby felt the need to see how she would cope without him. They could still see each other without living together. She would explain her feelings to him later.

"When did Spen confess?" Jensen asked Parky, in his 'Mr I'm-in-charge' voice.

The car swerved slightly - luckily the road was clear of other traffic. "Spen's confessed!" Parky gasped.

"You didn't know?"

"No. God, I had no idea!" Shaking his head he went on. "Spen, Woody and Mark were all taken in for questioning early this morning but that's all I know. My God, I can hardly believe it – Spen of all people." He made a whistling sound through pursed lips. "So that's why Bob asked me to come and collect you. I thought it was because you wanted to come back and I'm the only one who still has a car."

The rest of the journey passed in silence. Abby couldn't help but be aware of Jensen's displeasure at her decision to stay at her apartment. The space that had appeared between them vibrated with his disapproval. Once she'd explained everything, he would be fine again.

Jensen gave directions and soon Parky pulled up outside the house where Manolis and Agathi lived.

"Do you want me to come in with you?" Abby felt she had to ask.

"No, go and get settled, I'll come around later and take you shopping. You will probably need bread and milk." he offered grudgingly, still not fully prepared to make up with her.

"Thanks." Leaning across she kissed him gently on his firm cheek, her lips tasted his aftershave lotion.

Parky roared off as soon as Jensen disappeared through the gates. "Looks like the boss is in a snit. I might as well take you shopping now."

"Better not, I don't want to anger him any further."

"Don't be silly, I don't mind and it will be one thing less for you to do." Ignoring her wishes, he turned the opposite way to her apartments.

Sitting back Abby decided to let him get on with it. Once back at her rooms she intended to get changed and spend the rest of the day on the beach. If she got her shopping now, she needn't hang around waiting for Jensen to turn up.

Lost in thought, it was a while before Abby realised it seemed to be taking longer to get to the hypermarket than when Jensen had taken her. She peered out of the window, noticing for the first time that the road looked unkempt and apparently free of other traffic.

Leaning forward she asked, "Do you know where you're going?"

Parky grinned boyishly at her in the driver's mirror. "Thought I did, I could've sworn that this was a short cut."

"And is it?"

"I hope so. If not, I'll turn around in a mile or so."

Abby settled back down. This was typical of Parky.

Her first real doubts came when the car began to slow. Looking through the windscreen, she saw a dilapidated farmhouse immediately ahead.

"The road seems to end in front of that building."

"Just what I was thinking, it looks a good place to turn around." Parky brought the car to a halt outside the house.

"Fancy a look around while we're here? I need to find somewhere to have a wee first, give me a minute or two." Opening the door, he got out.

The sound of cicadas filled the air with their incessant song, if it hadn't been for the little insects the silence would have been oppressive. Without the engine to power the air conditioning, it soon became stifling in the car. Abby opened her door to let some almost nonexistent air in. Parky seemed to have been gone an awfully long time for what he needed to do. She considered switching the engine back on but when she glanced at the dashboard she couldn't see the keys.

Damn! Parky had obviously taken the keys with him so starting the car was out of the question. Fanning her face ineffectively with her hand, she tried to ignore the sweat running between her breasts and down her back.

Come on Parky, this isn't funny.

Minutes passed. Fissures of fear crawled along her nerves - it was so remote here. Parky's penchant for getting into trouble, at the front of her mind, she worried something had happened to him. Maybe he'd fallen into a disused well and broken his leg, or hit his head and been knocked out. Anything could have happened in a crumbling old building like that.

Sighing with annoyance, Abby climbed out of the vehicle and set off in the direction she'd last seen Parky heading. Out of the car, the sun's heat caused her to hunch forward as though hit by a tremendous blow - it was very, very hot today. She took a few steps away from the car. Apart from the noisy cicadas, she could discern no other sounds.

"Parky," she shouted. Only the sound of chirping greeted her. Turning slowly she called his name over and over without receiving any response. Heat shimmered, the glimmer mocked her peripheral vision fooling her into thinking she could see movement.

Stepping over fallen masonry and skirting the longer grass, she made a slow circuit of the building. Stopping to peer down what had once been a well but now ended in packed dirt a few feet from the rim, she heaved a sigh of relief. At least he hadn't hurt himself falling down there.

She tried calling him again without success. Really worried now, she contemplated entering the dilapidated building. Although broken down in places the main part of the building looked fairly sturdy.

Could he be lying injured inside?

Stepping through the rotting doorway, she had a brief view of a large, rubbish strewn room before a sharp pain exploded in the back of her head. Stars spun before her eyes then blackness descended just as the floor rushed up to meet her.

Abby could hear someone groaning in the distance but her leaden eyelids refused to lift. Her throat felt so dry, swallowing she realised two things, one, the groaning had stopped and two, she was lying flat on her back. Liquid dripped onto her lips, she licked them greedily. More water cascaded, opening her mouth she received a much needed drink.

Excess water ran along her jaw and into one of her ears, she moved her hand to wipe the liquid away. A sharp pain zigzagged through her head causing nausea. Taking a few deep breaths she tried again. Her arm refused to move and her wrist hurt. Puzzled, she attempted to use the other hand only to find the same reaction. Realisation dawned, suddenly freed eyelids flew open.

Something which had once been soft but was now lumpy supported her back. The sagging, flaking ceiling overhead looked as though it might fall at any moment. Tilting her aching head she saw that her hands were cable tied above her head and secured to the ornate, rusting, metal headboard of the bed on which she lay. Wiggling her legs she sighed with relief - her feet were still free. Carefully lifting her throbbing head she looked toward the foot of the bed.

Parky stood casually replacing the cap on a water bottle.

What the hell!

CHAPTER TWENTY-THREE

"Parky?"

His wide grin bordered on evil. "Surprised?"

"What's going on?"

Pushing his wayward hair off his face, he laughed. "Come on Abby, a bright girl like you can do better than that."

Confused, her brain at first failed to respond to the evidence of her own eyes. Several moments later everything clicked into place.

No, it couldn't be!

"You're the one who kidnapped me!" she accused. Struggling to sit up, the cable ties bit painfully into her wrists. *Ouch!*

"Got it in one, aren't you a clever girl," he mocked.

"Why? What have I ever done to you?"

"You - nothing – Stone plenty. Unfortunately you're a casualty of war, a victim by association if you like," he snarled. "Taking you from him hits him where it hurts, so to speak."

"I mean nothing to him, please let me go," her voice rose sharply.

"Don't be so silly Abby, how can I release you now?"

"I won't tell anyone." Ready to make any promise to get away she said the first thing that came into her head.

"Of course you would, probably sooner rather than later." He tossed the half empty water bottle on the bed beside her.

Her involuntary flinch caused the bands to tighten, cutting into the soft skin of her wrists. Scalding fear raced through her veins.

Is he going to kill me now?

The thought once planted wouldn't go away. *Oh God, I need to distract him somehow.*

"Did you kill Willie?" *Oh no, no, she hadn't meant to say that out loud.*

The bed creaked as he sat down heavily beside her.

Abby's already overwrought nerves screamed with fright.

Parky's face held abject sorrow, leaning forward he looked into her eyes. Abby prayed he could not see her terror.

"I didn't mean to." His sudden little boy's voice was almost a whisper. "It just sort of happened."

What!

Swallowing her fear, Abby sought to keep him talking - anything to delay the inevitable.

"Tell me about it," she failed to keep the tremor out of her voice.

Taking a sighing breath, he closed his eyes and started talking.

"Willie and I left the taverna together. I'd had too much to drink and needed a pee. Willie said if new guests were expected at the apartments, near the harbour, then the key was left in the door for their arrival. We decided to see if we could get into one of the rooms to use the loo. The only door with a key was on the top floor at the end of the building."

"My apartment," Abby whispered.

Parky opened pain filled eyes. "Your apartment," he confirmed. "I used the bathroom first, then Willie. When he came out he had my passport in his hand – I must have dropped it. Anyway, he said he'd needed a laugh so he'd looked at my passport photo and that was when he realised it had a different name to the one I was using." He sighed heavily, looking around the dingy room as though reliving the experience.

In spite of being at the mercy of a killer and in physical discomfort, Abby was intrigued by Parky's story.

"Why were you using a false name?"

His gaze snapped back to her face, his eyes flashed with hatred.

Oh crap!

"Because I didn't want that bastard, Stone, to know the son of the man he'd killed was a member of his crew," he snarled.

Jerking to his feet he began to pace the room.

Jensen killed someone? On no!

Shocked into silence, Abby waited for the man she knew as Parky to continue his tale.

He didn't disappoint. "Before I could think of a cover story Willie moved outside to the balcony. When I joined him I saw Stone walking up from the harbour. Willie, the stupid bastard, was signalling to Stone. I ducked behind Willie then pulled him down and wrapped my hands around his neck before dragging him back into the bedroom.

"When I saw Willie lying unconscious I panicked, Stone was about to appear and I had no time to hide the body. There was a heavy pan sitting on the hob so I took it and hid in the bathroom. When Stone walked into the room I whacked him one."

He gave a crazy crackling laugh. "I enjoyed that. Then I had a brainwave, I could frame Stone for Willie's death. I'd seen the snapped washing line so I collected it from the balcony and wrapped it around Willie's neck a few times. I thought if I covered my finger-marks with the rope then the police wouldn't know I'd done it. He was hardly marked, so I thought the plan would work."

Covering his face with his hands Parky started weeping. His loud, anguished cries filled the room, the sound completely at odds with the manic glee of a few moments ago.

Any hope of getting out of this alive fled, Parky was obviously insane. Abby lay quietly, not wanting to attract his attention. Time passed slowly, his grief seemed to go on forever.

Although marginally cooler inside the old farmhouse, the heat was still stifling, sweat rolled from her body to soak the old mattress. The trickle running down her face caused her skin to itch. She could remain still no longer. Pain lanced her skull like being stabbed with a thick knitting needle as she turned her head sideways in an effort to wipe her face dry on her extended upper arms. Parky was too wrapped up in his own unhappiness to notice her actions.

After a while barely whispered words escaped from behind the barrier of Parky's fingers. "Willie wasn't dead you see. I thought I was strangling a corpse but he put up a fight. The gurgling noises he made were horrible. I knocked him out in the end – I couldn't have finished him off otherwise."

A shiver of revulsion quivered through Abby, cooling her as nothing else could and causing the fine hairs on her body to stand to attention.

Oh God! Oh God! I'm going to throw up. She'd never heard anything so grotesque.

Dropping his hands Parky looked directly at Abby, his eyes full of remorse.

"It was hideous. I'm ashamed of what I did." He seemed to be asking her forgiveness.

Unbelievable!

Swallowing bile, she soothed, "I know you didn't mean to." It seemed to be what he needed to hear.

"No. No of course I didn't." Coming over to the bed he sat down next to her again. "I used a wet dishcloth to wipe the ends of the rope and other things I remembered touching, then I left. I threw the cloth over the hedge on the way back to the taverna." His mercurial mood switched again as he smiled and shrugged. "You know the rest of the story."

"Not really."

Crap - her stupid mouth had run away again.

"What else would you like to know?" He sounded so sane, so normal, as through they were having afternoon tea and a little chat.

Here goes – in for a penny, in for a pound. He was going to kill her anyway.

"What happened to Moonie and Bilbo?"

Fists clenched, eyes wild, it seemed that he would finish her off there and then.

"God knows what happened to Bilbo, it was nothing to do with me. Moonie though – that was me. I knew Stone was on his own, I'd just taken him some coffee, so I thought I'd try and frame him again – my first attempt had so obviously failed.

"I took Stone's tie and sneaked up behind Moonie when he was leaning out of the launch doorway. I only meant to mark his neck then push him overboard but the stupid idiot struggled and fell out. He grabbed my bracelet as he fell so I had to hold onto the tie for a while to try to shake him off, in the end the clasp snapped and I let him drop."

Abby suddenly remembered Parky wearing a thick-linked, silver chain when Jensen interviewed him shortly after Willie's death. The small suspended lock had caught her attention as each time Parky put his hand to his hair it made a slight swinging motion. The bracelet must have been the glint of silver which Jensen recalled seeing.

Running a shaky hand over his face he went on. "I didn't know he couldn't swim, I only meant to mark him before returning the tie."

Outside a car door slammed. Neither of them had heard the vehicle approach, they'd been so wound up in the story.

A hot, sweaty hand slammed onto Abby's face, she tasted blood as her teeth caught her top lip. One of her nostrils was completely covered, the other only partially. Struggling she attempted to drag air into small space available.

"Abby. Abby are you in here?"

Jensen's voice – Abby sagged with relief.

Thank God! Oh thank God!

Twisting her head she, tried to throw off Parky's hand. The pressure on her face increased – she could no longer breathe. Red mist danced behind her eyelids, she watched as a creeping darkness devoured the edges of a diminishing crimson circle.

Coughing and gagging, Abby returned to consciousness. Breathing deeply, she forced her eyes open. The sickening smacking sound of flesh hitting flesh accompanied by vicious swearing assailed her ears. Jensen and Parky were fighting.

I need to help.

Twisting around she managed to survey every part of the ruined room - she was alone.

Where were they?

The room was nothing more than a large platform, a mezzanine floor which ended a few feet from the side of her bed. Broken wooden remains of what had once been a balustrade bordered the edge of the platform like a row of rotten teeth. At the far end, a newel post leant drunkenly at an impossible angle with a broken wedge of banister still attached.

Shuffling up the mattress until she could see the thin white cable ties around her wrists, she attempted to free her hands. One of the ties wasn't quite so tight, by tucking her thumb into her palm then folding her fingers around the digit, she managed to slide her hand through the loop.

Abby rubbed her liberated hand on her thigh to alleviate the redness and stinging pain caused by dragging her skin through the narrow, sharp plastic.

Freeing her other hand became a useless task, the gap was too small. Small cuts soon bedecked her wrist and she suspected there would be bruising later.

Sliding off the filthy, stained mattress she grasped the headboard and pulled. Inch by gruelling inch the heavy bed, which she suspected had not been moved for many, many years, screeched nosily towards the edge of the raised area.

Soaked in sweat and aching all over, Abby could eventually look down into the room below.

The fight continued, although both men seemed on the verge of exhaustion, one moment it looked as though Jensen had the upper hand - the next Parky appeared to be winning. Abby stuffed her fist into her mouth to stop from calling out and perhaps distracting Jensen.

Jensen pounded Parky with his fists while Parky tried desperately to defend himself. Both fighters were covered in filth and splattered with blood. Parky's hand shot out with speed and clipped the blade of Jensen's cheek. Jensen swore and smashed his fist forcefully into the taller man's jaw. Parky flew backwards, his skull slammed off the exposed brick wall with a sickening thud. Slowly he slid down to slump on the dirt packed floor, his seemingly unconscious body looked as boneless as a rag doll.

"Have you knocked him out?" Abby yelled.

"Well hello beautiful." Jensen gave her one of his devastating smiles before glancing down at Parky. "It looks like he's out for the count." He peered up at her through a trail of blood leaking from a cut on his brow. "Are you alright luv?" His expression was pure self-satisfaction.

He'd enjoyed that fight!

"Yes fine. What about you?" her tone was cool.

Using the bottom of his shirt, Jensen wiped it across his brow, smearing the fine fabric with the blood and giving Abby a great view of his hard flat stomach. Examining his grazed knuckles, he gave her a boyish grin.

"Great, never better."

Men!

"Come down." He pointed to Abby's left.

Looking along she noticed a large metal ladder propped against the rim of the floor. "I can't get down that."

"Now Abby, this is not the time to be frightened of climbing down a ladder. After scaling the high chimney in the caves, this should be child play," Mr Bossy told her in no uncertain terms.

He held out his arms, his face softening as he slipped into cajoling mood. "Hurry up, I need a cuddle."

"I can get down – it's the bed that can't."

"What bed?"

"The one my hand is tied to."

"You're tied to a bed?" A look of pure horror crossed his face. "He hasn't touched you – has he?"

"No of course not! Come and free me. Bring something sharp enough to cut a cable tie."

Jensen joined her a few moments later. Using his yachtsman's pocket knife, he swiftly cut through the tie.

Rubbing the pins and needles from her wrist, she stood. Her earlier anger at his boyish pleasure forgiven, she slipped her arms around his neck and pressed her cheek against his. Jensen's wonderful male scent filled her nostrils as she hugged him.

"I thought I'd never see you again," she whispered in his ear.

"Me too." Disentangling himself he kissed her lips briefly. "We need to get out of here."

A loud crash made them leap apart. Dust billowed up from the room below.

Bloody hell!

Placing a hand over her heart, which hammered like a piston engine, Abby sneezed several times.

Jensen looked over the edge of the platform muttering a selection of foul words.

Pivoting, Abby could see what angered Jensen.

Oh no!

Parky stood hunched in the doorway with one arm thrown across his ribs as though supporting them. Wiping his bloody nose with the back of his hand, he glared upwards.

"This is not over," he warned. "I'll get you if it's the last thing I do."

Still holding his ribs he staggered out of the doorway.

Leaning further over, Abby identified the source of the loud bang. Strong metal ladders lay amid the decaying wooden remains of the original staircase and balustrade which littered the dirt floor of the lower room.

CHAPTER TWENTY-FOUR

Several things went through Abby's mind at once, mostly to do with whether Parky had brought his gun with him and, if he escaped, what would he try next. What she actually said was, "How are we going to get down?"

"I'm thinking," Jensen growled.

"I'm only asking."

"And I'm only telling."

God I hate it when he says that.

Moments later Jensen relented. "Sorry luv, I didn't mean to snap." He pulled her toward him, tucking her under his arm. "I've got a few things on my mind at the moment."

"Tell me about it."

He smiled at her attempt at sarcasm. "You're the most important thing - I can't believe I've got you back." He dropped a light kiss on top of her head.

"How did you find me?" She snuggled closer.

"Captain Georgallis rang Manolis whilst I was there. He wanted to know if Manolis knew where I was. The policeman who was supposed to be guarding the corridor outside our hotel rooms had been found unconscious in a locked cleaner's cupboard."

"Parky?"

"Well we didn't know it was him at that point but we suspected it could have been Willie's killer. I thought it might still be Spen as he had been taken in for questioning that morning along with Woody and Mark."

"That's what Parky told us."

"Exactly, although it wasn't true, I found out later that no-one had been arrested," Jensen sighed. "It would seem that Parky used Bob's phone to send us the phoney message. He had me completely taken in."

"Me too. He seemed genuinely surprised when you told him about Spen."

"Yes, that car swerve was some stunt."

The door to the building creaked open. Jensen tensed, as they both turned toward the noise.

Parky reeled through the gap holding a burning branch aloft. Grinning up at them, he waved the makeshift torch as though in greeting. Sparks flew in all directions, some even landing on his bare arm - he ignored them.

"Looks like your day's about to get even hotter, Stone," he taunted. Limping across the floor he thrust the branch into a dense pile of sticks and wood splinters - remnants of the old staircase.

Leaping back as the wood immediately started to smoulder, he laughed gleefully. "Let's see you get out of this one."

"Just one more thing Parky," Jensen called down. "How did you know that we were staying at that hotel?"

A look of pure cunning crossed his features. "I followed the dickhead policeman. He led me straight to you."

His manic laugh sent chills through Abby.

Parky hobbled away slamming the door behind him. It rebounded against the sides of the warped frame, bouncing back to leave a small gap. A short while later Abby heard a car drive away.

Running to one of two small, high windows situated on either side of the room, she was relieved to see that it was no longer glazed, although in places jagged pieces of glass still clung to the rotting frame. Once they were removed, there would be enough room for her, and hopefully, Jensen to be able to wriggle through.

Jumping up and down, glass shards crunching beneath her feet, she tried to see out. Finding it difficult to see anything other than a canopy of blue dappled with green leaves, she ran to the other, similarly damaged, window which offered only a view of the cloudless sky.

"Come and lift me up so I can see through the windows, there could be a tree close enough to climb down," she shouted, trying to keep the panic out of her voice.

"Shush." Jensen watched the smouldering wood closely.

Stopping what she was doing she stared at Jensen's back.

Did he actually tell me to shush?

"Don't tell me to shut up. We need action – now," her voice rose higher, as did her temper.

"Wait – let me think."

"Wait!" she shrieked. "Wait for what? It may have escaped your attention but there is a fire underneath us and this is a very dry wooden floor. I don't know about you but I don't have any intention of becoming barbecued meat," she yelled at his unyielding back.

"Calm down and lower your voice. God, you can be so loud sometimes," he spoke as though talking to a small child.

Ohooo! How dare he speak to her like that? Of all the…!

Her mouth opened and closed but no sound came out.

Jensen swung towards her, his decision made, an 'I'm in charge' expression on his beautiful face. "Here, give me a hand with this mattress."

"The mattress? What for?" Moving to the bed she had a horrible feeling that she knew exactly what he intended to do.

"We're going to use it to smother the fire. The wood's still smoking so the flames haven't quite caught hold. If we aim it well the weight of the mattress should snuff out the fire before it gets started."

It sounded like a plan.

"And if we miss?" She grasped the corner he'd indicated was hers.

Determined deep blue eyes stared at her across the stained ticking, their intensity instilling confidence.

"We won't miss."

Abby gave mental cheer on hearing the loud thunk of the heavy mattress hitting the floor. Lying on her back, chest heaving, nails torn, breathless and covered in sweat, she took a well earned rest. Having used her feet to lever the mattress over the edge, she'd been unable to watch it fall.

Turning her throbbing head, she looked towards Jensen who lay in the same position a few feet away. "We did it," she whispered.

"Yes but did it work?" Getting painfully to his feet he supported his lower back while he stretched. "God I'm so stiff, that fight has really taken it out of me. I bet I've got bruises in places I never knew I had."

Walking to the edge of the platform he peered over. "It's landed directly on top of the fire, not a spark to be seen." Wiping sweat and blood from his cut brow, he motioned for Abby to join him.

"You first."

"What?"

"I want you to jump first."

"Jump where?" She knew exactly what he meant and she had no intention of complying.

"Would you prefer I threw you?"

"Why are you so bossy?"

"Why are you so argumentative?" He ground his teeth. "Abby we don't have time to discuss this, the mattress will break your fall," he tried to persuade her.

"We aren't discussing it though, are we? You're telling me what to do – again." She backed away; afraid he would simply pick her up and throw her.

"We need to move quickly, we seem to have killed the fire but who knows what's going on underneath, the mattress could burst into flames at any time."

Oh!

"Now I'll lie on the floor on my stomach and lower you over the edge by your hands. When you fall throw yourself forwards to protect your back. Now – are you ready?" His tone said quite plainly that he was not prepared to negotiate.

Shaking with trepidation, Abby managed to nod.

"Right let's do it."

It was over before she knew it. Standing near the door Abby watched Jensen lower himself by his arms before dropping to the floor. He rolled to his feet and grinned like a schoolboy. "That didn't do my bruises any good but it was fun."

Men!

The sight of his hire car wiped the smile from his face. Every tyre was flat and the windscreen shattered.

"This just gets better and better."

"You're insured aren't you?" Abby pushed past him to peer in the driver's window. "Got any painkillers in there, my head's killing me?"

Jensen gave the car bonnet a sympathetic pat as he approached Abby. "As a matter of fact I still have some the doctor gave me the last time Parky whacked me one. There should be a bottle of water as well. The car has its own first aid kit - everything's in the glove compartment."

After Abby washed the tablets down with disgusting tepid water, she stuck a sticking plaster over the cut on Jensen's forehead and gently rubbed Arnica cream over his knuckles to help reduce the bruising.

"What about a kiss to make me feel better?" He pursed his lips.

"How old are you?" She grinned at his childishness.

"How old would you like me to be?" He gave her a sexy smile.

Laughing, Abby turned away. "Let's get out of the sun first. There's a large Mulberry tree over there with plenty of shade." She pointed to the side of the farmhouse where a weathered chair and broken table sat under the sheltering branches.

"Don't attempt to sit on the chair," she warned Jensen as he joined her. "It looks as though it's about to collapse, your weight would destroy it completely."

"Are you saying that I'm fat?" he teased.

"You know that's not what I meant." Sauntering around him she ran her fingertips lightly over his chest and biceps. "No. Not fat at all. Rather a fine male specimen I would say."

"But still too heavy for that chair?"

"Yep."

"I'd rather stand against the tree."

His warm arms wrapped around her as he walked her backwards until the rough bark of the tree supported her shoulders, buttocks and calves.

"I'd like to claim my kiss now." His mouth descended.

Placing the palms of her hands against his shoulders she held him off. "I don't remember actually promising you a kiss," she laughed.

"I really need to kiss you, don't make me beg." He ground his hips against hers leaving her in no doubt of his intentions.

"How can you have sex on your mind after what we've just been through?" she accused with a smile.

"All the excitement seems to have travelled to other parts." He pressed himself against her again for emphasis.

"Well this is your lucky day because I need to kiss you too." Her hands slid slowly upwards to link behind his neck, bending her elbows she pulled him forward until their lips met. Long, hot, lingering kisses full of relief and joy at their escape soon turned to smouldering passion as his tongue and hips moved in unison.

Releasing her, Jensen pulled her tee-shirt over her head, his returning lips nibbling the newly exposed skin of her neck and chest. "I have lots of sore places for you to kiss later," his throaty whisper vibrated against the swell of her breast.

Shivers of anticipation ran along her nerve ends. Every time they made love seemed like the first time, she would never forget this man. No-one had ever made her feel the way he did, everything about him was irresistible - from his devastating smile to his sexy voice. The very thing she'd feared had happened – she fallen totally and utterly in love with Jensen Stone.

Hands busy with Jensen's obstinate belt buckle, scorching heat flooded as he sucked in his already flat stomach in an effort to aid her. Soft body hair tickled her knuckles as one hand slipped inside his waistband. Jensen almost purred.

Oh boy!

Then he was standing a foot away, frowning as he listened intently. Coming out of her sexual haze Abby realised she could hear a vehicle approaching.

Eyes wide with shock, she managed to whisper, "Parky?"

"Could be." All signs of Jensen the lover disappeared as he snatched her shirt off the ground. Grasping her upper arm he pulled her behind the concealing bulk of the tree trunk. "Best not to take any chances in case he's been to collect his gun."

Crap!

She struggled into her tee-shirt, arms tangling in an effort to get dressed quickly.

The vehicle crunched to a halt. A car door slammed, followed closely by another.

"Jensen?" A voice, Abby recognised as belonging to Manolis, called.

"Miss Grainger?" Captain Georgallis added his own query.

Together they stepped out from behind the tree.

CHAPTER TWENTY-FIVE

Abby ended up staying with Jensen on his boat after all. With Parky on the loose and all her belongings in the boot of his hire car, it was the only place she could go. She intended to store enough memories of these too few precious days to last her a lifetime.

After searching the yacht, to make sure Parky hadn't hidden aboard, the police allowed Jensen to take the boat out a couple of miles and drop anchor. The crew were to take it in turns keeping watch to ensure that no-one attempted to board.

On the mainland the police had mounted a full scale search for Neil Parks or Nigel Parkinson as they now knew his name to be. Enquiries at local car rental companies had confirmed that someone of that name had used his passport to hire several different vehicles over the past week and the address he'd given was that of Abby's current apartment.

Dinner over, Abby lay on a large sofa still wearing her flowered playsuit, her head rested in Jensen's lap.

"Did you know Parky's dad?" It had taken her all afternoon to find the courage to ask him.

Sighing, Jensen ran jittery fingers through his curls. "I knew an Ian Parkinson about three years ago," he admitted.

"And?" Abby prompted.

"And – I think he might have been Parky's father."

Oh no!

"Why did Parky think you'd killed his dad?" her voice only just above a murmur as she gazed up at his strong, clean-shaven jaw, the only thing she could see from her current position.

"Ian Parkinson was one of my clients. He liked to invest heavily and not always wisely. I tried my best to steer him towards more secure stocks but I wasn't always successful." He sighed. "He wanted to buy some stock, which had been rising steadily, in a large IT company. I felt they'd become too expensive and that their market value had peaked but he was adamant that he wanted them. I tried to explain that the prices were likely start to fall and he could end up losing a lot of money, the value had raised too far, too fast."

A bit like their relationship! Had their romance also risen too far, too fast – could they expect a fall?

"He refused to listen; convinced the value would continue to rise for a little while longer. He planned to sink thousands into buying them and then sell a few weeks later when they were worth more. I refused to buy them on his behalf as it was against my instincts to do so.

"I heard later that he'd asked another firm to purchase the stock for him. Days later the shares started to drop in price, selling them would have meant huge losses so he held onto them. Apparently he'd sunk every spare penny into buying stock which continued to devalue. He hung himself about three months later."

What? No wonder Parky was angry.

"Oh my God, that's terrible." Abby sat up.

"That's the luck of the stock market – unfortunately. Parky must have thought I'd bought the shares for his father because up until then I'd been his dad's stock broker."

"So Mr Parkinson's death was nothing to do with you?"

"No. If he'd listened to me he might be alive today."

"Poor man, poor Parky."

"Yes it's very sad."

"I wonder why he waited for three years before coming after you."

"Revenge is a dish best served cold. He must have thought his best chance to cause me damage would be to try and get close to me. While biding his time he learned everything he could about sailing a large yacht.

"I don't normally hire crew under the age of twenty-one because I need people I can trust. Parky will be twenty-one next month - he seemed like a level headed young man so I took a chance with him." His short laugh was almost a groan. "I couldn't have been any further out in my judgement - a less *level* headed person would be hard to find."

"You're right there. I think he has some sort of split personality disorder."

"It looks that way doesn't it?" Running the tips of his fingers down her cheek he gazed into her eyes. "Let's talk about something else."

Abby couldn't help but smile. "Like what?"

"Like you extending your holiday and staying here with me." Tender lips brushed hers - a gentle persuasion.

Tempted beyond belief she kissed him back. "Sorry. I'd love to but I have to be back at work on Monday."

"Ask for an extra week or so to recover from the horrors you've endured." Hot breath played across her lips as he spoke between kisses.

"No can do. The boss is on holiday next week and I'm in charge while he's away." Rubbing her nose softly against his she sought to distract him from trying to persuade her to stay. It would do no good to prolong the sweet agony. Her holiday was coming to an end – she had to go home. This time next week Jensen would be a wonderful, but painful, memory.

Before then there was tonight, tomorrow and the day after that. "Is it bedtime yet?" she whispered.

He chuckled. "I think it might be. I like the fact that you're insatiable." Picking her up, as though she weighed next to nothing, Jensen walked across to his stateroom.

Abby opened the door for them, Jensen back-kicked it shut.

"I've still got those sore places that need your attention." He gave her a comical leer.

"I'll have to see what I can do to make them better." she promised with a smile.

Placing her on the bed, he gave her a long lingering kiss full of promise.

Neither of them heard the slight swish as the wardrobe door, directly behind Jensen, opened.

"Well isn't this cosy," Parky said sarcastically kicking Jensen in the buttocks so hard he sprawled helplessly across Abby's body - cutting off her involuntary scream. Instead she gave a long drawn out groan of pure fear.

Parky pointed his gun at her face, his arm still cradled his ribs – she suspected, no hoped, that one or more of them were broken.

"Any more of that noise and I'll use this," he threatened.

Abby swallowed nervously. "Jensen didn't buy those shares for your father," the words came out very loud. Lowering her voice she went on. "He warned him not to buy them because the market was sure to drop."

"Is that what he told you?" Parky forced a laugh. "You might be naive enough to believe him but I'm not."

"It's true." Jensen struggled into a sitting position. "Why would I lie?"

"To stop me from shooting you both." Parky pointed the gun at each of them in turn.

"It's over Parky, everybody knows you killed Willie and injured Moonie." Jensen attempted to position himself between the gun and Abby. "What good would shooting us do?"

Using the nozzle of the gun, Parky waved Jensen back to his original position. "I'll have revenge. That's worth going to prison for."

"Even if you misguidedly think that I had anything to do with your father's death, Abby is innocent, all this happened long before I even met her."

Parky sneered. "I might simply shoot her so that you'll know what it's like to lose someone."

Oh holy crap!

"I thought you liked me," fear made her voice quiver.

God she sounded pathetic.

"You preferred Stone to me." He seemed genuinely hurt.

Jensen raised his eyebrows – this was obviously news to him.

"Come on, let Abby go. It's me you want to punish."

Abby's courage returned she squared her shoulders, a sure sign she intended to do battle. "I'm not going anywhere without you," she told Jensen in no uncertain terms.

"Don't argue," Jensen growled.

"I mean it..."

"Stop!" Parky terminated the quarrel. "I will say who stays and who goes and you're both staying."

"We're just indulging in a bit of *pillow* talk." Abby hoped Jensen would pick up on her clue and remember their pillow fight.

"Yeah only pillow talk," Jensen confirmed.

Before Parky could form a frown at the bizarre turn the conversation had taken, Abby snatched a pillow off the bed and threw it at him. At the same time Jensen leapt to his feet making a grab for Parky's wrist.

Nearly deafened by the sound of gunshot, Abby's nostrils were unexpectedly assaulted by the terrible smell of burnt feathers, other small, pure white feathers swirled around like a sudden snowstorm. Kneeling in the centre of the bed, she peered through the blizzard towards the two struggling men trying to see what was happening.

The bedroom door crashed against the wall as Bob Simms and Spen burst into the room. Within minutes Jensen held the gun while the two crewmembers contained Parky between them.

"You okay Sir?" Bob's question was edged with concern.

"Not really." The gun clattered to the floor as Jensen slumped down on the bed, the front of his pale blue shirt covered in blood.

"Jensen," Abby shrieked.

Parky used the moment's shocked surprise to throw off Bob's restraining grip. Using his free hand he punched Spen soundly on the nose and fled out of the door. Bob chased him, yelling for other crew members to help. Spen clambered unsteadily to his feet and followed them out.

"Where are you hurt?" Abby ran her hand over Jensen's chest until she located the bullet wound below the hollow of his left shoulder, too near his heart for her liking. Bright red blood flowed from under his body, turning the once white sheets crimson.

"I need to look at your back. Do you think you could roll onto your right side if I helped you?"

Gasping with pain Jensen lifted his wounded shoulder off the bed. Abby pushed gently trying not to hear his groans. Swallowing her shock, she quickly took in the larger exit hole in his back. Lowering him carefully she tried to smile encouragement. "It looks like the bullet has gone straight through."

Gritting his teeth Jensen nodded. "That's good isn't it?"

"Yes, yes of course, very good." Abby wasn't so sure, there was too much blood. Superstitious, as always, she crossed her fingers.

Bob dashed back into the room puffing and panting. "Parky jumped over the side Sir," he told Jensen. "We swept the sea with flashlights but it's too dark to see much."

"Never mind Parky, Jensen needs a doctor - now." Abby held a wad of bunched up sheet under the hand pressed against Jensen's chest. Her eyes pleaded with Bob to do something – anything.

"Let me see him." Bilbo limped into the room aided by Mark who carried a large first aid box under his other arm. "The police launch is on its way with a doctor aboard. In the meantime I'll do what I can."

Bilbo packed the wounds and made Jensen comfortable until the doctor arrived. Abby sat at his side holding onto his hand as he lapsed into unconsciousness. "Everything will be alright," she told him over and over again, in an attempt to convince them both of something that seemed more and more impossible as time passed and the doctor did not arrive.

"Don't die darling," she whispered. "It will be hard enough having to live without you in my life but living without you in the world would be unbearable."

Once white bandages slowly turned a deep red as Bilbo's packing could no longer cope with the amount of blood escaping from Jensen's still form. Fat, hot tears ran freely down her face to drip off her chin as she watched the colour fade from his face and his breathing slow.

"Oh please don't die – please give me the chance to tell you how much I love you."

CHAPTER TWENTY-SIX

Jensen was in theatre having surgery to repair the bullet-holes. Captain Georgallis returned Abby's handbag and case which had been recovered from Parky's abandoned hire car.

Using the shower off Jensen's hospital bedroom, she washed her hair and changed into a pair of navy cut-offs and a white top with red flowers. Jensen might like to see her wearing something cheerful when he came around. The possibility that he might not recover did not bear thinking about.

Waiting by Jensen's allocated bed in the private room, Abby was shocked when he was eventually wheeled in.

Oh no! Please no.

Unconscious and defenceless, his toffee coloured hair in disarray, a large white bandage, with a thick tube protruding, swathed his bare chest and shoulder, he looked much younger than his years.

Oh my love!

Two male porters slid Jensen's inert body from the metal gurney onto his hospital bed. He was so pale, so un-Jensenlike, in his pale blue hospital shorts.

Abby choked back a sob.

A female nurse hooked him up to the machines around the bed. Using the thick tube sticking out from under his bandage, she attached him to a drip.

Pumped full of antibiotics and painkillers, Jensen slept soundly as he received blood through a vein in his chest. Abby had been told that this was called a central line transfusion and the tube was thicker than the usual cannula tube fed into the arm, this way Jensen would receive the life-giving blood slightly faster than normal.

Sitting on a hard blue plastic chair, similar to one's in the waiting room, Jensen's large hand resting in her much smaller one, she listened to the whir of the machines monitoring his every breath, his heart rate and other vital signs. He was strong and the indications were good but he was still seriously ill.

Turning her head at the soft swish of the door, she smiled at the sight of Bob entering the room.

"Are you still here Miss?"

"Abby."

"Abby then. Don't you think it would be a good idea to have a lie down - you've been here since last night?"

"I'm fine. I don't want to leave him until I know he's completely out of danger."

"What about something to eat then. It's nearly lunchtime – have you even had breakfast?"

"I'm not hungry." Lifting Jensen's hand to her mouth she brushed his knuckles lightly with her lips. "How can I eat when he's like this?"

"How can you not? You know what he's like, there'll be nothing the matter when he wakes up and learns that you haven't been taking care of yourself." Sitting down in the matching chair on the opposite side of the bed, he continued. "I'll be for the high jump as well for not looking out for you. Come on Abby, there's a good canteen here, go and at least get something to eat."

Later, having half eaten a meal which had looked delicious but tasted like cardboard, Abby returned to Jensen's side and Bob had departed. Her energy exhausted by the shock and worry of the last hours, her eyes refused to stay open. Pulling her hard chair even closer to the bed she allowed her head to rest beside Jensen's hand.

The squeak of Jensen's drip stand moving on the rubberised floor woke her. Looking around she saw a nurse changing the empty blood bag for a full one. A quick glance at the large white clock on the wall told her she'd been asleep for over an hour. Still groggy, she moved away from the bed while the nurse checked his vital signs.

"How's he doing?" Almost scared to ask, she crossed her fingers behind her back.

"At the moment he's just the same. His body is fighting shock and infection. The bullet somehow missed his ribs but the surgeon has inserted a metal plate to support the partially shattered scapular, or shoulder blade. Once he's had this new bag of blood we will know better, until then it's simply a waiting game."

"So we could know later today?" Her heart lifted.

"We'll see."

After the nurse had gone, Abby returned to her chair.

"Please come around soon." she whispered. Picking up his hand she stroked the tanned skin, her fingers playing with the silky smattering of hairs. "I couldn't bear to lose you so you'd better fight as hard as you can. Come on Mr Bossy, you're always in charge – remember?"

The loudly ticking clock and the bleep of the machines were the only answer she received.

Come on open your eyes.

During the course of the next hour, Woody and Spen dropped by to see how Jensen was doing. After they'd gone Bilbo and Mark arrived, the three of them chatted as they sat around the still form lying in the pristine white bed.

"He's best asleep." Bilbo tried to lift the negative atmosphere which invaded the room as time passed and Jensen remained in his comatose state. "The food in here's awful."

Mark laughed and Abby smiled.

"Remember Moonie." Mark covered Abby's hand with his own as his concerned, brown eyes looked deep into hers. "It took days before he woke up and he's fine now."

She smiled her thanks at his attempt to cheer her.

Leaving Jensen in their care, Abby made another foray to the canteen for a large cup of coffee; she even managed to eat an egg and cress sandwich.

Back in the sickroom she stared out of the window as the blue sky slowly darkened towards another night. Tomorrow she must return home, her plane was due to take off in the late afternoon. How could she leave if his condition worsened?

A different nurse interrupted her musing. Watching her efficiently checking on Jensen and changing the blood bag again, Abby felt a lump form in her throat. She could not have spoken if she'd wanted. Another bag gone and he looked no different - he hadn't even moved.

Did this mean that he might die? She didn't dare ask.

Alone with Jensen she paced the small room, stopping to fling open the window. He loved fresh air, being on the deck of the Cassandra Rose, walking through the pretty country lanes surrounding her apartments and lounging on her balcony Jensen always spent as much time as possible outdoors.

Maybe the air would help revive him. Abby resumed pacing, every now and again she bent to kiss his cheek and check he hadn't awakened. Her efforts were wasted, his condition remained unchanged.

Disheartened, she sat close beside him and, as she'd done earlier that day, she laid her head on the bed. Tiredness swept over her in waves, eventually unable to keep her eyes open any longer, she fell into a deep sleep.

Awaking with a sense of deja-vu, she heard the familiar squeak of the drip stand. Stretching, she turned slowly expecting to see one of the nurses. Parky stood behind her, the soft glow from the light, located above the bed, illuminating the manic gleam in his eyes.

Leaping to her feet, she positioned herself between the madman and the utterly vulnerable Jensen. Astonished at the sight of the man who'd shot her lover she did not, at first, notice the dark stain pooling at his feet.

"How did you get here? We thought you'd drowned." As usual the words were out before she could restrain them safely behind her teeth. Chills ran down her spine at the sound of his soft, almost apologetic, chuckle.

"I 'borrowed' a rowing boat from the harbour and when I got close to the yacht I simply dropped anchor and climbed aboard. Those two goons, Spen and Woody, were too busy talking to notice me." He shrugged. "After I jumped into the sea I hugged close to the yacht so I wouldn't be seen. After a while I swam to my boat and rowed ashore." He grinned at her. In the semidarkness of the room his perfectly white teeth seemed at odds with his deeply tanned face.

His face darkened as his mercurial temperament changed directions. "It bloody hurt, that bastard Stone's done something to my ribs."

Abby noted that his arm still supported his chest.

Flicking his hair off his face in a now familiar gesture, he looked beyond her to the man in the bed. "Not long now," his tone was sombre.

What? What did he mean?

Machines whirred to their own tempo, the clock ticked the seconds away, but in the background Abby detected a new sound. Within seconds she registered the meaning of the steady plop, plop, plop. Glancing at the drip stand she saw that the cannula was no longer attached, the bag of blood bled out onto the floor.

"How long have you been here?" Her voice was an anguished whisper.

"Long enough," he grinned and gave a lopsided shrug.

Rage flooded her body with scorching heat. A red mist of hate temporarily impaired her vision. Without taking any time to think things through she grabbed the large, plastic water pitcher off the bedside cabinet and threw it in Parky's face. Half full it hit him squarely on the forehead, knocking him momentarily off balance. Abby launched herself behind the jug.

The force of Abby's weight added to his current unsteadiness and the steadily building pool of blood beneath his feet caused him to crash to the floor. Abby knelt astride his stomach and smashed her small fists repeatedly into his face.

Screams reverberated around the room. It wasn't until a male nurse lifted her bodily off her enemy that Abby realised she was the one making all the noise.

Parky, taking advantage of the army of medical staff who'd suddenly appeared, got swiftly to his feet and backed hurriedly away.

Abby, spotting him, yelled at the male nurse holding her wrists. "Don't let that man get away, he's the one that shot Jensen."

Parky scrambled further back, the blood soaked soles of his shoes slipping and sliding as he tried to get away. The window ledge caught him hard on the top of his thighs. Losing his balance completely, his arms wind-milled frantically as the weight of his upper body mass pushed the window further open. He disappeared into the night with a cry.

Standing at the selfsame window, arms wrapped tightly around her body, Abby watched the sun come up, too afraid to try to sleep again.

She'd been told that Parky had not survived the fall but her mind refused to believe it. Every-time she'd thought the danger was over and started to feel safe, Parky would appear again.

The room had been restored to normality, the floor cleaned and Jensen had received both painkillers and antibiotics. Parky had arrived too late, as Jensen had already been topped up with enough blood to survive.

Hearing a sound, she darted towards the bed.

"Hello beautiful," Jensen greeted her, his wonderful voice throaty with disuse.

"Hello lazybones, how are you feeling?"

"There's nothing wrong with me that a kiss wouldn't cure."

Under her lips his mouth felt warm but unresponsive – he'd fallen asleep again.

Later, Jensen, propped up with pillows, ate a light lunch, his expression leaving Abby in no doubt of what he thought about the taste.

"I have to go shortly." Tears pricked her eyes as she picked her handbag off the chair and checked her passport and ticket were tucked safely away. Everything was in just where they should be - she replaced the bag.

Fork halfway to his mouth, Jensen returned it to his plate. "Go where?" his words were threaded with surprise.

"You know where. I have a plane to catch," she checked her watch, "in four hours." Blinking tears away she dared to look at him. "It will take over an hour to get to the airport and nowadays they like you to be there three hours before you fly.

"You can't go now. I need you here." He appeared flabbergasted that she would go now while he still needed hospital care.

"I have to go. I've already explained this to you. You're going to be okay. The doctor tells me that after a bit of rest and relaxation you'll be fine. You're shoulder will knit together in a few weeks but when the stiffness wears of you'll be..." She trailed off at the look of abject hurt in his remarkable blue eyes.

"You'd better go if you want to catch your plane," he said coldly, pushing his barely touched plate, roughly away. "Don't let me keep you."

"I'll keep in touch."

"Don't bother."

Eyes burning with fresh tears, she snatched up her bag and ran out of the room.

CHAPTER TWENTY-SEVEN

Replacing the bedside telephone in its cradle, Abby sighed deeply. The conversation she'd just had with Bob Simms would be her last. They'd enjoyed several chats in the month since she'd returned home. Today she'd been told that Jensen had made a good recovery, and even though his shoulder was still strapped up, he'd returned to work a few days ago. Bob would now only have limited contact with him.

Utterly devastated, her heart continually aching over the loss of Jensen, Abby had somehow managed to live and work as normal. If anyone had noticed that she smiled less and the bags under her eyes were due to crying herself to sleep each night – they were too polite to say so.

Jenny knew of course. Abby could never keep anything from her inquisitive sister. Apart from the fact that they shared a flat - Jenny was her best friend. Without her sister to confide in, and provide much needed comfort, Abby wouldn't have been able to cope.

Lying on her pink satin bedspread, she fought off yet another crying bout. Jensen was well again - she needn't worry about him any more. It was time to put the ill-fated holiday behind her, to try to forget it ever happened. Today was the start of the rest of her life.

Coming to a decision, she swung her feet to the floor; it was Saturday night so no work tomorrow. She would have a shower, dress up and go out with friends - she might even go on to a nightclub later. Too many nights had been spent brooding at home. Jensen was getting on with his own life – she needed to get on with hers.

Sometime during her shower, Abby's brave idea to hit the highlife washed down the drain with the soapsuds. After drying and styling her hair she stepped into her old comfortable jeans and pulled on her comfy sweater, the one which felt like wearing a cuddle - she needed it tonight.

The sound of the doorbell peeled though the house. Abby heard Jenny bounding to answer it. Her boyfriend, Dan, was picking her up and they were meeting friends at the pub. Abby had been invited but wasn't feeling up to pretending to be sociable.

A few moments later Jenny bounced into the room grinning from ear to ear.

"Sis there's a guy sitting in our living room with a heavenly face and a voice that should come with a government health warning, and he's asking for you."

Shocked surprise ran through Abby, making her incapable of speech.

No it couldn't be – could it?

"I'll meet Dan outside, it's a warm evening. Don't wait up I expect I'll sleep over at Dan's tonight." Jenny smiled and kissed Abby's cheek. "Good luck sis," she whispered.

Jensen stood as she entered the small sitting room a few moments later, having taken the time to change her top and apply some lipstick.

"Hello Luv."

Oh God! Her lower body clenched with longing at the sound of that word.

The sight of him stole her breath away. He looked wonderful, thinner maybe, but still outrageously handsome. A white sling supported his arm, taking the pressure off his healing shoulder. The need to touch him was overpowering.

Hello my love. I've missed you so much.

Regaining control of her breathing and desires, she steeled herself to resist him. "How are you?" Even to herself she sounded stilted. Inside she was unravelling.

"Good as new – apart from my heart." He placed his hand on his chest.

"Your heart?"

Oh no - had it been permanently damaged by the bullet?

"Yes I think it could be broken." He gave her a lopsided smile and raised his eyebrows. "How's yours?"

Oh!

A huge smile spread over her face. "I think it might be broken as well," she admitted.

Jensen opened his free arm and Abby walked into his warm embrace.

His kiss was as devastatingly emotional as she remembered, it conveyed joy, vulnerability and undisguised need.

His lips left her mouth to trail quick searing kisses over her face. "Why did you leave me?" he whispered his breath hot against her ear.

"You know why. I had to go to work, I explained it to you." Tilting her head she gave him access to her neck.

"I thought I meant something to you." Uncertainty tinged his words even as his searching lips moved onto fresh territory.

If only he knew how much.

"You do." Abby's lower regions melted as sizzling desire took hold.

"Do you still want me as much as you did?" His mouth now hovered above hers.

"How can you doubt it?" Rising up on her tiptoes she closed the small space between them.

In her predominantly pink and typically female bedroom, Jensen appeared terribly male. His grin when he noticed the fairy lights twirled around her white, wrought iron headboard made her smile.

"No, really?" He raised his eyebrows.

"Yes really. I'm a very girly girl," she defended her choice of décor.

Cupping a breast through the silky material of her top his eyes darkened with desire. "I'm very aware of that." He scraped his nail across her nipple causing it to tighten. "How about we get naked?"

Oh yes please.

Abby helped Jensen to undress before removing her own clothes. She insisted he wear his sling whilst they made love, she needed him to get better as soon as possible.

Poised above him, Abby slowly worshipped his body with her mouth, her actions showing more than words just how much he meant to her. At last she covered him lip to lip, chest to breast and hip to hip.

Jensen's free hand gently stroked her back from shoulder to waist to buttocks. Abby shuddered with longing knowing that their joining, when it came, would be wonderful. This gentle lovemaking was unlike anything she'd experienced before, this time she knew how much she loved him and what it meant to be without him.

By the time he entered her she was ready to explode, but even with his limited movement, Jensen still managed to be in control, driving her mad with long, slow strokes before guiding them both toward a mutual toe-curling climax.

Oh boy!

Much later they lay wrapped closely together in her single bed.

"This won't work you know." Abby tangled her fingers in his damp chest hair.

"What won't work?" Jensen seemed to be only half listening.

"Us," she tugged hard.

"Ouch!"

"Are you listening?"

"Not when you're spouting rubbish. Why wouldn't our relationship work?"

"Because you're from a posh background and I'm a secretary at a small toy factory. My parents both work and they live in a tiny semi which they bought years ago. Plus I'm a northern girl and you're a southern boy."

Jensen chuckled before replying, "I'm a northern boy too. My parents live about forty miles from here in the council house I was brought up in."

What? No way!

Astonished, Abby suddenly understood the odd northern words which he often slipped into his conversation. "But your posh voice?" she queried, propping herself on an elbow so that she could see his face.

"Elocution lessons. I was a bright kid and won a scholarship to a really good school, my parents paid for me to have lessons during the summer holidays before I started my new school."

"And your parents really live in a council house?" She couldn't believe it.

"Yes. I bought it for them years ago and had it decorated and modernised. I wanted to buy them a big house but they wouldn't have it. All their friends live on the estate and their neighbours are great so they didn't want to move. Instead, I send them and some friends on several holidays a year and make sure that they always have a decent car." He shrugged. "I would do more if they'd let me."

"How did you become a millionaire?"

"At school I loved anything to do with mathematics and statistics, as I grew older I became interested in the stock market. After Uni I was lucky enough to get a job with a broker and I used my wages to invest some of my own money. I did very well. Later I was headhunted by a London Stockbroker and the rest is history as they say. Enough about me, it's time to stop talking."

"Are you tired?"

"No, bits of me have suddenly become very interested in staying awake." Pulling her down towards him he gave her one of his sensational kisses.

"You're very greedy." Abby gently bit his bottom lip.

"I've a lot of time to make up. I've dreamed about this for a month."

Oh wow!

Drawing apart, he traced her face gently with his fingertips. "I love you so much I don't know how I could ever live without you."

"Do you love me or are you half in love with all the excitement and adventure attached to our romance?"

Me and my big mouth! Why had she asked that? Why didn't she just accept his words?

"I love you totally. The adventure I could've done without. How can you doubt for a millisecond that I don't love you?"

His expression told her everything she needed to know.

"I'm sorry. I love you too. I was only asking."

"And I'm only telling."

God, she loved it when he said that!

OTHER BOOKS

AN EXCLUSIVE AFFAIR

An interview to die for…

A borrowed speedboat, with a virtually empty tank, lands accident prone, reporter, **Nicole Fisher** on a small uninhabited Greek island. Uninhabited except for an elusive and dangerously attractive millionaire, a man every journalist, worth their salt, dreams of interviewing.

Ryan Gregory, cosmetic manufacturing magnate, was cold and wet when he'd witnessed the short, bald man with the umbrella do his macabre Mary Poppins impression. When he also saw the face of the man who had just shot, 'Mary,' in the chest, he knew that he was in trouble.

When nosey journalist, Nicole, stumbles into Ryan's island hideaway, wet, dirty and hungry, she is last person he wants to see. Ryan does not need the distraction of having this maddeningly desirable girl in close proximity. Allowing her to give his whereabouts away is not an option, she is staying for a few days whether she likes it or not.

Nicole only wants to escape the building sexual attraction, and unaware that there is a contract out for Ryan, and that he is in hiding, she leaves a message on her answering machine – with terrifying results.

AN EXCLUSIVE AFFAIR IS AVAILABLE NOW

Find out more about the author and upcoming books online at
www.trishapyle.co.uk

Printed in Great Britain
by Amazon.co.uk, Ltd.,
Marston Gate.